CASSIE MINT

The Very Merry Mob
The Complete Series

BLACK CHERRY
PUBLISHING

First edition

ISBN: 978-1-915735-45-4

Cover art by Cormar Covers

This book was professionally typeset on Reedsy. Find out more at reedsy.com

Contents

I

Mistletoe Mobster

Description

I'm all set for a quiet holiday season.

Then a handsome mobster drips blood through my bookshop.

Fair enough, he's not being sloppy—there's a stab wound in his side. And once I get past his stormy eyes and his dangerous smile, I'm not scared of the mobster.

I *like* him.

Color me charmed when he stands guard outside my shop every day. And when he helps me hang the mistletoe? Forget it.

But this isn't like the cozy romance stories on my bookshop shelves. The mobster brings trouble, and now there's a target on my back.

He swears he'll protect me, no matter the cost.

But who's protecting my heart?

Leah

⚬୧ঌ৶ঌ৶ৎ⚬

Two weeks ago

It's always quiet in the bookshop after hours. The street outside is still loud with the roar of passing cars and bursts of drunken laughter from the nearest bar, but in here, it gets nice and sleepy.

Maybe it's antisocial of me, but this is my favorite part of a shift: dimming the welcome lights in the doorway and flipping the lock, then turning back to the maze of bookshelves. My own private wonderland.

What should I watch with dinner tonight? There's that new drama on Netflix, or I could listen to a podcast—

A thud rattles the door, and I leap back with a shriek. A shape moves behind the glass.

My heart pounds in my throat. "...H-hello?"

I'm not opening that door. Not for a million bucks. Not while I'm all alone in this shadowy bookstore, and I've never thrown a punch in my freaking life, and the laughter from

5

the bar down the street sounds extra harsh tonight. I creep closer to the front door, my hands clammy where they grip my sweater sleeves, and peer through the frosted glass window into the gloom.

A shadow moves across the door—a pale face, staring back with wild eyes.

"Gah!" I stagger back again, horrified, and dash toward the phone on the store counter. I've never been much of a runner, but you'd better believe I'm hustling now. I'm ready to vault clean over the new releases table.

"Please." A man's voice drifts through the door, deep and rough around the edges. He thumps the door again, but gentler this time. "I'm hurt. Let me in."

Right. That's got to be serial killer 101: make your hapless victim feel sorry for you so she opens the door willingly, then kill her gruesomely on the floor of her own bookshop. I don't think so. We don't have that Crime Fiction section for nothin'.

"I'm calling 911," I yell, and it's part warning, part an offer of help. "I'll tell them to send an ambulance."

"Fuck. Don't do that." The man lets out a string of curses, low and angry, and drops his forehead against the door. It rattles again, and I wince, creeping closer with the phone in my palm.

Why haven't I called yet? If this man dies on my doorstep, it's on me. I can see the headlines now: *Local bookshop haunted by doorstep ghost.* Business has been hard enough lately, but with a body count? Forget it.

And yet...

It makes no sense, but something about the stranger outside stills my thumb. It's like his voice was familiar somehow, or his being here gives me deja vu. Like we've met before, or his coming here was always going to happen.

Spooky.

"Buddy, if you want medical help, that's how it comes."

"Not your buddy," the man snarls, then cuts off with a groan. Crap, he really sounds like he's in pain. "Got my own doctor. Let me come in and call."

I pull a face he can't see.

Does the mystery man sound trustworthy? Nope, not at all. All I know is I don't want to let a stranger in the store— but I don't want to send away a hurt person, either. Choices, choices.

What would Aunt Karen do?

My fingers tremble against the lock. "If you try any funny business, I'll scream so loud it bursts your eardrums. And— and I'll bash your head in with a hardback. Got it?"

A huffed laugh blurs into another groan. "Got it. Come on, open up."

I must have lost my damn mind, because I do it: I flip the lock and swing the door open.

Huh.

The man on the stoop is tall and broad shouldered, dressed all in black with snowflakes settling on the lapels of his coat. His clothes are tailored and well made, and his dark hair and stubble are fancy—hey, maybe he could've offered me a million bucks after all, he looks that slick.

The stranger slumps against the door frame, eyes glittering as they stare into mine. The cold's whistling in past him, cutting straight through my clothes.

"Um." I clear my throat, nerves squirming in my belly, and wave an arm at the store. "Come in."

I still have the phone, squeezed tight in my fist until the

plastic creaks. I could still call 911. It's not too late.

Because what kind of person doesn't want you to call an ambulance? No one you want in your bookshop after hours, that's for sure.

Damn it, Leah.

I've made a dumbass move, but it's too late to take it back. Just need to see this through, and hopefully I'll finish the night with a caramel hot chocolate and not in a shallow grave.

Don't need to make it easy for him, though.

"Leave that open," I say when the man goes to close the door behind him. "And, um. Keep your distance."

The words feel so rude as I force them out, but his mouth quirks with something like approval. "Smart girl." Then he takes a step, and all the humor drains from his face, leaving nothing but ashen skin and stark lines. His body is so tense, *my* muscles are aching in sympathy.

Can't fake pain like that.

"There's a chair over here." I lead the stranger on a slow, agonized procession through the shelves to the kids' area where I read aloud to them every Saturday, and point at the bright orange velvet armchair on its polka dot rug. When he lowers himself down with a hiss, I shove the phone into his hand. He took way too long to cross the bookshop, and his breathing is ragged.

Wow. I really hope he doesn't die here. What do you even do with a dead body? Aunt Karen would know. Heck, she's probably made a few.

I nod at the phone. "Call your doctor. You're dripping blood through my store."

8

Leah

I'd love to be a Florence Nightingale figure. A person with an iron stomach and unflappable sense of calm, who bandages wounds without a single twitch. But when the stranger leans back in the armchair, peeling his coat open and showing a dark shirt soaked with blood, my tongue is suddenly way too big in my mouth.

"You gonna throw up?" He watches me closely as the phone rings, the handset propped between his shoulder and ear. Apart from his ashen skin and shallow breathing, you'd never know he's hurt. "I can take it from here. Bring that kit over and go."

Ass. He thinks just 'cause I let him in, he's free to boss me around? Well, Aunt Karen left me in charge, and I don't take that responsibility lightly. The first aid kit rattles in my hands and I force myself to walk forward. "I'm not leaving you in my store unattended."

The man huffs. "I'm not going to steal your shitty notebooks. Relax."

9

I hate this guy.

"They are not *shitty*." I ordered them from a glossy catalog last month. Took me ages to pick out my favorites, and they've sold like hot cakes ever since.

My knees hit the polka dot rug, and the man's eyebrows bounce up his forehead. Heat crawls over my cheeks, and I know how it looks, but I'm kneeling for first aid reasons. That's all. "They're hand-tooled Italian leather. Now let me see."

A faint coppery scent fills the air when he shifts, peeling his coat open wider—the wound's just above his hip on one side, the blood turning his dark shirt the color of tar. The sticky fabric clings to his body like a second skin, and I breathe through my mouth as I fumble the first aid kit open.

"Hey."

I glance up, but he's not talking to me. He fires off rapid instructions in Italian to the person on the phone, his stormy gray eyes never leaving my face, and my stomach swoops under the force of his gaze.

Definitely mob.

I frown at the stranger. He smirks.

Then he hangs up, and the motion of tossing the phone to the rug makes him stiffen again, cursing under his breath. Sweat beads his forehead, and his lips look way too pale.

Oh, hell no. This mobster is not dying in the kids' reading area. Such bad vibes.

Rocking back on my heels, I slap my thighs. There are goosebumps beneath my black tights, but I blame the cold. "I have vodka upstairs."

That helps with pain, right? And with cleaning a wound? That's what they use in the movies, anyway. I may have lived my whole life before now through books and other stories, but at least I've learned a thing or two.

But the man rolls his eyes. "Don't insult me with shitty booze."

Well, then. I tilt my head, voice hard. "Maybe you should wait out on the sidewalk after all."

Because if there's one guarantee, it's that this stranger is nothing but trouble. He's already dripped blood through my store and stained my vintage velvet armchair, and the frosty air from the street outside keeps gusting through the open door. Every now and then, a flurry of snowflakes whirls through the shop and makes me shiver.

A burst of laughter echoes from the bar a few doors down. I swallow hard against a surge of foreboding.

What am I doing?

Seriously, how did I get here?

Maybe he can sense my plummeting mood, because the man sighs softly and leans forward an inch. A hand spreads over his chest, and I try not to notice how strong and masculine it is, with those long fingers and squared knuckles and that expensive watch.

A signet ring glints on one finger. Is he married? He's still watching me with those gray eyes. "Forgive me, bella."

He shouldn't call me that if he's married... but then I'm sure plenty of criminals step out on their wives. Their moral code is not a top priority.

Doesn't matter. Lethal wound. Focus.

"I'm not trained or anything." Band-aids and rolls of gauze and antiseptic wipes slither everywhere as I dig through the first aid kit. "I mean, I did a day course last March, but I don't *really* know what I'm doing." I hated every second of that course, too. They showed us this slideshow of gross household injuries and I nearly threw up. "Your doctor's coming soon, right?"

"Yes." The man unbuttons his shirt with stiff movements then peels it open wide, and I fight the urge to wolf whistle. He is *fine*. Sculpted and trim with dark hair dusting his chest, and his stomach muscles may be tensed from the pain, but they're giving me all kinds of inappropriate thoughts.

He hisses between his teeth as the fabric clings to the wound before giving way. Blood oozes from the cut, thick and gloopy. Gross.

"Just slow the bleeding. He'll do the rest."

Ugh.

Okay. Okay.

My face twists into a grimace as I press a cotton pad against the bloody gash in the man's side. Heat washes over my knuckles, and he grunts, abs twitching, then spreads a warm palm over mine and drags me firmer against his skin. "Press harder, bella. It's deep."

It's a stab wound is what it is. Nothing else it could be. "Did you deserve it?" I ask, voice strangled.

I mean, most people don't just get stabbed for no reason—and this guy oozes danger with his dark, expensive clothes, the glint in his eyes, and the way his powerful body sprawls in my armchair like a panther.

His smile has sharp edges. I can feel this man's pulse thudding under his skin. "Depends who you ask, I suppose."

I snort, because the thought of me asking around after this stranger is ludicrous. My survival instincts may be rusty, but they *do* exist, thank you. "I think I know better than to ask anyone anything."

His eyes glitter. "I knew I liked you."

Oof. I've always known there was a screw loose in my head; whenever I read a romance book or watch an adventure movie, I always crush on the villain. But how have I found myself alone in the store with a stranger after dark, pressing down on his lethal wound with butterflies in my belly? I should be scared, right? Or at least counting down the seconds until he's gone.

Instead I'm… *enjoying* myself, the nagging concern for his wound aside. I keep gnawing on my bottom lip, wondering how I can get him to say more in that deep, rough voice. He smells good, too. Like a citrus aftershave.

Okay, I've been quiet too long. It's getting weird. "While I have you here, shall I tell you about our winter special offers?"

The man tips his head back and lets out a rich laugh, and even though it must hurt his wound, we're both delighted when he looks at me again.

This is so surreal. I love it.

"I know you're not a notebook fan," I go on, gathering steam, "but I bet I can find the book for you. Is Crime your genre?"

The stranger rolls his eyes. "Too obvious."

"Historical fiction?"

He feigns a yawn. I chuckle, then remember to press hard against his wound. He grunts again.

"Sorry. Romance?"

My face heats as he reaches out and curls a lock of my brown hair around his knuckle, rubbing the strands with his thumb, and… crap. I've forgotten how to breathe.

"If you like."

Please god, let him not be married. "Okay, I give up. What do you normally read?"

13

"Threats, mostly." A smirk flashes across his face, here then gone. "But a man can change. Which is *your* favorite genre, bella?"

I start to answer, but across the store, the bookshop door slams shut. Footsteps thump along the carpet in quick strides, and a man appears between the shelves in an open black coat. He's gripping a leather medical bag in one hand and he looks pissed as hell.

With tanned skin and wavy dark blond hair, thick framed glasses and a square jaw, the man staring down at me is clearly very handsome.

Even more worrying, then, that I only have eyes for the sharp-tongued jerk bleeding all over Aunt Karen's armchair. "Um." I shuffle closer to the wounded stranger. "Is that your doctor?"

He's still holding a lock of my hair, and he tugs gently on the strands. "Yes, that's Raul. Don't worry about him, bella. He's a pussy cat."

He doesn't *look* like a pussy cat. He looks like an angry mountain lion in glasses.

I turn to the man stroking my lock of hair. We're closer than I realized, my body wedged between his spread thighs. "And *you* are?"

"Nico Falasca," the newcomer answers for him, striding closer and dropping his medical bag with a thump. "Since he's feeling so free with names." The two men exchange loaded looks, and my heart sinks.

Okay, I definitely know too much. Will they kill me for this? For helping?

Will anyone tell Aunt Karen what happened to me? Will anyone else even care?

14

I always figured my life would be quiet and cozy and kind of dull. Not that it would end with a watery grave.

"I'm Leah," I say, in case it humanizes me or whatever. "And, uh. I'm very good at keeping secrets, I swear."

Nico

"**D**on't even think about it." Raul's hands are much rougher than the pretty bookshop owner's, manhandling me into a better position on the display table. The wood is cool against my bare back, and pain lances down my side as I stretch out.

The neat stacks of hardbacks that were here before must have taken Leah a long time, but she cleared them with a single barked order from the doctor, piling them neatly on the store counter. Didn't complain about my getting blood all over another piece of furniture, either.

She's scrubbing at the stains on the armchair now with a bowl of hot soapy water and a cloth, pretending not to watch us through the curtain of her hair.

Her soft, silky hair.

Fuck.

She smelled so good when I had her close. Like brown sugar and spice. Would she smell like that everywhere if I peeled off her bottle green shorts and Doc Martens? Her slouchy white sweater that I already stained with blood? Is she soft and creamy all over?

"I mean it," Raul mutters, reaching into his bag below the table, then placing a whiskey bottle by my elbow with a thump. "Don't get attached. You know how that story ends."

Yeah, yeah. Are all doctors miserable as sin? I glare at mine as he tosses his coat over a nearby display stand then rolls his shirtsleeves to the elbow. Raul's knees crack as he crouches, rummaging in his medical bag, and I unscrew the whiskey bottle and prop myself up to take a long swig.

It burns all the way down, scorching a trail through my chest. I take another and another, because one thing's for sure: this is gonna hurt.

When I tip my head back with a groan, the ceiling is blurry. Better.

"This won't be fun," Raul promises, pulling out a fresh needle and surgical thread and a small bottle of clear alcohol.

Well, what else is new? I gulp down another swig.

"In the movies, they bite down on a strip of leather." Leah's voice makes me jump, and I glance up to find her by my shoulder. She chews her bottom lip—plush and pink; would look perfect wrapped around my cock—then slowly, like I'm a wild animal that might lash out, reaches out and cards her fingers through my hair.

Jesus Christ. I buck into her hand, the scratch of her nails sending shivers down my spine.

"You'll want to stay back," Raul says stiffly, and I know he wants her gone so he can have an empty space to work. It's clear from the rigid set of his shoulders and the way he keeps glancing at his bag—at the *other* tools he keeps in there.

If he lays a finger on her, I'll shatter both his kneecaps.

17

Drunk or not, I'll do it. *No one* touches Leah.

"This is going to hurt him, even with the whiskey," Raul tells her, unscrewing the clear alcohol. "Nico might thrash. Go on home and I'll take it from here."

"I *am* home." Fuck, she looks cute when she's angry. Leah's cheeks are bright pink, and she's squaring up to the doctor even though she's pint-sized. He could squash her like a bug.

Don't like that thought. I hook a finger through her belt loop and tug her closer, my head fuzzy. "You live here, baby?"

If Raul rolls his eyes any harder, they'll get stuck pointing at the back of his skull.

Leah ignores him, still scratching my scalp. Feels like heaven on earth—worth the stab wound, that's for sure. "Yeah. There's an apartment above the bookshop. I live up there."

"Alone?"

Raul shakes his head as he threads the needle, but I'm just checking. For security reasons.

"Yep. Since my Aunt Karen left, it's just me." When Leah leans down, the ends of her hair tickling my bare chest, I breathe in a chestful of brown sugar and spice. So good.

Her voice is soft in my ear. Husky and private. "And that's not a wedding ring on your hand, is it, Nico Falasca?"

"Nope," I agree happily, swigging the whiskey one more time before laying flat with a thump. "No ring, baby. I'm all yours."

"For fuck's sake," Raul begins, but we both freeze when Leah's hands land on my belt buckle. She's not—is she—? In front of *Raul*?

"Bite down on this." I relax against the table again as Leah pulls my belt from its loops. The leather whispers against fabric, my hips lifting an inch to help her out, and I can't meet

Raul's eye. I know what we both thought for a second there.

He'll never see her that way. I decide on the spot: he'll never get a single goddamn glimpse of her like that.

Leah is *mine*.

The leather creaks as I bite down, sinking my teeth into the belt. That does help, actually.

"Ready?" Raul asks, peeling the cotton pad off my wound.

Glancing around, I catch Leah's wrist and put her hand back in my hair. Then I screw my eyes shut and nod.

Fingernails scratch at my scalp.

Ready.

* * *

"You know you can't keep her."

The street blurs past the tinted car windows, snowflakes pattering against the glass. I'm still woozy from the whiskey, cracking the nearest window to gulp down fresh air, but my head's clearer now. Getting a stab wound stitched up is sobering like that.

"Keep who?"

I wanna play dumb, but Raul's not buying it. His knee keeps jiggling, and he's staring at me with his arms folded over his chest. That magazine-worthy hair is all rucked up from running his hands through it, and there's a smudge on the right lens of his glasses.

Our doctor has had a long night. Yeah, that's on me.

"If Santo finds out you gave our names like that, that you linked us with a stabbing, he'll wipe her out."

Cars rumble past on the street, engines purring. "Then he'd better not find out."

I say it lightly, but I know Raul hears my unspoken words. If he gets Leah hurt, I'll kill him without a second thought, loyalty be damned.

"For fuck's sake, Nico." Raul pinches the bridge of his nose, the way he always does when he has a migraine coming on. I'd feel bad if he didn't keep threatening Leah. "What am I supposed to tell Santo?"

"Tell him some asshole got me by the docks, and you came and stitched me up in a bookshop. Tell him to send a clean up crew over there. And… tell him the owner was out."

"Nico."

"She won't say anything." I know it surer than I know my own name. "Leah won't cause us any trouble. Trust me on this."

Her touch was so soft in my hair. Did she really ask if I'm married, or did I dream that part?

The car slows for a red light, and I tip my head back against the leather seat, trying to remember every detail of the bookshop owner. She was a fiery little thing, all soft curves and pink cheeks. A quick thinker, too.

Thanks to her my belt's rolled up, studded with teeth marks and stuffed in Raul's medical bag. Maybe some other asshole can chew on it soon.

"You know if he finds out we lied…"

"I'll take the fall."

Raul gusts out a sigh, and I know I've won when he takes off his glasses, polishing the lenses on his shirt. His question is an afterthought. "Was it the Bulgarians again?"

I pause, because I forgot about this. In the haze of meeting Leah, I left out a key detail.

"No. It wasn't them this time." My throat is dry as I turn to stare out of the window, my head pounding from the whiskey. I've got a bad feeling, and it's not just the freshly stitched wound.

"It wasn't the Serpicos, either. This was something new."

Leah

P *resent day*

Nico Falasca thinks he's so sneaky, but I *see* him ducking inside that bus stop over the way. For the last two weeks, he's been hanging around my bookshop like a stupidly handsome ghoul, spying on me from different spots on the street.

First it was the bar three doors down, his coat collar turned up against the wind as he leaned against the brick outer wall, cigarettes glowing like fireflies between the teeth of the smokers all around him.

Then it was the neighbor's fire escape. Then an open topped bus trundling past. One afternoon, he even sat chatting in the barbershop over the road, watching me through the window as the old fella trimmed his hair, bold as anything.

Honestly. Don't they learn how to lurk properly in the mob? Pretty sure Nico's not supposed to grin at me this much, shrugging like he meant to get caught.

I don't mind him hanging around. Not really. Not now that I've accepted he's not here to kill me or shut me up—that if anything, Nico Falasca seems... protective.

A few nights ago, I forgot to lock the front door before checking on all the shelves. He crept up and did it on my behalf, the *thunk* echoing around the empty bookshop. I stood there waiting in the darkness, but he didn't come in.

Sure wish he'd talk to me. What's the point in lurking if he keeps his distance forever?

"Is there blood in this?" A harried voice floats across the store, and I stiffen behind the counter. Crap. I thought I got it all—I scrubbed all night at the stains until my hands were raw, and I swear the next evening when I came home from my barre class, the store smelled like extra strong bleach. A gift from Nico, I figured.

I even sewed a new cover for the reading armchair. Emerald green velvet, good as new.

My heart pounds against my ribs as I force a polite smile. "Blood?"

A redheaded woman with a severe bob and a bored teenage son holds up a new release from the Crime fiction table. "Yes, is there violence in this book?"

I squint across the room at the title: *The Butcher of Oslo*. The letters are steel gray, etched over the image of a snowy white street criss-crossed with crimson footprints. "Um." I fiddle with my cardigan. "Yes. But we have plenty of books without violence in our other sections..."

She's already turned away, hissing something at her son. Cool. That's cool.

If Aunt Karen were here, she'd whisper something hilarious and awful in my ear. She'd *love* Nico, too. Her next video call

23

can't come soon enough.

Does Nico have family? Are they also in the mob?

Will I ever meet them—you know, and live to tell the tale?

Can't imagine the mafia settling down to Thanksgiving dinner. Nor do I think Raul was my biggest fan, but in my defense, he was way too casual about threatening to kill me. Nico thought I didn't notice, but I did.

It's messed up that I want to see my mobster again so badly. Even Aunt Karen has better survival instincts than this.

* * *

The afternoon goes slow. Thursdays always do—they're sleepy days, when the traffic outside is muffled like the cars are wrapped in cotton wool, and even the ticking store clock seems lethargic. It's cloudy out today, with fluffy white snowflakes dancing on the breeze.

Is Nico cold out there in that bus stop?

No. Doesn't matter.

He's a grown-ass mobster; he can take care of himself.

For hours, I serve customers in a dreamy haze, taking breaks when the shop is quiet to neaten up the shelves and dust the display tables. The radio plays nothing but holiday tunes, and my jaw cracks every time I yawn.

Nico and Raul were exciting, I'll give them that. The hours they spent in my bookshop were the most alive I've felt in months.

"Excuse me." A man's deep voice pulls me out of my daydream, and I glance over from where I'm sorting the letter Ps back into alphabetical order. A customer stands in the center of the store, hands spread in a goofy plea. He's wearing a smart gray coat and a red tartan scarf, and on the spot, I decide he's probably a dentist. He has that vibe. "Any chance you know what five year old girls are reading these days?"

Hell yeah I do, and I'm already grinning, pushing away from the shelf. "Depends on the little girl. Is she into horses or ballet? Ice skating or softball?"

The man flushes pink. "Uh. Yes."

Figured.

I snort, leading the poor guy over to the kids' section, and already I'm more awake. This is my favorite part of running a bookshop: chatting with customers and finding them the perfect read, like some literary matchmaker. I'm so wrapped up in serving the maybe-dentist that I don't notice the tinkling bell of someone entering the shop. By the time footsteps prowl around the shelves, I'm kneeling on the polka dot rug and pulling glossy kids' books off the shelves.

"This one's super cute, it's about a mouse who opens a bakery—"

I cut off, glancing up at the newcomer. Nico leans against the bookshelves, watching me work with strong arms folded over his chest and a sour expression.

Guess he's not thrilled to find me kneeling at the feet of another man. But the shelves are near the floor, and what else am I supposed to do? Bend over?

"One moment, sir," I tell the mobster, widening my eyes.

Nico glowers. Seeing him up close again with that powerful body and stormy gaze makes me flush hot all over. Were his cheekbones always that sharp? The barber did a great job with his scruff.

"Oh, I don't know," the dentist laughs weakly from my other side, "I'm clueless about these things. This could take a while."

Oh dear.

That was not a wise statement.

Slowly, so slowly, the mobster turns his gaze on the other man. I wince, squeezing the book in my hand, and silently pray that my bookshop won't see any more blood stains this month. At what point do I become an accessory to Nico's crimes?

Soft and deadly, the mobster says: "Choose your book."

The dentist splutters, but I let out a relieved sigh.

Two minutes later, I'm waving goodbye to the harried man as he makes a beeline for the door, a brown paper bag of books tucked under one arm. Nico waits for him to leave, then strolls around the bookshop counter, invading my personal space like he owns it.

Jerk.

I really shouldn't like it this much.

But sure enough, my breath catches as he cages me in against the counter, gripping the wood on either side of my ribs, and as he towers over me, my head swims. I bite back a smile. "Why were you kneeling for him, *bella?*"

He's dressed all in black again today, his clothes tailored and speckled with snowflakes. Is the black a fashion statement, or is it to hide the inevitable blood splatters?

"For sexual reasons, obviously."

I grin as Nico glares, squeezing the wood counter behind me until it creaks. Definitely shouldn't provoke the mobster like this, but I can't help myself—and I know in my bones that he'd never hurt me.

Spank me, maybe. Boss me around, sure.

But hurt me? Nope, where I'm concerned, Nico Falasca is all bark but no bite. Just like I'm blustering about *sexual reasons* but I've never touched a man like that in my whole life.

"You are trying to make me jealous," Nico grinds out.

"Trying and succeeding."

In fairness, he makes it very easy. The mobster is wound tight, a muscle leaping in his jaw, and with his warmth so near my front, the faint scent of his citrus aftershave in the air, he's not the only one struggling to keep his cool.

There are only a few inches between us. I could spread my palm over his hard stomach; could feel the ridged muscles through his open coat, the fabric of his shirt warm under my touch. Could slide my hand lower—

"You need to be more careful." Nico speaks softly, scanning the bookshop over my shoulder, and oh yeah: the rest of the world still exists. There's a teenage couple giggling in the travel section, and an old man keeps peeking over at us from the new releases, scandalized at my behavior. Oops. "Don't tuck yourself away with strangers. They may not be who they seem."

My scoff is breathless. It's hard to think when he's this near, caging me in, his gaze dropping to my mouth before it shoots back to my eyes. The mobster is taller than me. Bigger, stronger, harsher. More *everything*.

"I hardly think that dentist was any kind of threat—"

"You don't know." Without warning, Nico grabs my wrist, holding my arm between us with two fingers on my pulse point. He watches me, eyebrows lowered, as my heart thrums faster. "The people who hurt me may have seen me take shelter here. They may come for you."

I swallow hard, tongue heavy. "Why would they do that?"

"To hurt me even worse," Nico says, like it's the simplest

thing in the world.

Um. What?

The radio splutters on the edge of the counter, a Christmas song crackling as it hits the second verse. The cheeriness is jarring. The shop door tinkles again, the old man shuffling out into the cold, and a wintry breeze gusts through the open doorway.

I did not sign on for this: threats and blood and feeling the hairs rise on the back of my neck. I snatch my arm back, but not before Nico feels my pulse spike in fear. He nods, all grim satisfaction now that his message has been received.

"You will regret helping me that night, bella."

Well, hell. Maybe I already do.

Except... no. I don't and I never will, because the alternative is too awful to think about: Nico Falasca left out on the frosty sidewalk outside my bookshop with a stab wound in his side, in terrible pain and unable to call for help.

The mobster jolts as I place both palms on his waist. The open sides of his coat brush against my forearms, and he's so vibrant, so solid, so *alive.* Surprise flits across his handsome face and makes him seem vulnerable, if only for a split second.

My thumbs rub against his shirt. "I won't regret it."

Nico lets out a slow breath.

"And you won't let anyone hurt me."

He pauses, then nods. So that's settled, right? Rightly or wrongly, I trust this strange man, and there's one more thing left to handle between us.

I jerk my head toward the cardboard box of holiday decorations on the counter, tangled string lights and tinsel exploding through the open top.

"Look there."

Nico frowns at the box of decorations, and I see it: the exact moment he spots the sprig of mistletoe snarled in the tinsel. One eyebrow lifts, and the corner of his mouth twitches.

"How festive."

His body is warm and sculpted under my hands. Has his wound healed well? If I pressed my front against his, would it hurt? "I'm deciding where to hang it. Any ideas?"

"Behind the counter," Nico says immediately, plucking the mistletoe from the box. He spins the sprig between his thumb and forefinger, seemingly fascinated by the white berries and dark leaves. "Or better yet: upstairs in your apartment. Somewhere only I can find you, Leah."

It's the first time he's used my name today. I bite my lip, giddy feelings bouncing around my chest like firecrackers, and when he holds the mistletoe over my head, one eyebrow raised, I just about die on the spot.

The sounds of the bookshop fade away as Nico lowers his head. There's no radio, no whispering teenagers, no rumble of traffic outside. There's only the hitch of my breath and the rustle of our clothes. My gasp as his mouth meets mine.

…God.

Nico Falasca kisses like a very bad man.

I was not prepared, because there's nothing polite or gentle about it, nothing to ease me in—he's all heat and nipping teeth and the scratch of his stubble against my cheeks, strong hands roaming up and down my sides like he owns me, the sprig of mistletoe tossed on the counter and forgotten. Nico feasts on me, hungry and harsh, and all I can do is sway in his powerful arms, some part of my brain desperately wondering how I got here.

Never mind that I'm at work, or that we've only met once

before. Never mind that kissing this man is a really, really bad idea.

I'm lost, whimpering and breathless. When Nico's tongue rubs against mine, I melt like a snowflake hitting hot water.

His dark chuckle floats through my brain and I fight my way back to reality, tearing my mouth away and slumping against the counter. Jeez. So much for dignity.

My chest heaves beneath my sweater dress, and I feel like I just ran twenty blocks. What is there to say after that? Oh, yeah.

"Raul's gonna be so pissed off."

Nico smirks, but he doesn't look flustered at all, the big jerk. He tucks my hair behind my ear, his touch lingering. He's standing a lot closer than before.

Can he feel how I'm burning up? Does he sense how slick I am between my legs, aching and needy? How badly I want him already?

The knowing glint in his eyes says yes, he knows exactly how riled up I am, and he's smug as hell about it.

"So you'll stay behind the bookshop counter," Nico says, like we never paused our earlier conversation for a sprig of mistletoe. "You won't wander off behind the shelves with strange men."

"And you'll keep spying on me like a weirdo," I return, cranky and embarrassed by the change of subject. Did our kiss really not affect him? Not at *all*? Was it just a festive game? "Until you get bored or I call the cops, I guess."

Nico tilts his head. "You won't call the cops."

It's not a threat the way he says it. Nothing like Raul's veiled promises of violence that night, the doctor glancing longingly at his medical bag. He's simply stating a fact and daring me to contradict him.

I fold my arms. "And you won't get bored." My words are more confident than I feel.

The shop is quiet behind us. Deserted at last, with only the bookshelves and window display to witness my jangled nerves.

Nico gives one final gentle tug on my hair before strolling toward the exit. "Take care, Leah. I'll be watching."

Nico

˜˜˜

When Santo tells us all to meet in his study for a drink, that sounds like fun—but it's never fun. It's always business with Santo De Rossi.

Business with the finest Italian brandy in the world, but still. You'd be an idiot coming to the compound hoping for a good time.

"Raul. Update."

I stifle a yawn down at my end of the table. Usually, I'd be up nearer the boss, but I've been relegated down this end with the meatheads. Punishment for letting myself get stabbed, I guess.

It's not unreasonable. Walking along the docks whistling was a rookie error, but it's extra hard to concentrate down here with Gianni's cologne stinging my nose.

"The Bulgarians are laying low..."

Raul always sounds so goddamn serious when he gives his reports, like he's reading the eulogy at a funeral. Snore. Though I guess I should be grateful, since two weeks have passed and Santo still has no clue about my bookshop beauty.

Leah's safe. Sweet and sexy.

Mine.

The doctor leans back in his chair as he speaks and I squint along the table, fighting to concentrate.

It's so warm in here with the fire. Stuffy, baking us in Gianni's cologne. Will it draw attention if I get up and crack a window?

"...following up on a lead, but it's not much to go on..."

Oh, come on. Can't I just have been stabbed by a random piece of shit? Some desperate asshole with nothing to lose, out prowling for shits and giggles down by the water? I've guarded Leah for weeks now, and there hasn't been a single peep.

Why has everything gotta be a goddamn conspiracy?

"Nico." The boss's voice is low and measured. He never has to raise his voice, Santo. He speaks with the absolute certainty that we'll listen.

I straighten in my seat. "Yes, boss."

"I hear you've been wandering off lately." Seated at the head of the table, Santo swirls his drink, watching the liquid catch the light. With his dark hair and sharp jaw, his open shirt collar and the shadows under his eyes, a stranger might mistake him for any one of us. Overworked and hardened by life.

Not for long, though. Not once Santo's piercing blue eyes land on you. Then you're rooted to the spot, a bead of sweat trickling down your spine.

"Care to share?" The boss's mouth quirks in a half smile, but there's no humor there.

I fight a full body shiver and blurt, "I'm not stepping out," like a prize idiot.

No shit. Only a fool would go behind Santo De Rossi's back, spreading our secrets around the town. Even suggesting it is a death wish. A few seats down from the boss, Raul closes his eyes, like he can't stand to watch this car crash a second longer.

"I never said you were." That velvet voice could give a grown man nightmares. I force a grin like this is all a hilarious joke, like the boss isn't staring at me without blinking. "But where have you been?"

My mouth is so dry.

Can't tell him about Leah. Won't do it. I'd rather end the night at the bottom of the river than sell out my girl. And you'd think I'd have seen this coming, you'd think I'd have an answer queued and ready, but I've been all tangled up in thoughts of Leah and now I'm paying the price.

My back is damp beneath my shirt, my stitches hot and itchy in my side. When I clear my throat, it's way too loud, but Raul speaks before I can force out a lie.

"He met a girl."

…Molten rage.

It courses through me; fills me up and cooks my skin. How fucking *dare* he. Any harm that comes to Leah, I'll repay to the doctor ten times over—I don't care how many times he's saved my life.

"She's nothing," I say quickly, the lie bitter on my tongue. Leah's *everything*, but Santo De Rossi doesn't need to know that. The less he knows about her, the better, because god forbid that Santo might think I'm too distracted. "A piece of skirt, that's all. I'll stop seeing her, boss."

Santo leans back, stroking his jaw, still watching me. Always watching. Studying me like he sees inside my skull, all my most private thoughts splayed out for him to read. The fire dances in the grate beside the table, casting golden light across the room, lighting up the bottom half of the De Rossi family oil paintings.

Right now, they're a bunch of over-intimidating legs. Not a helpful observation. And I'm all ready to push my chair back, to fall into a defensive stance, but Santo clicks his tongue.

This time when his mouth twitches, there's a flash of warmth. A rare sight for our ice cold leader. "Check in more often, Nico. No more secrets, but keep your girl. I'd hate for you to sulk around the compound with a broken heart."

Low chuckles echo around the room and I huff a pained laugh of my own. As if I'd ever go to the boss for comfort. To get drunk, maybe, but to mope about Leah? Never.

She's too good for any of this. I don't even want her name spoken in this house.

"Gianni." Santo's moved on, his gaze tracking further along the table. "Talk to me about diamonds."

As the conversation moves along, I'm not the only one sinking an inch down in my seat, tension bleeding from my frame. Up near the boss, Raul plucks his glasses off his nose and polishes them with a scrap of cloth from his pocket, frowning at his hands as he works. His stupid Hollywood-looking mouth is all pouty, like *he* has a right to be mad.

I'll kick his ass for this. Near miss or not, he risked Leah.

Hey, Raul's a doctor. He can fix his own scrapes.

* * *

Leah's street quietens down at night, especially once the bar closes its doors. The occasional cab trundles past, splashing through shallow puddles, and lamplight bounces off the wet sidewalk.

The snow's melted again. Hope Leah wasn't too excited about that. If I could boss the weather around for her, I would.

Over the last few weeks, I've chosen my favorite guarding spots. Some nights I like to keep watch from her neighbor's fire escape; some nights I pick my way over the roof. Tonight, with fear still coppery on my tongue, I wedge myself right in her shadowy bookshop stoop, a meat shield against the world.

"I knew it."

Raul's voice is no surprise, but it's definitely not welcome. His footsteps smack against the sidewalk, and he's agitated when he reaches me, cheeks flushed like he's been slapped.

Hey, the night's still young.

The doctor came out without a scarf, his collar open to the wind. He'll catch a chill waltzing around like that.

"Go home, Raul. Or better yet, go and finish selling me out to Santo. Asshole." I know I sound petty, but I can't help grumbling, pressing my back harder against Leah's door. If he wants me to stop protecting her, he'll have to peel me off the painted wood.

Can't believe he told the boss about Leah. Doesn't he realize she's more important than any of us?

One day this prick will fall for a woman of his own and have his whole world turned upside down—and I will laugh.

"I knew you had a screw loose, Nico, but this is bullshit. If Santo finds you here—"

"The boss gave his blessing." My smile is unpleasant. "Didn't you hear? You should really listen when he talks, Raul. You might miss something important."

"He gave his blessing for you to keep screwing some random woman that you don't care about." Raul jerks his chin up at the silent windows high above us, dark and slanted with moonlight. Leah's apartment. "That's not what this is, and don't try to tell me I'm wrong. I'm not fucking blind."

I lean closer, peering at his glasses. It's childish, but I can't help myself. "You sure about that?"

Raul's curses echo down the empty street, and I grin, settling back in Leah's stoop.

No one's getting through me tonight. I already spent way too long away from here—hours and hours at the compound, when anyone could've got to her. Unacceptable.

"It's been weeks." Raul's only saying what I've been thinking lately, but I'll never admit that. "If they were going to come for her, they'd already have tried it."

"We don't even know who they are."

If there is a *they*. If my stabbing really was the opening gambit to some grand conspiracy. If this isn't just Santo getting paranoid as he approaches midlife.

A drop of rainwater drips down the back of my neck, sliding under my collar. I suppress a shudder.

"If you don't like it, Raul, learn to mind your fucking business—"

A muffled thump drifts down from Leah's apartment, followed by the tinkle of breaking glass.

"Nico!"

I'm already kicking the bookshop door open, splintering the wooden frame. The dark shelves whip past in a blur, and I snarl as I take a wrong turn, sprinting into the travel section instead of to the back of the shop.

After tonight, Leah and I will have words. If she wants to set up her store like a goddamn maze, I need a map or something. A trail of red string on the carpet.

"Shit!" There's a crash behind me, and a landslide of books hits the floor. I dart past Raul wading through a sea of hardbacks and lunge for the door to Leah's apartment in the back wall.

Unlocked.

Did she leave it like that?

Footsteps move overhead, the ceiling creaking.

Go, go, go. My chest is ready to burst as I take the stairs four at a time, wrenching myself up with the handrail. I don't bother trying to sneak; don't have a plan.

I need to get to Leah.

And I've known fear before. Plenty of times in my life, I've tasted that special sourness on my tongue. I've felt my heart thump and squeeze inside my chest, and the panicked ringing in my ears is all too familiar.

But when I burst into Leah's apartment and find my girl kicking and flailing on the living room rug, a bald man crouched over her with gloved hands wrapped around her throat...

My brain goes blank.

There are no thoughts. No voice of reason in my head. Nothing beyond raw, animal instinct and the need to tear this fucker limb from limb. His surprised grunt as I wrench him off my girl—that ends with a crunch of bone. I splatter his nose across his face, beating him until each ragged breath gurgles in his throat. I pound him into mincemeat on the rug until his body is limp and my knuckles sing with pain, and it's only Raul shaking my collar that brings me back to earth.

"Nico! Nico, don't kill him, you prick. The boss will want

to question him."

The doctor's voice sounds like it's coming from far away, but finally, it filters through the thick cloud of rage in my brain. I blink sweat and blood from my eyes and glance over at Leah.

Oh.

Shit.

My girl is huddled by a chintzy armchair, clutching her throat and staring at me in horror. I shake out my stiff hand, feeling sick.

It's worse when I look down at her attacker again. Worse, because now I see him through her eyes—see the brutality of what I've done—and because I want nothing more than to keep going.

See what I mean? Leah's too good for any of this.

"Check him over," I rasp, swiping my upper lip on my sleeve. My coat is tacky with specks of the other man's blood. "His pockets, I mean. Don't you dare give him first aid."

"Obviously." Raul crouches by the unconscious man, pulling a pair of latex gloves from his inner coat pocket. He wriggles them on, snapping them against his wrists, then begins feeling along the man's limbs, checking his pockets with a wrinkled nose.

"H-he... I got up to get a glass of water, and he..."

Leah's rocking slightly, still clutching her throat. Her long, brown hair has exploded from its braid, and her red sleep shirt has twisted around her body, sliding off one shoulder.

I move to shrug off my coat, then think better of it. Don't want to get any blood on Leah, so I fetch her a padded blue winter coat from her front door hook instead, my movements robotic.

"Put this on." Can't look at her. Can't see that horror in her pretty green eyes. "You're shivering."

The apartment is quiet except for the rustle of her coat and the shaky scratch of her zipper. "Thank you."

I aim my question at the wall. "Did he hurt you? Besides your throat, did he hurt you?"

Don't care about Santo's questions. If this man hurt Leah worse than we already know, I'll put him in the ground.

"N-no."

Thank god. My shoulders drop an inch, and I let loose an exhausted sigh. Never would have forgiven myself.

"But your knuckles…"

My fingers ache like hell when I straighten them out, inspecting my ruined hand with a blank expression. Over by the attacker, Raul hums and pulls out a small stack of crumpled polaroids from the man's front pocket.

I walk over, gut tight.

"Old school." Crouching by the doctor's side, I'm glad for the distraction. The first photo is of Leah's bookshop—no surprises there. The second is a shot of my girl stepping out of her front door, probably taken from inside the bus stop shelter.

I'll change her name. Get her in some witness protection program. Or hell, I'll go begging Santo for help, cap in hand.

Whatever it takes to keep her safe.

"You're here. Figures." Raul drops a photo of me on the man's chest, disinterested. Then there's one of Diego, Santo's brutal right-hand man, followed by a photo of the doctor himself, peering through his glasses at a restaurant menu.

Raul freezes, the last photo crinkling in his suddenly tight grip. I frown, leaning closer. "Who is it?"

The doctor doesn't speak. Not sure he can right now. He tilts the photo to show me the next face on this hit man's To Do list, and the pieces thunk together in my aching brain.

Raul's monk-like existence, never showing the slightest interest in either men or women.

His caution around Santo, tip-toeing around our icy boss like there's something unspoken on the line.

His habit of calling at the compound, checking in way more than we're commanded to, sometimes sleeping there for weeks at a time—and the tension rolling off him now in crackling waves.

"The boss's little sister, huh? You're brave."

Raul's hand twitches, the photo of Allegra De Rossi crumpling in his fist. He sniffs and puts it down slowly, with far more care than any of the others.

Well, this is too rich. "You're asking for a one-way trip in the trunk of a car, doc."

"You think I don't know that?" Raul pinches the bridge of his nose. Migraine alert. "I need to get her out of the city."

I roll my eyes. "Hypocrite."

As if Santo would go for that. As if *Allegra* would either. She's a spitfire, raised and hardened in our world, more likely to kill a hit man than to fall victim.

Not like my Leah. Sweet, innocent, too-good-for-this-bullshit Leah.

My bones ache as I push to my feet. I hold out a hand to the huddled young woman, trying not to wince at the fear still pinching her face.

"Come on, bella. You'll be safer at the compound than here." I ignore Raul's harsh snort, and plaster a reassuring smile over my face. "Our boss won't hurt you. Not when I explain everything."

Not when I make whatever trades necessary to ensure Leah's safety. Not once I sign away whatever's left of my soul.

Leah doesn't move, and I'm so fucking hollow. Tumbling into an abyss. I risk a step closer, and at least she doesn't scramble back, but god. Her face is so pale.

"Let's go, baby. You can see the holiday decorations at the De Rossi mansion. The boss doesn't scrimp on a Christmas tree, you'll see."

Leah looks dazed as she stands, wobbling on her bare feet. She blinks toward the shadowy doorway to her bedroom. "I should change…"

"Just put on shoes." The faster we get her to safety, the better, and Raul clearly isn't worth shit now that he's seen that photo of Allegra. He's staring down at the hit man with a hard jaw and empty eyes, and I wouldn't be surprised to learn tomorrow that the good doctor snapped the man's neck. "I'll take care of everything else, okay?"

"The shop…"

Leah's trembling. That's not just cold.

"I'll take care of it. Shoes, baby."

It's a small victory when she stumbles toward the bedroom, but man do I need it.

What a night.

Leah

∽⚬𝒪𝒪⚬∽

N ico calls up a car, muttering instructions into his phone while I huddle beside him on the sidewalk. Behind us, the front door to my bookshop hangs crooked on its hinges, the frame splintered where someone kicked it in.

"Don't worry about that." I don't realize Nico's hung up the phone until he takes my chin, turning my gaze away from the ruined door. The shop was a wreck inside, too. What will Aunt Karen say? "I'll fix it all, I promise."

Gray eyes bore into mine, willing me to trust him.

I do. God, of course I do.

And he must have been worried about that, because Nico's shoulders relax an inch when I step closer, winding my arms around his waist. He puffs out a warm breath against my hair, then crushes me close against his chest. Cradles me like something precious.

"You'll keep an eye out for bad guys, right?" My words are muffled in his coat, my voice hoarse from getting choked out

43

by that hit man. Nico's already fussed over my throat about a dozen times, making Raul check it again and again.

He scoffs. "I *am* a bad guy, bella. But I'll protect you, yes."

Mm. It didn't truly sink in before tonight: the fact that Nico's in the mob. That he's dangerous; maybe violent sometimes. That he breaks laws and has probably killed people. The image of that battered attacker flashes before my eyes, his face swollen and bruised, broken teeth scattered across my rug.

Gross. I'm so not cut out for this.

"Your teeth are chattering."

I press the frozen tip of my nose against Nico's throat below his stubble. "Sorry. It's cold out."

And I'm freaking out, but hey. No need to go on about it.

The stars glitter high above us in the night sky. Snowflakes whirl on the breeze, but they melt away to slush the second they meet the sidewalk.

"No white Christmas," I mumble.

Nico grunts. "Not yet. There's still time."

The way he says it, it's like he's going to march up to the clouds and beat the snowfall out of them. Well, he's got three weeks to do it.

"My Aunt Karen hates snow. Hates everything that's not a hot summer's day. She's on this year-long cruise at the moment, chasing the warm weather around the globe."

Nico rubs his chin on my head, his stubble rasping against my hair. "Is that why you're all alone?"

Well yeah, it was. But I'm not alone now, am I? Not anymore.

"She left me the bookshop, actually. It's technically hers; I'm just looking after it. Keeping everything ticking over, you know."

44

Why am I telling him this? Confessing my life story to this surprisingly sweet mobster on a dark city street. This must be so boring to him, and yet Nico presses a kiss to the top of my head.

"You're doing such a good job, baby."

Tonight's wreckage aside, I guess that's true—but now everything I've worked for is at risk. Freaking mobsters.

Leaning back a few inches, I ask him outright. "Is your boss gonna kill me?"

Nico's face shutters. "No."

"But if he decides to shut me up—"

"He won't. Not if I give him what he wants."

Lord save me from these roundabout answers. "And what's that?"

Nico sighs, and he looks a decade older than that afternoon with the mistletoe. "Leverage."

Huh? I'm kind of lost, but I don't get a chance to ask again before a black, fancy car pulls alongside us in the street, windows tinted and engine purring. Snowflakes hiss softly as they land on the warm metal.

Nico pulls open a rear door. Toasty air spills out, washing over my bare legs. "In you get, bella. Trust me on this, okay?"

...Okay.

I will.

* * *

It's a silent ride through the city. The partition is up, the driver a distant shadow, and the only sound in the car is the gentle whir of the heaters. Nico drums his fingers on his knee, staring resolutely out of his own window.

He hasn't looked my way once since we slid in here. Perfect.

"I know you're being all manly and mysterious, but we don't have to ride in silence."

Nico grimaces. He rubs his uninjured hand over his jaw, the stubble rasping. Still looking out his window.

"Nico," I say flatly.

He flicks a speck of lint off his knee. "You want the radio on?"

"*Nico.*"

My seat belt clicks undone, and I slide across the leather seats, the material sticking to the backs of my thighs. Really should have put on jeans or something.

For a big, scary mobster, Nico sure does look relieved when I scramble into his lap. He frowns down at me, gaze intent, like he's trying to commit my features to memory.

"Why are you being weird?" Better cut to the chase, because if tonight has taught me anything, it's that none of us can be sure we have time to mess around.

Stormy eyes roll. "I'm not being weird. I'm thinking."

"You're brooding," I point out. "That's different." Spreading my palms over his chest, I feel the steady thump of his heartbeat through his navy shirt. Nico stuffed his blood-spattered coat in the trunk, sliding in here in only his rolled shirtsleeves.

The leather creaks under my knees as I settle more firmly against him, straddling his thighs.

Thump. Thump. Yeah, that heartbeat's picking up speed; Nico's not the only one who can pull that trick. So if he still likes me, why is he acting like a stranger all of a sudden?

"Have you changed your mind? Do you want to take me back home?"

46

He blinks, handsome features sharpening. "Of course not. Why would you think that?"

"Because you'd rather stare out the window than look at me, you big goof."

"I thought…" Nico's face darkens, and he talks over my shoulder, gaze sliding away from mine. "I thought you'd want some space, after everything you saw back there."

Ah. Yeah.

The bloodbath in my living room; the unbridled rage as Nico beat my attacker to a pulp.

That was a lot, it's true.

He lets me grab his wrist, not hiding his knuckles from my inspection. The skin is torn and bloody, the joints swollen and bruised, and though every other part of the mobster is still, his fingers shake like they've got a mind of their own, nerves dancing from the pain.

"Ouch."

Nico snorts, a flash of humor in his eyes. "Yes. Ouch."

That's him: my Nico. I grin at him, relieved, and wriggle against his hard thighs to get comfier. And up until this moment, I've been focused on working out what's wrong, but now that I know we're okay…

It's a very nice lap. Strong and steady and warm beneath my bare thighs, exactly like I've been dreaming it would be.

Game time.

There's no script for this situation. No list of instructions for seducing your rescuer in the back of a moving car. I'm winging it, flying blind, and Nico watches with open fascination as I raise his injured hand to my lips.

I drop a feather-light kiss on each of his knuckles, holding his gaze the whole time.

His chest heaves; my breaths come shallow. And with each brush of my lips, my body wakes up a little more, nerves crackling and heat pooling in my belly. What's that myth about brushes with death being a huge turn on? That would explain why I've been wound tight since the very first night I met this man. Flustered and too hot under my clothes.

"Thank you, bella." The mobster sounds strained. His throat bobs, and his free hand shifts to rest on my thigh as I skate my lips over his last knuckle. "Raul never kisses it better."

Ha. Maybe it's no myth after all.

"I'm not scared of you, Nico." Doubt flickers in his eyes, but it's replaced with crackling heat when I grab his other hand and draw it under the hem of my sleep shirt. It's a baggy red men's t-shirt, faded and stretched, the lettering worn, but I swear nothing has ever felt sexier as Nico pushes it up my thighs.

My hands tremble as I yank my coat zipper down, shrugging my arms out of the sleeves and letting it fall behind me into the bottom of the car. Then I'm balanced on the mobster's lap, knees sinking into the leather seats beside his hips, and all I'm wearing is this scrap of old fabric and a battered pair of old sneakers.

"Whose shirt is this?" Nico asks pleasantly, and he is such a bullshitter.

"It's from a thrift store, Falasca. Stand down."

The mobster grins, sharp and dangerous, and a thrill skitters down my spine. Seriously, what is wrong with me?

"Good. I already beat one man unconscious today."

Yeah, he did—to save my life. My teeth dig into my bottom lip, and I'm already rocking my hips forward, urging his fingers to get where I want him to go. "There's no need to be jealous."

Seriously. Now that I've tasted *this*, how could I ever settle for less?

Nico hums, mouth quirking up when his fingertips skate between my legs. I gasp, gripping his shoulders for balance as he says, "No underwear, bella."

Nope, and it's just as well, because they'd be soaked through. Nico slicks his fingers through my wetness, the traitorous evidence of how far gone I am, then swirls light circles over my clit.

Oh my *god*. Teeth clenched, I tip my head back to the ceiling, because he's barely touched me and already my whole body is on fire. That injured hand lands on my thigh, gripping possessively. Kneading and squeezing.

"Shit." I'm rocking against his hand, whining like I'm out of my mind. Hey, maybe I am. "Nico, touch me. Touch my pussy."

The mobster is calm as he slides two fingers down to my entrance, and that composure doesn't break until he pushes inside me, the tight fit making my head swim. Surprise flits over his face.

"Fuck," he mutters, and I huff a laugh, thighs burning as I rise and fall over his hand. My body is adjusting to the stretch, muscles aching and nerves tingling. Feels so freaking good, and I can't help picking up speed. Can't help pushing down harder onto his fingers, especially when his thumb swipes my clit.

"Yeah. See, there's *really* no need to be jealous."

His groan echoes around the quiet car, and Nico tips forward, hand twisting beneath me. I expect him to rest his forehead on my shoulder, but instead he *bites* me, gentle but possessive. Holds my shoulder between his teeth.

Such an animal. And my heart thunders behind my ribs; I'm breathing in short gasps, slickness spreading over my inner thighs.

I'm too hot. Too sensitive. Too desperate to do anything except moan, stomach muscles twitching as I ride the mobster's hand. Can't even feel the ache in my throat anymore—can only feel pleasure, rising hot in my body like a wave.

"*Nico.*"

"I've got you, baby." He's let go of my shoulder to speak, turning his head to lick my bruised neck. "You're so pretty, letting loose like this. So desperate for me to make you come. Isn't that right?"

My heartbeat's thumping in my ears. "Uh-huh. Please, I want to come."

Nico hums and licks me again. "You sound so good when you beg."

This time, as I rise up over his lap, Nico crooks his fingers inside me and rubs at a spot on my inner wall. With his thumb on my clit and his hot breath on my neck, it's—I feel—*fuck*.

"That's it."

The city lights blur through the car windows. My mouth drops open on a silent scream. I'm flying apart, exploding into a million tiny pieces, and when I float back to earth, Nico's watching me with a half smile. He draws his hand out from under my sleep shirt, tugging the fabric back into place.

"You're a work of art, bella." He brushes a gentle kiss over the corner of my mouth. "And whatever happens—you were worth it."

Nico

Usually, when I bring an outsider to Santo's place, it's strictly business. Maybe a local lawmaker wants to cut a deal; maybe an industry big shot has a mutually beneficial arrangement in mind. Maybe some asshole just needs a good scare. Whatever it is, I'm vigilant but bored. I don't get *nervous*.

I'm nervous now. It's not even my damn mansion, yet I'm self conscious as the car swoops around the circular driveway, the big house lit up by golden lights in the bushes.

It's not like I chose the manicured hedge maze and fountains in the grounds, or all those stuffy old oil paintings inside—Leah will get that, right?

Two men in dark suits linger by the entrance at the top of stone steps. They're familiar, but I can't remember their names. Nobody important.

"Santo's not so bad." Can't seem to stop running my mouth, giving my girl a never ending pep talk. I started about half a mile back and haven't stopped for breath. "He only kills people who really deserve it."

Leah snorts, but she's pale as she climbs out of the car behind me. Her eyes go wide, and she tugs down the back of her sleep shirt as she stares up at the mansion, the breeze fluttering the fabric against her thighs.

"Um. I really don't want to flash this guy, Nico."

No, I do not want that either. In fact, go ahead and file that under Nico Falasca's Worst Nightmares.

I turn and fish her coat out of the car. "Tie this around your waist."

Better. Okay.

Our footsteps echo against polished tiles as I lead Leah through the grand hallways. She winces every time her sneakers squeak against the floor and I grab her hand, wrapping her fingers in mine.

"He'll love you," I lie. Santo De Rossi is not exactly warm and fuzzy, even with us in his inner circle. Maybe he's different with his baby sister, but if so it's only behind closed doors.

Leah slides me a look.

"Okay, well he'll tolerate you. But *I* love you."

She brightens at that. And have I really not told her yet? Guess I thought it was obvious. Nico Falasca doesn't lose his mind over some lightweight crush, that's for sure.

It's a long, intimidating walk to Santo's quarters, past statues on plinths in alcoves and the musty *tock, tock* of a grandfather clock. This route is designed to show off the De Rossi wealth and power, to make visitors feel about three inches tall, but I don't want that for Leah. She's tiny enough already.

So I distract her with murmured promises, brushing her dark hair over her shoulder. "You like hearing that I love you, baby? Well try this on for size: I'm gonna make you my wife.

I'm gonna marry you and put little Nicos in your belly."

Leah wheezes a laugh, shaking her head, and I'm not fucking joking but hey—whatever helps.

"You want a diamond ring, bella? Or are you less traditional?"

"A diamond ring would look so weird in the bookshop," Leah muses, "but maybe I don't care."

I squeeze her hand. "Atta girl."

We cross a lobby with a grand staircase, and I'm so wrapped up in my own thoughts that I nearly forget the Christmas tree in the center of the floor. Leah pulls me to a halt, grinning at the sight of string lights and the scent of balsam fir.

"Hey, look." The branches have tiny red velvet bows scattered on them. "You weren't kidding—the mob boss really does like Christmas."

"This is one of the smaller trees, too." I lean close, talking in a stage whisper. "Whatever you do, don't tell Santo's enemies that he loves mulled wine and old carols."

Leah's laugh bounces around the lobby, but we both freeze when a cold voice drawls from the landing above us: "No, that would be... unwise."

"Boss," I rasp, my heart suddenly thumping faster. Oh, god. He heard that. Was it a mistake bringing Leah here?

Far above, Santo De Rossi rests one hand on the polished balustrade, watching us with a cool expression. It's late, but he's still dressed in tailored suit pants and a crisp white shirt, a gray embroidered waistcoat hugging his sides. Those glacial eyes take in Leah's sleep shirt and old sneakers, then linger on her hand clutched in mine. Did I seriously think I could ever hide this from him?

"This is Leah. She's the, uh—"

53

"Piece of skirt?" Santo tilts his head.

Out of the corner of my eye, Leah raises one eyebrow. I tighten my grip on her hand.

"Bookshop owner," I say instead, way too late. "She saved my life that night when I got jumped, and she was attacked tonight by someone with pictures of all of us. Raul, me, Diego and Allegra. Contract killer, unaffiliated. Raul's got him."

Maybe if I keep talking, Santo won't ask any more questions—and I'll never have to face Leah about that piece of skirt thing.

"No photo of me?" Santo asks lightly, still staring at my girl with a laser focus.

"No, just your inner circle. And Leah, so I guess they think she's one of us. Someone's trying to send you a message, boss."

Whoever it is, they've signed their own death warrant, because Santo De Rossi does not take well to attempts at intimidation. The last idiot who tried to make our boss dance to some other man's tune got cubed inside his favorite fancy car.

Guess there *is* a grand conspiracy. Christ, I hate when Raul's right.

Santo is quiet for a long moment, contemplating, and with each second that passes, I can breathe a little freer. I know our boss, and if he meant Leah harm, he'd have done something already. Besides, he's not even looking at her anymore. He's gazing into the Christmas lights on the tree, expression distant.

I steal a glance at my girl, because even though I've known Santo all my life, I'm not blind—I *know* that he's a handsome motherfucker, and power can be a hell of a draw. Plenty of girls around here make heart-eyes at the mob boss all the time, much good it does them.

Does Santo even have human urges that way? I've only ever seen him hungry for priceless artworks or power, never for sins of the flesh.

Though as we wait, a faint scent drifts into the lobby from the direction of the kitchens: the sugar-sweet smell of baking cookies. Not very intimidating, but a sweet tooth is Santo's only weakness.

"You're still here." The boss shakes his head and blinks down at us, resurfacing from whatever mental game of 4D chess he was playing this time. "What do you want, Nico? Keep the girl if you want, but don't get distracted. This is no time to be sloppy."

Here we go.

I clear my throat. "Her name is Leah, and I want to hide her here for a while. It's not safe for her back home while she's a target."

Dark eyebrows bounce up Santo's forehead, because how often do I make demands of the boss? Maybe never. "I can see that you are… attached, Nico. But I don't have time to babysit an outsider. It seems we are at war."

"I'm right here," Leah says loudly, and I grimace as she goes on: "And I don't need babysitting. I run a successful business and I saved Nico's life, and I can entertain myself, thank you very much. Jerk," she adds under her breath.

Silence.

Thick, painful silence.

"She didn't mean that," I start to say, but Santo holds up one hand.

"Yes, she did." The mob boss watches my girl for a long moment, and my stomach doesn't unknot until cool humor

55

flickers in his eyes. "Keep her around, then. She suits you."

I go to usher Leah from the lobby before he can change his mind, but Santo's voice makes my shoulders stiffen.

"Oh, and Nico? She's important to you, then?"

There it is. He won't let her stay otherwise—and if I agree, Santo will have more power over me than ever.

Leverage. Everything is goddamn leverage in our world, even back when we played games and got scabbed knees together as little boys. What Santo's really asking is: what will I do for him in return for her protection?

Anything. I'll do anything.

"Yes," I rasp, my voice loud in the lobby. String lights pulse on the tree, and I lead her to the doorway, my chest tight. "Leah is very important."

Leah

"What happened back there?"

Nico's quiet as he leads me through the De Rossi mansion, and I've had about as much awkward silence as I can stomach. There are so many polished stairways and chandeliers; so many grand rooms and fancy paintings. Super efficient staff beetle everywhere, even this late at night, and none of them catch my eye. It's unsettling.

"Nico, what happened back there? What did you two agree on?"

Because I'm not an idiot, you know. Even I could tell there were two conversations happening back in that lobby, one out loud and one unspoken.

What trade did Nico make? Why is he so quiet and grim now?

"It's nothing, bella. Santo was just checking that you're worth it."

Worth *what*?

"This is it," Nico says before I can ask, pushing a heavy

door open. We're somewhere near the top of the mansion, what feels like miles and miles from the entrance. There's less power-move decor up here, and the halls are lighter, their paintings calm. "These are my rooms whenever I crash at the compound."

Crashing somewhere implies a night on the sofa with a crick in your neck, but when I follow Nico into the suite, my mouth drops open. There's a four-poster bed and a blue silk chaise lounge; French windows leading to a stone balcony overlooking the grounds. A dish of grapes on the coffee table makes my stomach rumble, and Nico squeezes my hand one more time before letting go.

"Make yourself comfortable. It could be a few weeks before it's safe for you to leave again, but until then you can ring for anything you need. There are always staff around."

He nods at a bell on the nightstand. An honest-to-god tiny bell.

What the hell.

"I'll have clothes sent over from your place. Or would you rather all new stuff?"

Nico strolls to the closet, muttering under his breath, and throws the wooden doors open, his shoulder blades shifting under his tailored navy shirt. The mobster's body is lean yet so powerful, barely leashed by his clothes, and I flash back to the image of my battered attacker for the millionth time. Blood stains and broken bones.

Goosebumps prickle over my bare limbs. I nearly *died* tonight.

And this man saved me—then paid some mysterious price for his trouble.

Fitting my fingers over the bruises already staining my

throat, I swallow hard, wincing at the pain. My eyes burn, but I blink those tears away.

"Nico." He's rummaging through a chest of drawers, I guess looking for something I could wear. "Nico, please tell me what happened back there."

His hands slow, but he keeps digging. Doesn't turn back to me as he says, "Santo needed something in return for letting you stay."

"That leverage you mentioned earlier?"

"Exactly."

My mouth twists, and I kick off my sneakers one by one. Earlier, I was way too spun out to remember socks, and my bare toes curl against the rug. I tug my coat sleeves from around my waist too, tossing the puffy jacket onto the chaise lounge. "So he'll hurt me if you don't keep in line—that's what you're saying."

Nico's sigh is dredged from three floors below. "Nothing that crude. It's complicated, bella, but the more ties we have to Santo, the more secrets and pressure points he knows, the tighter we're snarled in his web. So when we need him, nothing comes for free, see? He'll help me, but first he needs an admission. Something he could use against me in a pinch."

"Me."

The drawer thunks closed. "Yes. You. It's the ultimate insurance, because now that your happiness is on the line, he knows I'll do anything. As far as Santo is concerned, I'm a puppet handing over another string."

That sounds awful. How can I possibly be worth *this*?

Nico strides to the glass doors, throwing them open so that cold, fragrant night air rolls in from the De Rossi grounds. His gray eyes are shadowed, his stubble dark on his jaw, and the navy shirt is open at the collar, the first hint of chest hair peeking through the gap. So freaking handsome.

"You know the real kicker, baby?" Nico's gathering steam, getting agitated as he rakes up his hair. "It's all unnecessary, but Santo's messed up. He can't see that Raul and Diego and me—he doesn't need to collect dirt on us. We're not gonna stage some coup; we're just plain loyal. Shit, I wouldn't be surprised if he has a mental file on his baby sister too. It's fucked up."

It really is.

Staring out at the gardens, my mobster looks so tired. "He'd never do it, you know. To others, maybe, but not to us. Santo thinks he's this unreachable ice man, but deep down, that fucker cares."

Remembering the cool way the mob boss stared down at us in the lobby, I purse my lips. If Nico says so.

"And you're sure…"

Wow, my throat really hurts. It's tight and aching, and I wince as I force the words out.

"You're sure this is what you want? You're sure *I'm* what you want?"

Finally, Nico stares at me properly, eyes hard. "What the fuck are you saying, Leah? Of course I'm sure. I'm not leaving you out there unprotected, alright? You're *mine*."

His.

My belly swoops, and I smooth down the front of my sleep shirt as the mobster prowls closer, throwing off his morbid mood like a heavy coat. He circles me like prey, and all my senses prickle to life.

"This other stuff is all bullshit, okay?" Nico tugs gently on a lock of my hair; he leans in and sniffs my neck, humming with

60

satisfaction. He's so freaking primal as he circles me, and it heats my blood. "Don't get distracted with Santo and hit men, Leah. There's always some drama playing out in this world; always something to fret over, but forget it. This is about us. Eyes on the prize."

In my rumpled sleep shirt, with my bruised throat and mussed hair, I don't feel like much of a prize.

Nico stops directly behind me, brushing my hair forward over one shoulder. He bends down and scrapes his teeth against the back of my neck, warm breath misting over my skin. A harsh kiss follows, with a swipe of his tongue.

Jeez. I sway on my feet, woozy already.

"Nico…"

"Remember what I promised you, baby?" He kneads my stiff shoulders, thumbs digging into the tense muscle until I moan. "A ring on your finger and little Nicos in your belly. You think Santo De Rossi's scheming means shit to me compared to that? He can collect his leverage all he likes. Me, I'm playing the long game."

"With Santo?"

"With *you*." Nico's stubble rasps against the side of my neck as he kisses me there, strong hands sliding down to roam over my body. He traces my waist; my ribs; my soft stomach and the swell of my tits. He lingers there, squeezing and pinching until I moan again, breath coming in short pants. "This is what really matters. Hell, this is *all* that really matters. Don't you see that?"

I sag against the hard planes of his chest. "Um. I guess so?"

"You *guess* so?" This time, Nico pinches my nipples so hard I gasp, a bolt of heat spearing through my lower belly. My knees are wobbly, and he's taking most of my weight already.

"You guess so? I don't like that, bella. I don't like that at all."

"Sorry," I wheeze, laughing as the mobster scoops me up, carrying me bridal style to the giant four poster bed. And I'm wearing a faded sleep shirt instead of a wedding gown, but it sure feels like a vow when Nico lays me down, gentle and reverent, the mattress firm against my back.

Standing beside the bed, Nico plucks his next shirt button undone, gazing down at me with those stormy gray eyes.

"Open your legs, baby. I'll *make* you sure."

Lips bitten and heart hammering, I slide my thighs an inch or two apart.

The mobster stares at me, expression flat.

I huff a laugh and slide my legs wider, but as I do, anxiety spikes in my chest, and I can't help babbling: "I've—You—I've never done this before."

Nico looks viciously pleased as he climbs on the bed by my legs, settling his shoulders between my knees. "I know."

"But if I'm not good at it—"

Nico waves an airy hand, his ruined knuckles extra swollen in the lamplight. "Not gonna happen. But it doesn't matter, does it? We've got our whole lives to find our rhythm."

Well… yeah. I guess so.

And I'm running out of reasons to stall, which is so nuts, because I want this so badly my bones ache, and yet if I get it wrong… if I'm not what he's expecting…

I want so badly to be worth it. Nico is already everything I've dreamed of.

Except the destruction of my bookshop, I guess—but hey. Everyone has flaws.

"You're already perfect." Nico kisses the inside of my knee, inhaling the scent of my warm skin. He shifts closer, flipping my sleep shirt up my thighs. "Sweet and soft and so pretty when you blush. You gonna make those little noises for me again, baby? Fuck, you're already slick and shining. How long have you been aching for me?"

Forever. Whole ages of the earth.

"Since the first night I met you. Since I knelt beside you in my shop."

Nico growls, nipping the sensitive flesh of my inner thigh. A broad fingertip traces along my seam. "I remember. We're gonna recreate that night sometime soon, bella. You on your pretty knees, fussing over my body, yanking at my belt. Sucking on my cock, nice and greedy. Kissing it better."

Hang on. "I never sucked—"

"You would have." He sounds so sure, rubbing his bristly stubble against my thigh and touching me firmer now. Delving between my folds. "If Raul hadn't come in, you would have."

Ugh. Is he right about that? Nico had a freaking stab wound, but... maybe. I *did* want him already back then, and there was something special about the connection sparking between us. Something that felt like fate.

Either way, the thought of it has me arching on the bed, cheeks hot and fingers scrabbling against the sheets. He's only got one fingertip on me, skating through my wetness and circling my clit, but it's enough to steal the breath from my lungs.

Never been this flushed and desperate. Never *needed* so badly in my life. And Nico's right—all the drama and danger and power plays with Santo De Rossi, it's all faded away to a low hum. Nothing matters in this moment except Nico's teeth nipping my leg, his thumb swiping over my clit as he

63

pushes one finger inside me. The delicious stretch and burn; the way my hips rock up, automatic.

"Yeah, that's it." The mobster's deep voice is ragged. "Show me you like it, baby. Show me you want me too." A flick of his wrist, and that finger pumps deeper.

Uh, of course I want him too. Is that really in doubt? I want to ask but Nico's taking me apart with his hands, his tongue sliding between my folds. His breath is hot on my aching flesh, his teeth sharp wherever they nip, and he may not be gentle but he *is* perfect.

He's mine, too. This goes both ways, and I want to reassure him—and stake a claim.

Nico grunts, surprised, when I grab a fistful of his hair. I push him harder against my pussy, hips rising to ride his face. "You're mine, Nico Falasca. No one else's. Even your mob boss will play second fiddle, and don't you forget it."

The words take even me by surprise, they're so vehement, but Nico snarls his approval and plunges his tongue inside my pussy. Licks me from the inside out.

I groan, head grinding back against the mattress as I squeeze my own tits, and I'm lost. Nothing but a bundle of heat and instincts and sparking nerves, my body arching and falling in a wave. I shove my sleep shirt up to my neck, plucking and twisting my nipples, and I'm squeezing his head with my knees, making such low, desperate noises—

Nico sucks on my clit, fingers crooking inside me.

I go up in flames.

It's an inferno roaring through me, scorching my insides, and all I can do is gasp and shudder as Nico keeps licking. My thigh muscles twitch and my stomach clenches and god. *God.*

Is it always like this?

No time to ask, because as soon as my moans subside, Nico rises above me, expression stark, and yanks at his belt. He doesn't even bother to undress, just draws out his cock and strokes it once, rubbing his thumb over the head. It looks angry, flushed and red. So hard it must hurt.

"You gonna let me in there, baby?"

God yes. Can't speak yet but I nod, and even that tiny movement is clumsy.

Nico exhales sharply, then crawls over me, his body so broad and strong. He reaches between us to line up with my entrance, the fabric of his shirt brushing against the bare skin of my body.

And I'm all gooey and loose-limbed, still floating down from my high, marveling at how good it feels to be pinned beneath him. It takes two tries to make my arms work, but I wind them around Nico's neck.

His shirt collar scrapes against my forearms. Next time, I'll get him naked, I swear.

"Do it." I lick a patch of bare skin on his neck. "Fuck me."

The mobster huffs and grips my thigh—then pushes inside.

Nico

There should be angels singing or fireworks going off. Maybe heavenly trumpets blaring. Some kind of external sign, some proof out there in the world that Leah is *mine*, and she's this hot and slick, and this really is the best fucking thing I've felt in my whole life. I'm not imagining it.

"Jesus." I've barely pushed all the way inside her, nice and slow so it doesn't hurt, before my ears are ringing. Am I gonna survive this? "God, bella. You feel like a dream."

I'm already moving over her, thrusting deeper. Grunting like a beast. Pounding her down into the mattress, building up a steady rhythm, the four poster bed frame creaking.

"Jesus," I say again, and I guess my brain's fried. Can't think properly, can't make smart comments or crack a joke. All I can do is fuck deeper and deeper into my girl, my hips rolling like I'm trying to burrow to the farthest corners inside her. Thank god I already made her come, because I've barely felt her around my length and I'm already ruined.

66

Leah whimpers and moans beneath me, biting her lip and twisting my hair. I duck down and kiss her, and that's rough too.

She's *mine*.

"You feel this?" I angle my hips, rubbing a sensitive spot inside her. Leah cries out and yanks on my hair. "This is the only cock you'll ever need. You're my girl now, you understand? This is it, baby. This is it for us."

I *need* her to get this. Need for us to be on the same page.

Can't live without her. Leah's the goddamn air in my lungs.

"Do you like your man's cock?"

She moans, grabbing two fistfuls of my shirt. Squeezing and releasing the fabric, lost to the sensations building between us.

"Leah."

"Uh-huh." When she nods, her green eyes are glazed. Ankles hook around my lower back. "I love it. Never want you to stop."

Well, I might need water breaks, but that sounds good to me. I'm ready to fuck her all night until her moans shake the walls. There's no other rational thing to do with the angel who's fallen into my lap; no better way to celebrate that she's all mine, with nothing Santo or anyone else can do about it.

Tension coils at the base of my spine and I grunt, thrusting harder. My teeth find her shoulder and bite down.

I draw it out as long as I can, my control fraying with every ragged breath; pound my girl into the bed until she's damp with sweat and flushed all over, her legs twitching where they hug my sides.

Under my shirt, my stitches pull. I don't care.

"Leah." I kiss her hard, then groan when she sucks on my

tongue. "*Jesus* Christ. Leah."

The room is hazy. The lamplight blurs. All I can hear is my own thundering heartbeat and our matching short breaths; the creaking bed and the smack of our bodies coming together. I cram my hand between us, only remembering how wrecked it is when my knuckles twinge with pain.

Don't care. Nothing else matters but this.

Beneath me, Leah gasps and stiffens when I rub her clit.

She stays that way, taut and shuddering, and I ride her through every wave of sensation, her channel clamping down on me and squeezing tight. On and on and on—my girl knows how to take her pleasure. There's no air in the room by the time she sags back against the bed, and when I bury myself as I deep as I can go, when I finally let go...

It *hurts*, it feels so good.

"Leah," I say, face pressed against her poor, bruised throat, my body wringing itself out until I can barely remember my name. I flood her, take her, *claim* her.

"Leah." My whole body is buzzing when I finally collapse to one side.

I press a kiss to her shoulder: my miracle.

My future.

* * *

One week later

Leah clings to my hand like she might float away if she lets go. I know the feeling. Knotting our fingers together, I tow her through the chapel doorway, the blanket of stars above the De Rossi grounds replaced with the glow of hundreds of candles.

"In here. Quickly."

"What's the rush, Falasca?" She's giggling and breathless, one hand holding the long, white skirt of her dress above the stone tiled floor. "Are you scared Santo will hear that you borrowed his priest without asking?"

Ha. "No, I'm scared *you* might change your mind."

My tone is light, but my gut clenches at the words. The last week together has been a dream, the happiest I've ever been, and Santo's been rolling his eyes non stop at the way I've been floating through our strategy meetings like a love struck teenager. I've never been surer about anything in my whole life than Leah, but maybe she doesn't feel the same.

One week to a wedding—that's rushed, even in the mob.

Does she really want this? My steps slow down.

"If you want to wait a while longer, we can go back to the house. You can change your mind, bella."

But Leah snorts, and already I'm ten pounds lighter. "Shut up, Falasca. We're getting married tonight. I spent ages on this hair, and there's no way I'll fit in this dress after the holidays."

I drag my gaze down her body, hungry and appreciative. Oh yeah, she looks good draped in ivory silk. Like a goddess.

Leah tugs on my hand as we stroll up the aisle together. "Are *you* sure you don't want to wait for Raul to come back? He could be your best man."

I shake my head, because god knows how long the doctor will be away. He disappeared a week ago along with Allegra. No idea what's going on there, but I'll bet it's messy, and who wants to wade into that?

Besides, I made other arrangements. The priest is waiting at the altar, stifling a yawn at the late hour, and Santo's right hand man Diego stands beside him, ready to play witness. He rolled his eyes when I asked him for this favor earlier today, but the savage fucker is wearing a buttonhole. He's slicked back his dark hair too, and trimmed his beard. Softie.

"Don't we need two witnesses..." Leah trails off when a figure stands at the front pew, brushing down his embroidered blue waistcoat. Icy blue eyes glance back in our direction, tracking our progress. "Oh my god."

"I did ask about borrowing the priest," I confess as we near the front of the chapel. "Why push our luck?"

Santo smirks.

"Right," Leah rasps. "Ha. Okay. Well, then maybe you could hold this for me, Mr De Rossi?"

Santo blinks down at the tablet pushed into his hands, a grainy video feed of Leah's Aunt Karen playing on the screen. The older woman is squinting at the camera, decked out in a vivid purple kaftan, her image frozen in a grimace.

"Don't worry about the feed," Leah says brightly. "She's used to it cutting out, but I figured we should at least try."

The mob boss stares at the tablet, nonplussed. Diego claps him on the shoulder. "Good man."

The priest clears his throat, and the old guy sounds kind of strangled.

"Not a word about this," Santo warns the priest, low and deadly. We all move into position, Leah's hand still clutched in mine, and Santo aims the tablet toward us, his nose wrinkling in distaste. "I could have you all killed," he mutters into the stone quiet of the chapel.

"Mr De Rossi," the priest blusters, a flush creeping above his collar, but Leah laughs, high and bright, and the whole chapel feels warmer.

She'll fit in just fine, and more than that—she'll make us all better.

Especially me.

"Dearly beloved…"

Green eyes sparkle up at mine, and I squeeze Leah's fingers. Her diamond ring is safe in Diego's pocket, and nerves squirm in my gut. This is it. As the priest drones on, I wink at my girl and jerk my head up at the ceiling.

She follows my gaze then breaks into a huge smile, because high above us where I hung it this morning, there it is.

A whole bushel of mistletoe.

II

Silent Knight

Description

T he stern doctor broke my heart years ago.

Now we're holed up in a safe house for the holidays.

Dr Raul Ossani is the last man on earth I want to hide away with, even with a price on my head. Sure, he can stitch me up if something goes wrong—but what about my bruised heart? What about my damn pride?

This is a small, quiet house. We're trapped here together, all alone.

It doesn't help that the doctor keeps staring. That his touch lingers. That his *body* clearly wants me, even if his heart and brain disagree.

Maybe I'm looking at this the wrong way.

Maybe revenge is a dish best served… seductively.

Allegra

ne week ago

O I'm hunched over on my sofa, bare foot propped on the coffee table, frowning at my half-done pedicure when Santo prowls into my suite. Glancing up from the nail polish brush, I raise an eyebrow at my older brother.

Dark hair like mine, and the sharp De Rossi cheekbones. Hollowed eyes and the signature family exhaustion.

"You never knock. It's my bedroom, Santo."

He shrugs, surveying the furniture. "It's my mansion."

There's something off about him tonight. Something cagey. My normally pristine brother looks ruffled, the shadows under his eyes darker than ever, and there's a crease in his gray embroidered waistcoat.

A *crease.*

Guess the sky is falling.

The grounds are dark through the balcony doors, and my suite glows with lamplight. These rooms are more familiar to me than any place in the world, and I know every inch. Every piece of antique furniture, restored by master craftsmen and gifted by Santo; every famous painting on the walls. Everyone thinks that Santo displays his most impressive finds in the visitor areas in order to intimidate visitors.

I know better. He saves the best for me.

Swallowing hard, I sit back. Whatever has shaken the mob boss is not good news. Santo is a block of ice, hard and impenetrable, and yet tonight he looks lost in the center of my suite. He keeps gazing around, blinking hard as he drags his focus back to the present. That fearsome brain of his is working overtime, and I'm surprised there isn't steam coming out of his ears.

"What is it?" I cap the nail polish with only three toes painted red. "Maybe I can help."

Santo stares up at the ceiling. "Yes, you can."

Oh, I don't like that. "On my terms," I clarify. "I'll help on my terms."

Because I'm not one of Santo's pawns to be pushed around his mental chessboard. I understand this business better than anyone, present company excluded, and I don't do grunt work. Life's too damn short—especially in our world.

"You need me to get info?"

Santo shakes his head, slow and thoughtful. He's still staring at the ceiling over my shoulder.

You know, when I was growing up with no one in the world except this man, he protected me. Kept me safe from the wolves at our door. And he taught me everything he knew, even when I was a sulky, frightened teenage girl and he was a newly minted mob boss who surely had better things to do.

I owe Santo, no two ways about it. Doesn't mean I'll agree

to his requests blind. Because I *know* my brother, know him inside out and back to front, know him in a way that not even his inner circle do. And just because he cares about me, in his own stilted way… that doesn't mean I'm immune to his machinations.

"Stop scheming and spit it out."

Santo nods once, then looks me in the eye. "I'm sending you away for a few weeks."

Um. What? Over the holidays?

"There's a hit out on you."

Ah. My shoulders drop an inch, because at least my big brother is not simply sick of me. I hate that's where my mind goes, but I can't help it. I may bluster for the outside world, but there's a scared little girl deep inside me, and she is shrill as hell.

"Come on, there are always threats." I smooth over my flash of panic with a confident tone. "If you overreact every time some asshole tries to kill me, your men will think you've gone soft."

Besides, I can handle it. There are no less than six knives hidden around my suite, and always at least two on my person. No need to freak out.

"They stabbed Nico two weeks ago."

I scoff, blowing my dark hair out of my face. "Well, it's not like that's hard. And he was barely hurt! It was a flesh wound."

I already checked on Falasca. Such a baby.

"Raul said an inch to the left and Nico would be dead." My ears go hot at the doctor's name, but my features don't flicker as Santo goes on: "There was a second incident tonight, and the attacker had your photo. Don't brush this off, Allegra. I need you to be smart."

Smart. Fine.

I can do that.

"First, these grounds are completely secure," I begin, count-ing off my fingers, my foot bobbing with agitation against the coffee table. "If you're really worried, I can stay home for a few days. Second, Nico clearly dealt with the attacker, and third, I'm *always* on someone's hit list, as you well know. That's the De Rossi guarantee."

Santo understands that better than anyone, so why is he so freaking rattled?

A maid bustles past the open suite door and we both pause. My brother strolls over and closes the door with a *snick*.

That reminds me.

"You know, one day you're going to burst in here without knocking and regret your life choices." It's easier to grumble, shuffling over to make room on the sofa, rather than face the dread pooling in my stomach. Something's wrong.

The cushions sink as Santo sits beside me. Not touching—we are not a cuddly family—but close enough that I can feel his warmth. Draw some comfort.

"If that happens, I'll burn the mansion down," Santo says pleasantly.

Ha. Liar.

"I'm a grown woman, asshole."

"You're my baby sister." Santo's smile is sharp. "That comes with privileges."

"Like no dating life?"

"Like my concern."

Bullshit. Such bullshit. Not that he cares about me, I mean, but that Santo would ever burn down his precious mansion. This volley is comforting, though.

"It's the holidays, Santo." My plea goes unsaid. *Don't send me away. This is the only time of year we're a half-normal family.*

Santo clears his throat, and as he turns away, there's a flash of guilt in his pale eyes. "You'll be fine, Allegra. Raul will be with you."

…Raul?

My whole body flushes hot, misery clamping around my throat. My heart slams against my rib cage, more bruised with each thump, and I can't do this. I can't.

"I'll go with Nico," I rasp, fighting a whole new battle now. Sure, I'll hide out in a safe house for a few weeks if Santo insists, but not with the doctor. Anyone but him.

"Nico is distracted; his focus would be split. He brought a woman here tonight."

A woman? Since when? I blink hard, yanking my brain back on task, because we can gossip about Falasca's love life once we've safely ruled out Raul.

"Diego, then."

Santo sighs. He props his elbows on his knees; knits his fingers together. When he stares straight ahead with his face in profile, he looks like one of the carved stone statues in the hallway alcoves. "I know that Raul bores you, Allegra—"

That has never been the problem.

"—But he is reliable. If something happens, he can give you medical treatment, and I trust that he won't hit on you."

No, he won't. I hide my flinch at those words, because if Raul Ossani would hit on me, if he would allow himself even a moment of weakness, this wouldn't be a conversation. I'd leap at the chance to go away with him alone.

But the doctor made it clear a long time ago: he will never touch me that way. Never. And I can't stomach weeks of

81

being close to him, pining after a man I can't have, my body literally aching with how badly I crave him.

Seriously. Who wants that?

"I'll go alone."

"Allegra." Santo exhales and pushes to his feet. "Pack your things. You and Raul will leave in thirty minutes."

"But—"

"Do it." When Santo frowns down at me, my big brother is gone and the mob boss is back. Laying down the law. "This conversation is over. I need you gone while I deal with this threat, and I need to be sure you are safe. Your presence is distracting."

Ouch.

My eyes blur as I stare at my half-painted toes. The floorboards creak as Santo leaves the room, and I waste precious minutes relearning how to breathe.

Raul. Weeks alone with *Raul*.

My brother may be a famous criminal, but—surprise, surprise—he is also a huge asshole.

* * *

It's weird seeing Raul drive. Two hours into the journey, I huddle in the front passenger seat in silence, watching the doctor's hands flex on the steering wheel. Our headlights are alone on this stretch of highway, swooping in two ghostly beams along the tarmac.

We've been following the coast road all night, the ocean glimmering in the moonlight. This car smells like leather and the pine air freshener dangling from the mirror, and for a fancy vehicle, the heaters work like crap.

Usually, Santo's inner circle have drivers to take us everywhere—all the better to scheme together in the back. But the safe houses are top secret, so dear Dr Ossani is having a very long night. The dashboard clock says it's 02:58am.

"You need another coffee?" I should nap or listen to a podcast, but I can't resist needling this man. Now that we're thrown together with no escape in sight, Raul is an itch I can't scratch. "We could find an all night diner; get you good and caffeinated. Or would you prefer a sugar high?"

The doctor stares at the road as he says, "I'm fine."

Ugh.

The car engine is quiet as we zoom along the coast road, the mountains on one side and the ocean on the other. The moon is full tonight, waxy and cratered.

"I bet you hate this."

Shit.

Shut up, Allegra. Shut the hell up.

"Hm?" Raul glances over at me, his handsome face pinched with fatigue. With his wavy dark blond hair, black-framed glasses and square chin, Dr Ossani looks like he belongs on a movie set, not driving a mafia princess to locations unknown. "What do you mean?"

See, this is why I need to learn to chase myself into bed well before midnight every night. I need my full eight hours or I get weak and slip up. Say stupid shit.

"Nothing." My nails are glossy as I examine them, smoothed over with a fresh coat of nude paint. At least I finished all ten fingers before Santo dropped a bomb on my head. My feet didn't get so lucky.

The car is quiet. Raul grips the steering wheel hard, his knuckles bloodless.

"You think I hate this? Following your brother's orders?"

Nope. "Forget I said anything." Fiddling with the dials, I settle back in my seat, warm air wheezing from the car heaters. My head aches like a bitch as I close my eyes, body swaying as we round a bend.

This night sucks so badly, and I really don't want to think about spending the holidays avoiding this man, hundreds of miles from the only family I have. Sent away for being a distraction.

"Allegra."

It's tricky to roll my eyes while they're closed, but I manage it. "Yes, doc?"

There's a long pause, and I've nearly drifted off when he finally speaks. Raul's voice is deep and rich, and a single word from him always makes the hairs on my arms stand on end. Beneath my sweatshirt and tartan blanket, my traitorous nipples harden.

"I don't hate this."

I grunt. Hopefully he'll take the hint: Raul Ossani is the last man in the world I want to talk about feelings with. Should never have started this conversation.

Some words from him are like music to my ears, though. Like: "I changed my mind. Let's stop for coffee."

Raul

E ver since the car door slammed behind Allegra on the
De Rossi driveway, I've been stewing in a mixture of
relief and dread. Relief that against all odds, my plea
for Santo to send her away actually worked, and dread that
I'm the one he sent to guard her.

Diego wouldn't have touched the boss's sister, and he makes
a brutal bodyguard. He can't stitch up stab wounds, either,
which is clearly a useful skill around the mansion these days.
Why not send him?

"Take this exit." Allegra squints at her phone in the gloom,
the blue light washing over her delicate features. She has the
De Rossi pout, and the same shadowed eyes as her brother.
"There's an all night diner five minutes away."

Though they look similar, Allegra isn't as hardened by life
as the boss. She might pretend she is, but *I* see it.

The softness in her. The fear and the longing.

The next few weeks will last an eternity.

We pull up in a gravel parking lot, a neon sign flickering

above the diner entrance. "Classy," Allegra murmurs, but she's grinning as she throws the car door open wide, tossing her tartan blanket onto the dash. For a mafia princess, she's fonder of sweatshirts and sneakers than dresses and heels. Designer sweatshirts, but still.

"Stay close. Don't speak to anyone."

"No shit."

Allegra gathers her wild black curls into a high ponytail, the salty breeze tugging on her tresses. Securing a hair tie with a snap, she glances at me. "I didn't think you could enter places with such a high fat content on the menu. You gonna burst into flames if you step in there, doc?"

Hilarious.

I lead the way across the gravel lot.

We weren't followed on the drive. It's been forty minutes since we saw another pair of headlights, and they went in the opposite direction. No one knows we're here, but adrenaline still makes my heart race. Danger is an everyday part of our world, but when it's Allegra on the line...

I catch her wrist by the front door. Her pulse thrums under her soft skin, and I try not to fixate on how good she feels in my grasp. "I'll scope out the exits. You find a booth with good eyelines."

A loud huff. "This is not my first rodeo."

No, it's not.

"Are you armed?"

Allegra's smile is toothy. "Of course."

Good. Fine. Squaring my shoulders, I push inside the diner. A radio plays softly, crackling over the speakers, and there's an older man curled around a coffee mug near the window. The cook and the waitress lean together by the hatch, chit-chatting.

The windows are steamed.

At the sight of us, the cook shuffles back into the kitchens. Allegra tugs her wrist free and sashays toward a booth in the far corner.

"Hey, folks! A late one tonight, huh?"

The waitress plucks two menus from the counter and heads after Allegra, beaming at me on her way past, but I don't follow. The kitchen is warm and smells like frying oil when I slip inside.

I check the kitchen and both sets of bathrooms. Each booth and the cleaning closet. I finish up with a final lap around the outside of the building, then stride across the sticky checkerboard tiles and slide into the booth opposite Allegra.

"Well, there you go, honey," the waitress says to Allegra, one ample hip cocked. "Told you some fresh air would see your husband right."

The mafia princess smiles at me, deadly and slow. "Hi, baby. You feeling better?"

She's playing a role, but hearing her call me *baby* makes my stomach drop. So pathetic. "Much better. Thank you."

We order coffees and two waters, my leg jiggling under the table. Remembering Allegra's earlier dig about my diet, I order a basket of fries to share, too.

"How decadent," she says once the waitress is gone, tracing a scratch in the table with a polished nail. "It truly is a Christmas miracle."

With the diner secured and the De Rossi mansion hours behind us, I look at Allegra properly for the first time tonight. She looks tired, and thinner than last month. Swamped by her midnight blue sweatshirt, her shoulders sag with defeat.

Fuck, I hate this. I hate seeing Allegra's light dimmed by even a few watts, and I hate knowing that she'd be happier if Diego were here and not me. They'd be chatting and ordering burgers, telling each other awful jokes and savage stories. Is her low mood because Santo sent her away? Or because I have this effect on her?

For the record: I didn't always make her droop. Once upon a time, Allegra lit up when I walked into a room.

That was a long time ago. Now, the young woman across from me looks ready to take a hundred year nap.

"You can stretch out in the back seat after this," I tell her, shrugging out of my coat and folding it on the red vinyl booth seat beside me. "If you sleep the rest of the way, you'll feel better tomorrow."

"You have no idea how I'll feel," she says, tone bored.

"I *am* a doctor."

"But not a mind reader." Her smile is cool. "Anyway, you'll be the one trying to digest fat for the first time in a decade. Worry about yourself, Dr Ossani."

"I eat fat."

The waitress interrupts our bickering, thank god. Steam curls above both coffee mugs, and the water comes in a glass pitcher stuffed with ice and lime. The fries smell surprisingly good—hot, golden and salty.

"Enjoy!"

As the waitress strolls away, Allegra falls on the basket of fries like a hungry wolf. She stuffs three into her mouth at a time, leaning over the table, and ignores me completely.

I press my lips together, fighting a smile.

My own stomach growls with hunger, but I watch Allegra eat every single fry without coming up for air, sipping my own coffee and stretching one arm across the back of the seat. She vacuums up the tiny crispy bits too, pressing her thumb into the golden shards on the waxy paper.

"Told you."

I watch her lick the salt from her fingers, my whole body tensed with longing. Not for any damn fries—for *her.* For the lash of that little pink tongue.

"You talk a big game, Dr Ossani, but when the carbs come out, you sit there like a lemon."

A lemon?

"I'm not hungry," I lie. The truth is, I was hungrier for the opportunity to watch Allegra freely. To make her happy for a change, and to see her sit back with more color in her cheeks. "Drink your coffee."

Allegra scoffs, snatching up her mug. "Don't tell me what to do."

But her mouth twitches when she says it.

* * *

All of Santo's safe houses are nondescript from the outside. That's the point, obviously, but the mob boss couldn't resist adding more of his signature touches inside.

This house, for example, looks to passersby like a standard detached family home in suburbia, complete with white picket fence and a kids' basketball hoop above the driveway. But when you step inside…

Allegra yawns loudly, not bothering to cover her mouth. "Oh, look. Priceless paintings kept in the ass crack of nowhere. Classic Santo."

"There is a twisted logic to it, I suppose." I follow Allegra inside, shrugging off my coat and hanging it on the door hook. "Even if someone broke in here, they'd never suspect those paintings were real. The ultimate camouflage."

"And the sign of a man with an auction addiction." Allegra glances over at my chuckle, but she's not smiling. "Standard safe house procedures?"

Back to business, then. I nod, masking my disappointment. "Wait here while I secure the property. Then I'll leave you to get settled and fetch us supplies. Keep the door locked while I'm gone and don't open any curtains."

"Yeah, yeah." Allegra heaves her duffel bag onto the floorboards. "I practically grew up in these houses, doc. I know the drill."

That's true, though I've never considered before what that must have been like. Being shipped off to random safe houses at the slightest threat, far away from her only family; whiling away her adolescence in places like this, bored and lonely. It's not like her brother is the type to video chat.

No wonder Allegra looked mad enough to spit when Santo marched her down the mansion steps. This must be the last place in the world she wants to be.

The last place, with the last person. Guilt tastes sour on my tongue. Does she know this was my idea?

No, she'd have chewed me out for it already.

"Wait here, then." My body tenses as I slide past in the cramped hallway, all my senses on high alert like they always are around her. I'm hyper aware of the brush of her clothes against my side; the heat of her, close enough to reach out and touch. And I can't take back the conversation that brought her here—nor would I want to, not now that she's safe.

But I can at least do my job.

Allegra De Rossi will stay safe—I swear it. Safe from hit men, and safe from me.

Allegra

P Not to brag, but I am a boss ass bitch when it comes to safe house entertainment. Being locked inside with no daylight, no fresh air, and no change in company is no joke, and it takes strategy not to go insane.

Santo taught me that. Whenever I called him crying as a teenager, begging to come home, he told me in that cold, calm voice that I'm too smart to crumble to pieces. That the only way to overcome adversity is to *think*.

You can tell that Raul, on the other hand, hasn't had to hide out for long stretches before, because he's getting twitchy. Watching the clock each day like an amateur. He hasn't learned yet that counting each minute only makes it worse; that the only thing to do is surrender to the hazy soup of time. To stop doing and start being, as those zen enthusiasts say.

God, this sucks.

Under the tyranny of the safe house, I stop being the antsy, productive, driven Allegra that literally only Santo knows and loves. Instead, I become this: a woman in sweatpants and a tank top with two-day hair, laying on her belly on the living room floor, listening to a podcast about the Cuban Missile Crisis and doing a jigsaw puzzle. Could be worse, I suppose.

The floor creaks overhead as Raul powers through his daily workout. If I pause my podcast, I'll hear the faint *whoosh* of his breath with each push up.

I crank the volume instead, a raspy voice chatting about Kennedy's secret sex tunnels. No need to torture myself.

Because the doctor has found every excuse in the book not to spend time with me since we arrived. Over the last week, he's been more like an estranged roommate than someone I've known for my whole life, leaving the room after a polite exchange whenever I enter, and timing his kitchen visits for when I'm not there.

He must hate this too, if he's going to such great lengths to avoid me.

My chest pinches with hurt at the thought. I ignore it, slotting a puzzle piece into place with a sigh.

What did I ever do to him?

Okay, so I know what I did, but is a crush such a crime? I was eighteen and too young for the doctor—I know that now, years later. But I didn't throw myself at him or tackle him to the ground. All I did was corner him in Santo's study one night once everyone else had left, and gaze up into the doctor's eyes at the fireside… and beg for a goodnight kiss.

From the way he reared back, you'd think I asked him to bend me over the table in front of Santo.

Humiliation burns in my throat at the memory. Raul's horrified expression; my plummeting stomach. The way he's avoided me for years since. The ache in my heart that's never quite gone away.

Whatever.

Thirteen days when the world stood still... The cheesy opening lines of a new episode fill the living room, and I pause my phone then flop onto my back. There are plenty of options for entertainment here, and they all kind of suck, but that doesn't matter. The trick is to keep moving. Keep swimming in the safe house current, like Santo taught me.

Twenty minutes later, I'm pressing back into down dog pose on my yoga mat when there's a hoarse noise in the doorway behind me.

"Hey." I blow escaped strands of hair from my flushed face, fully expecting Raul to flee with barely a word. That's been our pattern so far, and I can see his legs between my knees. Behind him, the kitchen is in shadow. "I made extra risotto last night. There are leftovers in the refrigerator if you want them."

My hamstrings are tight, and I bend and straighten each leg one by one, ass pointed at the ceiling. Raul's voice is rough when he says, "Thank you."

And this is the part where he leaves, where his footsteps fade into another room—but Raul lingers in the doorway. I bite my lip, lowering to plank position, then flowing through a vinyasa.

"You can join me if you like," I say from cobra, my shoulders lifted from the mat, gaze fixed on the opposite wall. I will not look over. I will not screw up my postures with my need to see this man. "You ever do yoga, Dr Ossani?"

"Sometimes," he says quietly. "But I'm not as, ah… bendy. As you."

Huh. Stifling a grin, I arch back to down dog again, and I can't help myself—I wiggle my ass a tiny bit. Raul coughs, and I bite my bottom lip.

If I'd known this would happen, I would've worn skin-tight leggings, not baggy sweatpants. All the better to goad him with.

Through the gap in my legs, I can see the doctor from the waist down. He's in a slim white t-shirt and black sweats, the fabric brushing against strong thighs. A water bottle dangles by his side in a loose grip.

Is he flushed from his workout? If I licked his stomach, would it taste salty? Is there a line of dark blond hair on his abs?

"I'm going on another supply run today."

Blood slowly draining to my head, I roll my eyes. Figures he had a reason to linger, and it's not my peachy ass. But then Raul moves his hand, the movement deft, and I almost miss it—the doctor hiding his hard-on. Tucking it behind his waistband.

Oh ho *ho*. This asshole does want me! On a physical level if nothing else. He acted so high and mighty so when I begged for that goodnight kiss, but I freaking knew we had chemistry. And though it's a terrible idea, though this will only hurt me more in the long run, I've just found my new favorite safe house game.

Drive Dr Ossani mad. Keep him hard as stone for me, rigid and aching, and never provide any relief. Let's see how *he* likes it.

"You need anything from the store?"

"No, thank you," I say sweetly.

It's time to scheme.

* * *

I'm showered and primped by the time Raul comes back, safely changed out of my slobby workout clothes into leggings and a soft, slouchy purple sweater. If I come out all guns blazing in a sexpot outfit, he'll see right through my ploy. For this to work, I need to be stealthy. Need to get under his skin.

Besides, a coat of cherry-bomb lipstick goes a long way. I smile at the doctor as he shuffles sideways into the kitchen, laden down with grocery bags, and toy with the ends of my dark ponytail.

"No sign of trouble?"

See? I can make normal conversation. With elbows propped on the kitchen table and a half-drunk mug of green tea, I'm the picture of innocence.

Raul shakes his head, piling the bags in the center of the floor. "Nothing. I drove around the whole area, but couldn't find any cause for concern."

I bet he couldn't. No self respecting hit man would be caught dead in this suburban hellscape.

And it's not part of my devious plan, but I fritter away a few moments watching Raul put away the groceries. He's in casual mode while we're here, trading his standard tailored suit for dark pants and a navy sweater, and his ass is perfectly sculpted as he bends down to fish out a carton of milk.

It's almost… domestic. Being here like this with him.

I wince, rubbing a palm over my sore heart.

"You okay?" Raul glances over as he works, scanning me with an assessing eye. Doctor mode: activated. His gaze lingers on my cherry red pout.

I drop my hand. "Just indigestion."

Raul grunts and turns back to his task, and I chew on my bottom lip, heel swinging under the table. I'm sizing him up like a kickboxing opponent, trying to figure out how best to corner him and make him blush, when the doctor grabs the last bag and turns to me.

"I got you something."

Moi?

"My birthday is in August."

Raul's mouth tugs up at the corner. "I know."

"And Christmas is more than two weeks away," I say, though I don't know why I'm stalling.

The doctor shakes his head and holds out the bag. "Take it, Allegra. I thought it might help you pass the time."

I'm not the one scratching at the walls with each passing day like a feral cat, but sure. My chair scrapes back and I stroll across the tiles, putting an extra sway in my hips.

Raul gazes down at me intently as I pluck the brown paper grocery bag from his hands. A puff of laughter escapes me when I peek inside.

"You put on lipstick," Raul murmurs as I jostle the bag, surveying the glittery contents.

"And you bought me holiday decorations." Why does my stomach hurt? My throat is tight when I swallow, and I give him a wobbly smile. "Thank you. I love the holidays."

It's the one time of year when Santo slows down for a moment; when he puts family first.

Or it was, anyway.

"I thought tomorrow morning, if the risk assessment is good, we could go pick out a tree."

I feign a gasp. "And break safe house protocol? My, my, doctor. You really are bored." And I'm teasing him, but the thought of fresh air and some actual daylight on my skin is almost too blissful to bear. My whole body is screaming out for some good ol' vitamin D.

"I already ran it by Santo."

Figures. But a tree?

It's no family Christmas, but maybe this safe house will be less tragic with some holiday cheer. "Thank you," I say again, and my eyes are misty as I stare into the bag.

I don't realize how close we're standing until Raul touches my shoulder. It's a whisper of a touch, barely there at all, but I feel it like he grabbed hold and squeezed. My whole body warms up, my breaths suddenly shaky, and I sway toward him on the kitchen tiles.

What was the plan again? Oh yeah. I was gonna torment the doctor.

Instead, Raul lays a fingertip on me and I'm done for. Flustered and pink. And it's always been like this between us—the doctor has always been cool and reserved, completely unaffected by my presence, while I melt into a quivering puddle under the force of his bespectacled gaze.

It's so not fair, and it's humiliating, too. The paper bag crinkles in my grip, and I take a big step back.

"Thank you for these," I tell Raul's shoes. "I'll decorate tomorrow once we have the tree."

And I don't invite him to join me, even though he bought the supplies. I don't say another word, waiting with baited breath until the doctor is finally gone.

Then I sag where I stand, the grocery bag drooping in my arms.

So much for my schemes. I need to regroup.

Raul

❧❦❧

Guilt is lodged in my gut, sickly and hard. It's been there since the first day at the safe house, but it gets worse with each passing hour as Allegra retreats inside herself—and I get wound tighter and tighter with wanting her.

When I convinced Santo to send her away, I told myself I was doing the right thing... but what if I was wrong? What if there's no real threat, and I'm just making her unhappy?

It wouldn't be so bad if she were here with Nico or Diego, playing poker or arm wrestling, passing the time with the men she truly calls friends. Instead, Allegra stiffens when I get near; she falls quiet when I enter a room. Even after my gift earlier, she was stilted.

I hate this.

"No developments," Santo drawls in my ear, the phone clutched tight in my hand. "We're exploring new avenues, tracing the source of the hit, but these things take time. And I have many enemies."

If he's getting tired of me calling for daily updates, the mob boss is showing unusual restraint. Guess he wants to hear about his baby sister.

Sure enough: "Is Allegra eating well?"

My mouth twists and I wrack my brain. What did she eat for dinner last night? We've been cooking separately—another failed attempt on my part to keep some distance.

Well, either way, I've only been bringing healthy ingredients home. Allegra complained about it yesterday, tossing a cherry tomato at my head.

"Yes. And she's been doing yoga and listening to podcasts. Keeping occupied." Santo hums. "You could call her yourself," I risk saying, wincing at the kingpin's sudden frosty silence. "I know she misses you."

Santo is quiet for so long, I step away from my bedroom window, even with the curtains drawn. How long would it take for him to arrange a sniper?

"It was your idea to send my sister away." From Santo's pleasant tone, we could be discussing the weather, but I hear it: the undercurrent of threat. "Are you saying she'd be better off here?"

"No," I say quickly, and that lump of guilt lodges deeper. God damn me, but I need Allegra safe.

With me.

"I'm just saying that she'd probably appreciate a call," I say, pinching the bridge of my nose. I've got a monster of a headache brewing, and my eyes are hot and buzzing. "We're going for a tree tomorrow—"

"If it's safe," Santo interrupts.

"If it's safe," I agree.

On my life, I will never risk Allegra, not even to make her

smile. I can't do it. I *won't*. There are so many mistakes I've made with the mafia princess over the years, but a cavalier attitude to her safety is not one of them.

But it's been a week already, without a wink of danger. The real risk now is to Allegra's spirit, not her physical well being—and I am the worst person in the world to make her feel better.

A tree, I can do. Holiday decorations—fine.

But offering comfort? Testing my already paper-thin restraint by touching her? Drawing her close?

Not a wise idea.

"You are keeping your distance, aren't you, Raul?" It's like the mob boss heard each thought clanging shamefully around my head; like he can see the image of Allegra's cherry red pout displayed like a billboard in my brain. "We're discussing my younger sister. I'm sure I don't need to spell out any threats."

"No," I rasp, screwing my eyes shut as the headache rages through my skull. "No, you don't need to say it."

"Good." Just like that, Santo moves on, rattling off further business updates and instructions. He complains about Nico briefly, then mentions that Diego has fixated on a maid in the mansion.

"She's new," Santo grumbles. "And more efficient than most. It's so hard to find good staff these days, Raul. If he scares her off, I'll cut off his balls."

My soft laugh echoes through the bedroom.

"I'm sure that won't be necessary."

Santo grunts.

"Well, at least wait until I'm there to stitch him back up."

It feels good to joke. So often these days, the man we grew up with is absorbed by his criminal empire, his earlier humor subsumed by cold calculation. It's rare for the old Santo to appear, even briefly, but these flashes are good for my soul.

"Get some sleep, Raul." There's a distant rap of knuckles—Santo knocking on his desk. "If my sister gets so much as a paper cut tomorrow, it'll be your balls too."

* * *

"The nearest Christmas tree farm is five miles away." I pass Allegra my phone, maps loaded, before starting the car. I've already checked for car bombs and snipers; already cased the whole area. I was out before dawn, making absolutely certain that there is no risk to Allegra.

We're doing this.

Beside me, the mafia princess is practically vibrating with excitement. She's used to the high drama of the De Rossi business empire, to stolen art auctions and the flash of blades in the moonlight, but I guess a week of jigsaw puzzles has lowered the bar for adrenaline.

"I already looked up the different types of trees." Allegra kicks her feet onto the dash, clad in pristine white designer sneakers. She's in leggings and an oversized sweatshirt again today, holding my phone above her lap, but I can't relax.

The red lipstick is back.

"Apparently balsam firs are the ones that smell really good. We want that, right?"

Uh. Yes? "I assume so."

Our car winds slowly through the suburbs, carefully matching the speed limit. The car heaters wheeze out warm air, and the roads are empty. Good.

"Get an opinion, Dr Ossani. This is our big December outing."

It's wretched of me, but anytime Allegra refers to *our* anything, my heart skips in my chest. I cover my flash of longing by frowning out of the windshield. "I'm trying to keep you alive."

"How noble." Allegra slides down an inch in her seat, falling quiet, and I wish I could stuff those words back in my mouth. I like her chatter. It soothes me.

At the Jameson & Friends Christmas Nursery, Allegra waits in the car while I secure the farm. I'm thorough, checking every nook and cranny, but there's no tension in my neck; no hairs rise on my arms beneath my sweater. My instincts say: no danger.

That's good, obviously, but that guilt twists through my insides when Allegra finally climbs out of the car, pale and tired. I did this to her. Me and my paranoia.

"Pick whichever tree you like," I say, as though her brother isn't one of the wealthiest men in North America. As though a single tree could make up for all our years of awkward tension. As though I could ever atone.

Her reply is flat. "You got it, doc." Allegra strolls across the gravel lot and between two rows of Christmas trees, the ends of her dark hair fluttering in the breeze.

Heads swivel after her wherever she walks. Up and down the rows of Norwegian pines and balsam firs, Allegra strolls with her shoulders thrown back, up and down, drawing every man's eye. Each time some asshole in a thick flannel shirt or puffer vest stares after her, I tense, my heart pounding faster.

They could be dangerous. Could be the threat we've been waiting for.

Or I could be a jealous idiot.

And each time, Allegra strolls on, unhurt and perfectly safe.

103

That's our pattern: she wanders, they stare, I tense. Over and over until my muscles are aching like I've had a hard round at the boxing gym. Sick with worry, and a heartbeat away from slinging her over my shoulder and beating my chest like a caveman.

I keep closer than I need to, close enough to catches lungfuls of her scent. Close enough to block any attacks, and to give any men who get too near the stink eye. Same difference.

And fuck. I've never been a jealous man before, have never been a victim of my biology... but right now, if another country bumpkin licks his lips at Allegra—I'll burn this Christmas tree farm to the ground.

* * *

"Are you ready to head back, Allegra?"

Mine. Mine. Back off, she's mine. An hour later, the world's least helpful chorus is still circling through my brain.

There's a green, bristly tree wrapped and tied to our car roof, we've both had lukewarm instant coffees from the tin shack selling them from the parking lot, and Allegra's wandered to the bathroom three times. She's stalling, trying to eke out a few more minutes in the fresh air, and I hate to cage her again.

Allegra sighs, picking at her thumbnail.

We're sitting together on a lopsided bench, crammed like an afterthought in the corner of the Jameson & Friends parking lot. It's objectively a miserable place to sit, with the cold wind slicing clean through our clothes and no view except a few trucks and the coffee shack. It must have snowed here recently, but it's sparse and dirty, melting away in big heaps.

But Allegra gazes around us with so much longing, you'd

think we were lazing on a beach in the tropics. I shuffle an inch closer, hating my own weakness, but I *need* to be near her.

It's the safe house. All these hours spent in close quarters, far from Santo's watchful eye. My control is eroding.

"I changed my mind about the tree," Allegra says. "I want a different one."

I bite back a smile. "Bullshit."

She huffs a pained laugh, dropping her chin. "Five more minutes, then. The safe house can be... stifling."

Yeah. It really can.

And I'm the asshole who trapped her there, so I nod and shift against the bench, the chill seeping through my jeans. "You don't normally wear lipstick."

Allegra turns to me and smiles, slow and sly. A cherry-red pout shifting against her olive skin. "Do you like it, Dr Ossani?"

Yes. Too much. I like every single thing about her way, way too much.

I clear my throat, plucking off my glasses to polish them on my sweater. "Yes. It looks nice."

Allegra hums, and now I sense danger, but not from any hit man. The bench creaks as she shifts closer, her floral scent washing over me. "I think it would look good on you too, doc. Shall we test my theory?"

Huh? I blink at her, confused, as she cranes forward slowly and plants a hard kiss in the center of my cheek. Her lips are soft, her breath is warm, and her silky hairs tickle my nose. Allegra leans back and cackles, like I haven't just turned to stone.

Shocked, sexually frustrated stone.

My hand raises to scrub whatever mark she's left from my cheek—then I pause and lower it. Try to commit every sensation of the last few seconds to memory.

Two can play at this game.

Allegra's eyes glitter, watching me. They're the De Rossi eyes, ice blue and filled with intelligence, and they're clear even without my glasses. Boring into my soul.

"Oh, yeah. There it is. Red suits you, Dr Ossani."

Allegra

❦

Raul keeps the cherry lipstick pout on his cheek for the whole drive home, and I can't stop staring at it. It was supposed to spin him out, but now I'm the one with a low buzzing noise in my brain, glancing obsessively at the proof that I kissed Raul Ossani—chastely, but still. He didn't move away, even though I gave him plenty of warning, and he hasn't cleaned my mark off.

This is psychological warfare.

Where else could I leave little lipstick pouts on his skin? God, I just want to pepper them all over his perfect, tan body. One for each ab, stacked on top of each other in two neat columns. One on each hip. One in the hollow of his throat.

It's childish, but as I trail Raul back inside the safe house, the door thunking closed behind us like a prison cell, all I'm thinking about is how to torment him next. I need to regain the upper hand.

We set up the tree in the living room, my grocery bag of decorations at the ready. With holiday music drifting from my phone, I crack open a bottle of finest Italian brandy that I swiped from Santo's study before we left.

It's… nice. Hanging out together like this. Warm and companionable, like it was before I begged for that stupid goodnight kiss all those years ago.

Back then, Raul was the center of my world. My closest companion, despite being older and so serious, and the reason I didn't get too lonely when Santo was wrapped up in his work.

"It's two in the afternoon," Raul points out, but he accepts his brandy without complaint.

"Time isn't real in the safe house, doc." I clink our glasses together. "You know that."

As Raul tips back his drink, the strong column of his throat bobbing as he swallows, he *still* hasn't wiped my kiss-mark away. Has he forgotten about it?

No. As the doctor lowers his glass, he stares at me, and his cool gaze is knowing. It's a challenge, and it sends a bolt of heat straight to my core.

"Um." My voice is wobbly. Every time I think I'm in control, this man gets me all frazzled again. He's just so *much*, with his wavy hair that I desperately want to rumple, and his dorky black-framed glasses. The serious slant to his mouth, and those powerful shoulders. Gah. "Let's—let's get started."

String lights and glittery pine cones. Red velvet bows and dangly bells. Apparently Raul favors the classics of holiday decorations. Who knew?

I rummage in the brown paper grocery bag, cheeks flushed from the brandy and from how close the doctor is standing, and fight to keep my composure. We decorate slowly, sipping from our glasses and humming along to the carols, and for a blissful stretch of time, I forget all about my lost Christmas with Santo.

Safe house? What safe house?

This is the longest period Raul and I have spent together since our overnight drive, and it's truly tragic, but in this moment, I wouldn't trade places with anyone.

Except maybe that brandy glass. Feeling Raul Ossani's lips against my... uh, my rim...

I place my own drink down on the coffee table, shaking my head. Think I've had enough.

The lights glow between tree branches, and a slow carol drifts from my phone where it's balanced on the arm of the sofa. The safe house living room is always so boring and beige, like a middle range hotel with weirdly fancy artwork on the walls, but right now, there's something magical about it.

"Lightweight," Raul murmurs, and shivers ripple down my arms. "Santo will be pissed when he hears you tipped away his precious brandy."

"Don't tell him, then." I nudge my elbow into the doctor's side. His warm, muscled side. Oh god, this is the most we've touched in *years,* and we're pushing our luck, but I can't stop. Won't stop. "Snitch."

Raul's bark of laughter makes me feel like I'm floating. I flick one of the tiny bells dangling from the tree and it tinkles.

How many chances will we get like this again? How many moments alone back at the mansion?

I'm not crazy. I *know* what I've been feeling all day: the two-way tension in the air. The hungry glint in the doctor's eyes, and the possessive way he tailed me around that farm. Not like a bodyguard, but like a lover.

And sure enough: "I'll keep your secret if you keep mine." The doctor's voice is low. Gravelly.

"Dr Raul Ossani has secrets," I mumble, not daring to glance at the man beside me. Wishful thinking can be a real pain in the ass, you know? "Let me guess: sometimes you cheat when you do the Sunday crossword?"

"Allegra." Why do I love it so much when he chides me? "Look at me."

Ah. Yeah.

Just like that, my mood sours.

Three little words, but it's not so simple. Once I look at the doctor, he'll see the emotions warring in my eyes: the irritation, the resentment, and above all, the unbearable longing. I've always been an open book to this man, and it pisses me off.

I flick the bell again, harder.

Why should I let him see how I feel? I did that once before, and look where that got me. Rejected and lonely for years. Feeling like a prize idiot for ever thinking that this man, so much older and wiser than me, could ever want a spoiled mafia princess.

We've just settled into a fragile truce. Why ruin it?

And why should I be vulnerable again?

"You really won't look at me," Raul says, and I hate that he sounds hurt. Jerk.

"Let me ask you something, doc." I address the tree branches, but I know the doctor's hanging on my every word. He's barely breathing beside me. "If Santo told you tomorrow to never come near me again, what would you do?"

Raul is silent.

My chest burns, like there's acid seeping through my ribs.

Yeah. Thought so.

Because he may want me while we're here, safely away from

my brother's scrutiny, but Raul is Santo's man, through and through. Loyal to the mob boss, not his baby sister. What is he hoping for, a holiday fling?

I sigh, swatting at the branches one more time before turning to leave.

Raul catches my upper arm, his grip gentle. "Wait. I would— I would tell him no. If you still want me, Allegra, I'll tell him no."

I press my lips together, and there are fireworks popping off inside my chest. But he… he doesn't mean this. There's no way. "Santo tends to win his arguments."

"Not this one." Raul spins me to face him, and finally I see it: the honesty and devotion burning in his eyes; the determined set to his jaw. Holy shit, he *means* it. The doctor has finally unraveled, and this sight? It's magnificent.

"I'm yours, Allegra. If you'll have me."

I grip the front of his sweater, suddenly wobbly on my feet. "You could have had me *years* ago—"

"You were so young, sweetheart." Raul stares hungrily at my red lips. He's so much taller than me, so broad and strong. He smells like soap and balsam fir, and there are stray pine needles clinging to his sweater after carrying the tree from the car. "I have more than a decade on you. I didn't handle it well, I know that. But I thought you'd get older and want someone closer to your age; I thought you might want someone like Santo."

Ew. I wrinkle my nose. "Gross."

"You know what I mean." Raul slides one hand into my hair and I sway, already so woozy from his touch. He grips me steadily, and heat pools low in my belly. "You might want another mob boss. Someone who can give you the world."

Yeah, no.

I clear my throat, and I wait for him to meet my eye, because I need the doctor to feel these words down to his soul. "Ossani, if I want a criminal empire, *I'll* build it. I don't need to marry some loser for one like I'm chasing a dowry."

Raul's grin is like a blast of sunshine. It's all the fresh air and daylight I've been missing all week, and we're still so close, and this is happening. Holy crap.

When he kisses me, mouth slanting over mine, the doctor leaves no doubt about what kind of kiss this is. It's not *polite*. It's not friendly, and it's not an innocent peck goodnight. Nothing he could explain away to the boss.

It's so filthy it makes my toes curl.

"Mmph," I say against his mouth, kissing back hard. When Raul's tongue nudges past my lips, I suck on it and draw out a tortured groan, the doctor's sculpted shoulders trembling under my palms.

Perrrrfect.

Yes, this is a wonderful new game. And kissing this man is everything I've daydreamed about for years—so sweet it makes my head spin, so dirty that I can't catch my breath. See, Dr Ossani may look like a boy scout, he may seem like the calm, collected one, but I've always known the truth.

He is a very, *very* bad man.

But not bad enough, apparently, because when I reach for his belt, he steps back and breaks the kiss. "We shouldn't—the brandy—"

I roll my eyes so hard, they may get stuck pointing at the back of my skull. "You break literally so many laws."

"Not this one." Raul's gone all stern again, and I whimper, reaching out. He catches my hand, presses a kiss to my inner wrist, then lets go. "I'm never risking you, Allegra. Never going to make you unhappy."

"Well, you know what would make me happy right now, Dr Ossani? Riding your Hollywood chin."

"Allegra." Raul's exasperated, but it's undercut by the fact he still has the pout from earlier on his cheek. I reach up, trying not to sulk as I rub it away, and he says: "Tomorrow. With clear heads, I promise we'll do all that. You can, ah, ride my Hollywood chin for hours if you like."

Ah, crap. I can't resist those twinkling eyes; can't be mad at this bespectacled dork.

Not when he's finally taking this leap with me. Choosing *me*, and this sizzling connection we've always shared.

"Tomorrow," I agree grudgingly. "And if you change your mind…"

He kisses me again, deep and slow.

When we break apart, I'm floating somewhere near the ceiling.

"I won't change my mind. Now let me cook you dinner."

Raul

～～∘❦∘～～

Santo De Rossi may not be as psychotic as many others in his position, but he still has a ruthless streak a mile wide. Disobeying his direct orders to keep my distance from his baby sister… well.

I'd better be pretty fucking sure she's worth the danger.

I am, though. The younger De Rossi grew up a long time ago, and she's an incredible woman. Powerful and sharp-witted; Allegra is nobody's fool. God knows why I've taken so long to give in to these feelings for her, but now that I've done it, there's no turning back.

I've wanted her for years. My need for her has been a constant dull pain, like a throbbing toothache I couldn't treat, even when months passed while we barely exchanged a word. And I suppose I convinced myself that she'd moved on; that it would be selfish to dig up those hurt feelings again.

I'm done being an idiot.

Allegra is *mine*.

We pass a comfortable evening together, eating a linguini

114

dish my mother taught me to cook as a boy and flushing when we each catch the other staring. It's a sweet kind of torture, being this close and all alone and knowing that we *want* each other, damn it, but being held back by my own holier-than-thou rules.

Allegra keeps shifting on the sofa beside me as we watch a Christmas movie, her clothes rustling, impatient sighs leaving her lips. She's wound tight, and so am I.

Jesus. We've only shared one kiss, and already we're both losing our minds.

"I'd better turn in." I launch to my feet as soon as the movie ends, credits scrolling on the screen. Can't look at Allegra. If I do, I might crash to my knees and shove my face in her lap. "I, ah. It's—goodnight."

"Night, doc." When I risk a glance, Allegra looks way too serene. My nerves prickle.

She's planning something.

"I'll see you in the morning," I grate out.

Her smile curves up, and fuck. I'm already harder than granite.

* * *

"Update." Santo is brisk in my ear, his tone clipped. "Nico's *woman* has been badgering me to play checkers all evening, so you'd better have some fucking good news."

I raise my eyebrows at the bedroom wall. It's late at last, the longest evening in existence finally bleeding into the dead of night, and if I twitched those curtains aside, I'd see a blanket of stars glittering above suburbia.

Leah wants to play board games with the mob boss? Does

she have a death wish? Santo is *not* a graceful loser.

"We, uh." I shake my head, trying to dislodge the image of Santo playing checkers from my brain. "It went well. No trouble at the Christmas tree farm, and Allegra seemed happy."

Santo exhales. "Good. Keep her there a while longer," he says, and I tug at my collar, suddenly too hot, because the fact that Allegra doesn't have all the information—it's starting to feel like a lie. "We have a new lead. Have you ever heard of Governor Edwards?"

"Yes." A relatively new player on the scene, but ambitious. Cold. But nothing to do with us at this juncture, and the governor would be all kinds of unwise to rile the De Rossi boss without provocation. "Why are you looking into him?"

Santo hums. "Call it a hunch."

Okay. Our boss gets plenty of uncanny hunches, his superhuman brain working overtime to connect dots that no one else can see. So if he thinks something is off with Governor Edwards, the man is probably fishier than the harbor.

Not my main focus right now.

Pinching the bridge of my nose, I say it in a rush: "I'm going to tell Allegra the truth. That there were other hits put out, not just on her. She'd… she'd want to know."

Silence.

Long, cold silence.

"My sister is very willful, Raul." When Santo speaks quietly, his tone extra soft—that's our cue to hide under the nearest table. "Did you not hear my instruction a moment ago? I want you to keep her there, not chase her back home. Or have you forgotten this little trip was your idea?"

I screw one eye shut. "Even so. She deserves to know."

Santo snarls. "*No*, Raul."

"I'm going to tell her tomorrow. I'm sorry, but it's—it's done."

"You've touched her, haven't you?" His voice is low. Deadly. Shaking with anger. "Allegra is—"

"A grown woman." Jesus Christ, why am I confirming his suspicions? I'll be lucky to live through the night. But... I told her I was in this, and nothing stays secret from the De Rossi boss for long. "She's not a kid anymore, alright? She can make her own decisions."

Santo curses so loudly I wince, holding the phone away from my ear. When I listen again, he's still ranting.

"—dare to show your face again, I will tear it off with my *teeth*—"

He doesn't mean that. I hope.

"Goodnight, boss." And then, because apparently I have waved goodbye to my final scrap of self preservation, I add, "Good luck with checkers."

Santo's explosion of rage cuts off with a beep. The room is extra quiet, echoing with the mob boss's words, and I hold the phone loosely by my side, ears ringing and head pounding like a drum.

It buzzes again in my hand, and I send it to voicemail.

Santo will get over it. Probably. And in the meantime... at least we're hundreds of miles away.

* * *

Allegra's voice is soft and beseeching, drifting through the safe house walls. I pause where I'm reading in bed and strain to listen. Did I dream that? Am I hallucinating her now?

"Raul," Allegra calls again, soft and coaxing. "Will you come here for a second? I don't feel well."

I'm out of bed before my next breath, the book tossed behind me on the covers. Didn't even mark my page.

Tomorrow. We said we'd continue our... exploration tomorrow.

Is she really ill? Fuck.

The safe house hallways are carpeted and quiet. My bare feet pad past spare rooms and a shadowed bathroom on the way to Allegra's door, the painted wood sealed tight.

"Uh." I rap on the door, wincing. There's a rustling sound inside. "Everything okay in there?"

Allegra starts to reply, then breaks into a coughing fit. I nudge the door open, stepping into her dimly lit room.

She's bundled up in her double bed, so small under the covers. With her dark hair tied up in a messy bun and a black tank top clinging to her form, even while she's sick, Allegra makes my mouth go dry.

"You're not feeling well?" It's a relief to be able to slip into doctor mode. This, I know. This, I can handle. The faint floral scent of Allegra, lingering in the air, on the other hand... I inhale sharply before sitting on the edge of the bed. "Tell me your symptoms."

Allegra coughs, weak and scratchy. "I feel hot."

Pale blue eyes gleam as they watch me, and I rest the back of my hand against her forehead. Nothing. She's a little flushed, maybe, but that's all. I try her temple next, then the side of her throat.

Hm.

"What else?" I say, suspicions already half-confirmed.

"I have this cough." She demonstrates against her elbow,

dramatically feeble, then grabs my hand and presses it to the center of her torso. She draws it down her warm, tight body, arching under my touch, and her smile is so sly. "And my tummy feels all squirmy."

I lean back, exasperated, because I'm one more 'symptom' away from a heart attack. I'm also so hard in my pajama pants, I can barely think. "Allegra."

She catches my wrist as I move to leave, and nods at the clock on her nightstand. "Wait. Look, doc. It's tomorrow already."

I inhale sharply and glance at the clock face. Three minutes past midnight. Fuck.

"The brandy…"

"Was only a few mouthfuls, and it was many hours and two bowls of linguini ago." Allegra sits up higher, the covers pooling around her waist, and I glimpse a sliver of thigh. "Come on, you big prude. Did you mean what you said earlier or not?"

Did I mean it? That I want her?

Yes. With every atom of my being, yes.

Allegra laughs brightly as I crawl onto the bed, crowding her against the headboard. "Prude?" Her breath stutters when I catch her wrists, pinning them above her shoulders. "Don't forget who you're dealing with, sweetheart."

"The golden boy," she murmurs, and that is not what I meant, but she rocks up and kisses me, and every thought flees my brain. I kiss her back, savage and hungry.

Small hands escape, then roam over my chest.

Mine.

"I'm not going to hide this from Santo," Allegra pants between kisses as I tear the covers off, stripping the bed down to its sheets. Her legs are bare, her body covered only by the tank top and lilac lace panties. "So you'd better be sure, Ossani."

"I already told him on the phone." I smirk when she blinks at me, startled, and take the opportunity to grab her ankles and yank her down to lay flat. Allegra bounces on the mattress with a squawk. "Or he guessed, I suppose, and I confirmed it."

"Ugh." She's grimacing, but she can't hide the smile tugging on her mouth. "Why does my big brother know I'm getting laid before I do?"

Feels so fucking good to finally cover her body with my own. To grind down against the softness of her thighs, and feel her arms loop around my neck. "Santo knows everything. Now can we please stop talking about him?"

"Agreed." Allegra's teeth scrape over my jaw. "Oh my god, agreed."

She's hot and restless, arching up against me and stroking her feet along the backs of my legs; she tugs on my hair and scratches her nails on my scalp. Everything else in this beige, boring house fades away to nothing, and all I can see, touch, taste, *feel* is Allegra.

My Allegra.

We break apart from a long kiss, both breathing hard. I stroke the strands of dark hair out of her face and part her legs with my thigh.

Jesus. Even through two layers of fabric, she sears me with her damp heat.

"That's, um." Her stilted tone rings alarm bells in my head, and I lean back, peering down at her. The mafia princess—always so confident and wild—bites her bottom lip. Allegra looks *shy*. "Is there a cool medical way to tell you I'm a virgin?"

I pause. "You've—never?"

She huffs and rolls her eyes, and *there* she is. My girl. "Yes, that is the meaning of the term, Dr Ossani." And she's so flustered and cranky, a blush spreading up her throat, that I can't help ducking down and kissing her again, long and deep.

It's the easiest thing in the world to tip us over. Allegra swings on top of me with a squeak, grabbing two fistfuls of my white t-shirt for balance.

"That's fine." Obviously it's fine. We could end the night here and it'd still be the best night of my goddamn life. "But I seem to recall you mentioning my Hollywood chin."

Allegra laughs, startled. "You can't really want that."

I tap the top of my chest. "Get up here."

Her messy bun is lopsided, escaped locks of hair hanging past her shoulders, and Allegra's icy blue eyes are bright. As she crawls slowly up my body, I've never seen the mafia princess look so rumpled—or so beautiful.

Her knees sink into the mattress on either side of my neck. She's still in her lilac panties and tank top, but that's okay. One step at a time.

I force myself to meet her gaze and not stare like a starving man at the damp patch on her panties.

"This feels weird." Allegra grabs the headboard for balance, shifting forward to bring the juncture of her thighs above my face. "What if you suffocate down there?"

"Then I was weak."

I lick her through the fabric first. Mouth at her through the layer of her panties, because this must be a lot to process. And as Allegra's breathing changes high above me, turning from steady breaths to quick, shallow gasps, I stroke two palms up the back of her thighs and squeeze her ass.

"This is—I'm gonna take your glasses off."

I hum against her body, slipping both hands under her underwear. Her ass is soft and smooth, a perfect handful on each side, and I grip her harder as she slides the frames off my face. They're set on the nightstand with a soft clack.

I've always felt lost without my glasses. Half-blind and vulnerable as hell, but here with Allegra, I don't feel that automatic pinch of fear. I'm too busy yanking her panties aside and running my tongue up her seam.

"Oh!" She bucks, knocking me back into the pillow. "Oh my god, I'm so sorry—"

I growl, tugging her ass until she follows me down.

Sweet. Salty. She's slick and wet and perfect. Allegra is everything I've been dreaming of, everything I'd barely let myself imagine, and if I'm ever on death row, this will be my last meal.

She's just so fucking responsive, gasping and twitching with every lick, every nibble, and when I suck on her clit—

She *howls.*

My hips twitch up, humping the air.

Never want this to stop. Even as my tongue and jaw start to ache, even as my face flushes hot, I want to drag this out all night. I'm so hard that there's a stabbing pain in my stomach, but I don't care. Don't care.

Allegra whines, grinding down against my face, and this is what triumph feels like. I'm on top of the fucking planet. I've never been power hungry like most men in the underworld, but as Allegra yanks on my hair and lets out a rough moan, I'd lay waste to whole cities if it meant hearing that sound again.

"Raul." Love the way she says my name, so desperate and pleading. "Oh my god, Raul. *Please.*"

Alright.

Sliding one hand from her ass, down between her legs, I stroke a fingertip around her entrance. Allegra's thighs are sweat-damp and trembling on either side of my face as I breach her, pushing a finger slowly inside.

"Oh," she says, scrabbling for a better grip on the headboard. I stroke her inner walls, crooking my finger. "*Oh.*"

"You're going to come for me." My words are muffled, but I know she hears them. "You're going to come on my face, Allegra De Rossi, and you're going to stake your claim."

Her breath catches, and I suck on her clit.

Allegra stiffens above me, muscles shuddering.

On and on and on, I lick her. Driving her to new heights, then drawing out her pleasure. She twitches and moans; she cries out, her whole body flushing hot. Moisture floods my tongue, and I keep licking.

I keep going even when she slumps, too greedy to stop until she flops off me and collapses by my side.

"Have mercy, doc. Oh my god. That was…"

I wipe my chin, grabbing my glasses so I can gauge her reaction properly. "Yeah?"

"Yeah." Her icy blue eyes catch on the painful tent in my pajama pants, and Allegra smirks. "My turn?"

Jesus.

My heart's already thundering at a hundred miles an hour—and it's her first time. No need to rush. My mouth twists, mind racing, then I push onto my knees with a groan. "Let me just…" I kneel above her, flipping her tank top over her tits. Her perfect, pert tits. God. "May I?"

Those nipples are hard as two bullets, pointing at the ceiling, and when Allegra nods, I can barely shove my waistband down fast enough.

"This is probably degrading," she muses, wiggling to stretch out beneath me in a comfy long line.

I wince, gripping my shaft hard. "Do you feel degraded?"

"No." She tilts her head, and her smile up at me is almost sweet. "I feel... worshiped."

"You are." I grit my teeth, twisting my fist around the head, stomach heaving with each breath. "Fuck, Allegra. You are."

The mafia princess hums, happy as a kitten, and traces a single, teasing fingernail up my thigh. I choke out a low curse, curling over my fist, and jerk myself once, twice, three times— then paint the smooth, olive skin of her stomach.

"Sure hope you last longer when we finally fuck."

I shake my head, biting back a laugh. "Don't."

"Well, *you* can clean me up."

"Allegra." We're bickering again, teasing each other like we always do, but it's different tonight. Softer; filled with hope. And when I shrug off my t-shirt to wipe down her stomach, her wolf whistle makes me grin.

I trail kisses across both hips, then up to her nipples.

I'm going to kiss every inch of her. *This* will be my life's great work.

...Provided her brother lets me live.

Allegra

⚜

Diego answers the phone with a grunt. "What."

"Charming." I speak in a whisper, tip-toeing down the safe house stairs. Dr Raul Ossani is asleep in my bed, the worry lines all smoothed out from his forehead, and I don't want to wake him. "Did no one ever teach you how to answer a phone?"

My brother's right hand man huffs, and I can picture the exact way he'd glower at me right now, scratching his beard with one meaty, scarred hand. "Sorry, princess. What can I do for you at," he pauses, "two in the morning?"

Oops.

"Sorry. I know you need your beauty sleep."

"Allegra."

"How's Santo?" It's definitely pathetic, but I want an update on my big brother. He works so hard, and he never truly lets his guard down around anyone except me. I'm worried about what that means for his stress levels in my absence.

"You know I won't report on him." Diego sounds bored.

"I'm not asking you to spy on him, asshole. I don't care about work stuff. Just—how's *he* doing, you know? Is he sleeping?"

"I'll have to check my nanny cam."

Ugh. "Diego. If you can't answer one single goddamn question—"

"He's fine, Allegra." The mobster sounds irritated, and in the background, I hear the thump of a glass on a table. Oh, I *knew* I didn't wake him up. "What do you want me to say? Santo's the only one without a hit on him, so yeah, he's fine. Nico and I are good, by the way. Your friends with actual targets on their backs. Thanks for asking."

There's a long pause.

"Allegra?"

My lips are numb.

"Allegra. Come on, you knew that." Diego's words have an edge of desperation—like if he wants it enough, it'll be true.

"Who else?" When he doesn't reply right away, I drag one hand down my face, warping my features. A glance around me shows that apparently, I've found my way to the shadowed safe house kitchen. "Who got hits put on them, Diego? I want the full list."

His words are resigned. "You, Raul, Nico, me, and Leah."

"I... who the fuck is Leah?"

"Nico's wife."

I slump against the refrigerator, ears ringing. "Nico has a *wife*?"

"Yeah, but we think that her name on the list was a mistake. Nico was hanging around her bookshop everyday, and she got caught in the crossfire."

Who. Cares.

"So let me get this straight. You bitches all lied to me,

126

shipping me off to a safe house while the rest of you stayed home. Like I can't handle myself. Like you can't trust the stupid little woman to handle a hit."

"No, it wasn't like that—"

"And while I was gone," I continue, volume climbing with my rant. Because who cares about stupid Raul's stupid worry lines? He deserves them, the rat. "Nico got married without a single word, never mind that I've known him my whole life. Never mind that you just called us all *friends*."

Diego blows out a short breath. "Okay, so when you put it like that, it doesn't sound good. But we had orders, Allegra."

Orders.

Yeah.

I crouch down on the kitchen tiles, woozy with despair, replaying the last week in my mind. Replaying my whole freaking life.

Because these men that I call my friends, that I consider to be my chosen family, they will always, *always* choose my brother over me. And Raul...

I lurch to my feet, hanging up on Diego mid-sentence.

The doctor is the worst of them all.

* * *

Raul jogs out of the safe house in pajama pants and his white t-shirt, his dark blond hair rumpled and his eyes wide behind his glasses. He throws open the passenger door, stalling my getaway.

The headlights are ghostly, lighting up the garage door and the basketball hoop. So long, suburbia. See you never.

"Allegra? What the hell?"

"Hello, liar." I throw the car in reverse, giving Raul a rigid smile. "I just got off the phone to Diego."

The doctor's shoulders slump. "I can explain."

"Can you?" I gun the engine, peeling back down the driveway, and Raul curses before throwing himself in the passenger seat. The door thumps closed behind him. "Oh, good. That will pass the time."

"All our shit is in that safe house." The car lurches over the corner of the lawn as I spin us out onto the street in a screech of tires. The doctor winces. "And we're supposed to be discreet."

I suck on my teeth as we roar forward, loud enough to wake the neighbors. "Well, I know how committed you are to discretion, Dr Ossani."

I'm so pissed at this man I can barely think, and if I didn't know there was a hit out on him too, you'd better believe he'd be walking home barefoot. As it is, I want him safe behind these bulletproof windows—but silent. No, I don't want to hear a damn peep out of him.

But I'm quickly learning I don't get what I want.

"I told Santo yesterday that we needed to give you all the information. I told him I was going to tell you everything today, orders or no orders."

"How noble." I flick the heaters on full, then dial the temperature way down. I'm angry enough to steam over the windows. "But tell me, Raul: why should I believe a word you say?"

The leather seat creaks as he turns to me, reaching out to stroke my cheek. "Sweetheart—"

I smack his hand away. Trying to drive here, asshole.

"I bet you all had such a good laugh about it." My voice

is hollow, my stomach aching, and I don't know if I even believe these words, only that they keep spewing out of me like toxic waste. Poisoning the air in the car and everything that's happened between us. "Did Santo tell you to fuck me to keep me there?"

"Allegra, no." Raul sounds shocked, like I'm out of line for even thinking such a thing. Ugh. "He warned me to keep away from you. Come on, you know your brother would never do that. *I'd* never do that."

"I don't know either of you." The highway is empty, tarmac whipping beneath the car. My fingers ache from clenching the steering wheel. "Not really."

The doctor stifles a groan.

"It was my idea—taking you away to the safe house. Okay?" Raul leans close as he talks, one palm spread over the dashboard. "I know you can take care of yourself, and I know it was shitty, but I panicked. Couldn't stand the thought of anything happening to you, and all I could think of was getting you safe. So now you know everything, okay, Allegra? It's all out in the open."

Ha!

"Well, that's alright then." My foot shoves the pedal harder against the floor, the engine roaring as lights whip past on both sides. "You got caught out and confessed the final detail. That totally counts."

"Allegra." Moonlight washes over Raul's spread hand. Those fingers have saved lives—and made me come so hard my brain short-circuited. I hate that. "Please."

Nope. Even if I wanted to be reasonable right now—which I definitely do not—there's a tight ball of hurt in my chest, and it's throbbing. Hurts every time I breathe. I can't *think* like this.

"We're going back to the compound. I'm going to pack a bag, and you're going to let me, and I'm getting far, far away from you assholes, hit or no hit. And if you or Santo or one of his other lackeys tries to hold me there, I'll carve you up. Understood?"

Raul tips his head back against the seat, misery etched on his handsome face. "Understood."

Good. That's settled, then.

I flex my aching fingers against the steering wheel, and my palms are damp.

* * *

Santo is waiting for us when we roar up his driveway, arms folded as he stands at the top of the stone steps. The night sky is thick with dark clouds, and the only lights on the grounds are the electric ones in the bushes. I jerk the car, parking as messily as I possibly can, and hop out with one wheel teetering on the first step.

"Lovely," Santo calls, irritation snapping through his words. "How mature, Allegra."

God, I hate my brother sometimes.

Raul piles out of the car behind me, still barefoot in his pajama pants and white t-shirt, and the mob boss raises an eyebrow at the state of us. Don't know why he'd be so surprised—as if I'd let that rat bastard shower and change before driving us home.

"Allegra," Santo begins, winding up for a lecture, but I march past him. What's he going to do? Have me sent away against my will? So original. "*Allegra.*"

My big brother falls into step beside me, icy blue eyes checking me with equal parts anger and concern. "You are behaving like a child."

Am I? Sure, I'm huffing with every breath, and I'm so pissed off I can barely speak, but beneath the mood, I don't think I'm actually out of line.

Just in case, I force my shoulders away from my ears and speak politely. "I'm going away for a while."

"No," Santo says immediately, and my temper flares back up like he just poured a liter of gasoline on the fire.

"I'm not asking permission, asshole."

"You're still not going. It's not safe."

I wheel around in the center of the mansion lobby, throwing up my arms. Our words bounce off the tiles and up to the ornate ceilings, and I'm so tired and pissed off and sad.

"It's not safe for me *here*. Don't you get that?" My cheeks are wet, and I swipe at my face, annoyed. Behind us, a small crowd shuffles into the lobby, their eyes wide. There's Nico with a dark haired woman tucked under his arm; Diego and an exhausted Raul. A butler and a damn maid.

No privacy in this place. Never any space to fall apart.

"That's why I sent you to that safe house—"

"No, I mean it's not safe here with *you*. Or with…" I can't say Raul's name, my throat suddenly tight, but we all hear it. The doctor's name, weighing down my tongue.

Santo has turned to stone, his face wiped clean of any expression. I've hurt him, then. It's an olympic feat, but I can't even be glad about it.

I inch closer, lowering my voice so only my brother can hear. "You two, and even Nico and Diego… you break my heart when you pull shit like this. When you close ranks and

131

leave me on the outside. So how is a broken heart safe, Santo? How is that better than a price on my head? Nico and Diego are supposed to be my friends, and you're supposed to be my brother, and Raul—"

I cut off, and take two slow breaths. My eyes are blurry, my words coming out in a horrible croak. "This feels worse than any stab wound, Santo."

The mob boss scrubs one hand down his face, then glances over my shoulder. His eyes narrow at the crowd, and the word slices through the quiet lobby. "*Leave.*"

Hurried steps rush across the tiles.

"If you really want to go," he says slowly, "we'll make arrangements together. Not," he adds, one eyebrow raising when I start to argue, "because I want to control where you go. But it will be safer if you use my resources. You are still a De Rossi, Allegra."

Oh. My shoulders slump, and I'm dizzy with relief as I gaze at my cold, calm older brother. He's normally so unruffled, so impossible to bother, but right now his eyes are oddly bright.

"Thank you," I whisper.

A muscle leaps in Santo's jaw. He nods.

And there's a dull sense of peace as he leads me back outside to where the others are waiting on the stone steps. Nico presses a kiss to the strange woman's hair; Diego stares unblinking at the maid bustling past, her light blonde bob ruffled by the breeze. And the doctor... Raul watches me as we approach. The doctor stares like no one else in the whole world exists.

"Allegra." There's no sound when he says my name, but I see his lips move. My stomach gives a pathetic flop.

I look away.

132

"I need one of you to bring a new vehicle around." Santo scowls at the over-heated mess I left half on his steps, engine still ticking as it cools. "One that will bear Allegra's terrible driving. And," he whistles to the maid where she's ducking through the mansion doorway. She hurries back to our group, hands clasped in front of her plain black uniform dress. "My sister will need help to pack."

The maid nods and bobs a curtsy, but I'm not looking at her. I'm biting my lip as Raul sniffs and stares out at the grounds. He's got that empty, thousand-yard look in his eye, despair etched in the lines on his forehead.

My chest aches. I want to go to him so badly.

Why did I make such a scene?

"Say your goodbyes," Santo mutters, then strides away.

The night air is cold, nipped with frost, and our breaths freeze in chalky plumes in front of our mouths.

"It won't be forever," I say weakly, the doubt creeping in fast now. Raul looks hollowed out, the doctor's mouth pressed in a firm line as he frowns at the shadows. Does he think I don't want him? Surely he knows I want *him*, just not the lies?

Have I overreacted? Wallowed in my hurt feelings and taken things too far?

I *am* my brother's sister, after all. The De Rossi family is known for our dramatics, and our Thanksgiving dinners are non-stop fireworks.

But… perhaps I don't want that anymore. Perhaps I want something steadier; steady as a doctor's hands. I clear my throat.

"On second thoughts…" I begin, but a loud crack rents the air. There are several loud pops, and the stone tiles rush toward my face. A heavy body covers mine, squishing my torso into the ground, and there are screams. Yells. The screech of tires.

My cheek grinds against the frozen stone, and I'm stiff with shock. The body on top of mine is heavy, squeezing the air from my lungs, and I jab an elbow between its ribs.

"Raul?" I wheeze, calling out as loud as I can. "Raul!" Boots thunder past my nose, and there are more gunshots. I grit my teeth, bracing my palms on the tiles.

It takes all of my reedy strength, but I shove my human shield off to one side, grunting with the effort. Beside me, Nico has flattened his wife to the ground and kneels over her, gun jerking in his hand as he fires into the shadows. A few feet away, Diego kneels in front of the white-faced maid, blocking her with his body and speaking quickly into his phone as he draws a knife from his boot.

"Raul!"

He's behind me, sprawled on his back, staring glassy-eyed at the clouds, breathing hard. Blood soaks his shoulder, the dark, sticky fluid seeping through his white t-shirt.

"Help me!" I screech, and Diego's already here, slinging the doctor over his shoulder in a fireman's hold. He strides inside the mansion, the maid's wrist gripped in one meaty hand, and I follow them all, bile rising in my throat.

The world tilts as the door slams shut, and everything is sickly and wrong.

Raul.

Raul

It's not the first time I've been shot, and it won't be the last. Call it an occupational hazard. Everyone else in this mansion understands that, with Diego ducking out immediately to go after the attacker, but from the way Allegra keeps pacing by my bedside, you'd think I was an innocent office worker caught in a crossfire.

"How did this happen? You said the grounds were secure!" She tugs at her wild dark hair, my blood staining the front of her sweatshirt as she paces up and down. Up and down.

No one else speaks to Santo like that and lives to tell the tale, but the mob boss sucks his teeth and ignores his baby sister. He's in an armchair near my bedside, on the phone to security with one hand, the other holding a bandage against my wound.

"Keep the pressure," I force out, teeth gritted from pain.

Santo presses harder.

For all De Rossi's threats to bury me alive, I can't help but notice that he doesn't seem to want me dead. He's already summoned another doctor; already ruined his silk waistcoat with my blood.

Apparently the mob boss *cares.*

"I'm fine, Allegra. It didn't hit bone."

"Didn't hit *bone—*" she cuts herself off, shaking her head and pacing faster. If she keeps on like this, she'll wear through the floorboards and drop to the room below.

"It's alright. Really. No worse than Nico's stab wound a few weeks ago."

"Well, I don't care about Nico!"

"Charming." The man in question shoves through the doorway, shooting Allegra a sour look, but he's not really offended. We all know what she meant.

At least, I *hope* we all know. If I'm reading this wrong again, I'll put my head through a wall. When I thought I'd lost her for a moment back there...

"You're fine, Falasca." Allegra flaps a hand at the mobster, baring sparing him a glance. "And you got married without telling us. You can jump off a bridge for all I care."

You know, I don't think that's true. The De Rossis both like to pretend they're above sticky things like *feelings*, but who's hovering over me, pale with worry right now? Santo and Allegra, that's who.

"The other doctor is on his way." Santo's hand presses against my wound, steady and strong, as he tries to calm his sister. "And they've neutralized the threat. It's nearly over, Alle. You can wait in your room if you prefer."

She sucks in a deep breath, hands balling into fists. "I am *not* leaving him!"

Despite the pain, I fight a smile.

"He's fine." Santo jerks his chin in my direction. "Do you

136

see that smug expression? This asshole is fine."

Two matching pairs of icy blue eyes bore into me.

I raise my good hand in surrender. "I'm just glad she cares."

Allegra huffs, while Santo's nose wrinkles in distaste.

"Don't get any ideas," she snips out, marching to the doorway. "I have plenty of better places to be, Raul Ossani."

* * *

Exactly three minutes pass before Allegra storms back inside. "Not. A. Word," she warns, throwing herself down on the edge of my bed.

I nod, stark relief and amusement warring in my chest. For a second there, I thought she'd really gone, and who could blame her? Allegra was right to be furious. Right to call us all out on our bullshit—especially me.

I'll never strain our connection like that again.

"You will be fine," the doctor says as he prods at my shoulder. "The bullet did not hit bone, and it came out clean. Someone must help me, though, while I stitch."

"I'll do it," Allegra says quickly, scrambling into my lap. Santo curses under his breath and leaves the room, Nico swift on his heels. "Tell me what to do."

The old man hands her a pair of scissors. "Cut off his shirt. I need to clean the wound."

Allegra frowns, breathing steadily as she snips a careful line up the center of my torso.

"I had a dream like this once," I offer, trying to distract myself from the burning pain in my shoulder. "No old man next to us, though."

"Shut up, Raul."

"And you weren't half a breath away from leaving."

Allegra's face crumples, and she keeps snipping. "I'm sorry," she whispers, and I jerk back, head bumping against the wall.

"Why on earth are *you* sorry?"

"I would never have really gone. Not for long, anyway." The mafia princess looks miserable, and her face only falls more when she peels off my ruined t-shirt and gets a proper look at my wound. "If I hadn't thrown such a tantrum—if we'd only stayed at that stupid safe house—"

"Hey." I grip her thigh, squeezing as the old man tips alcohol over the wound. It stings like a motherfucker, so I focus on the glacial pool of Allegra's eyes. They're brimming with tears, but so beautiful. I could look at them forever, and I don't think that's delirium talking. "You didn't mean for any of this to happen. It's not your fault, sweetheart, and with those hits out, it was only a matter of time."

"But you're *hurt*." The word scrapes out of her, like she's wounded too. Like my pain is her pain.

I know that feeling.

"It'll heal. And I'll have a new scar to show off."

Allegra smacks my good shoulder, and I bark a surprised laugh. "Only to me, Raul Ossani."

Now that we can agree on. "Only to you."

The needle pricks my shoulder, the pain sharp and hot, but with the warm weight of Allegra on my thighs...

I barely feel it.

* * *

"You need rest." The old doctor stands in the doorway, bundled in his stiff black coat, leather medical bag dangling from one gnarled hand. A signet ring winks on one finger—another sign that he's well used to the underworld. "Tell De Rossi to stop running you all like dogs."

I choke back a laugh. "Yes, signor."

The doctor grunts and shuffles through the doorway.

Allegra chews on her bottom lip, her ass still balanced on my thighs. "I could talk to Santo if you like."

The door clicks shut as I stroke her cheek with my good hand. "I'm not scared of your brother, Allegra."

Do I have a healthy respect for the calculating mob boss? Certainly.

Do I think he'll harm the love of his sister's life? Not, I do not.

Besides, I grew up with Santo. I've bled with him; played cards with him; stitched his wounds; built his empire at his side. Nico and Diego, too. We're a cozy, twisted family.

The bed creaks as we shift, getting more comfortable, neither of us in any rush to move apart. The warmth of Allegra's body on my legs is the sweetest thing I've ever felt, and the room glows with soft lamplight.

"Did you see Diego with that maid?" Allegra whispers, smoothing her fingertips around the edges of my sling. "He looked like a cat with a mouse."

"Or Santo with a plate of cookies."

She snorts, dark hair fluttering against her cheek, and adds: "It's the same way you look at me."

"And how do I look at you, Allegra?"

I can't stop touching her; tracing the shell of her ear, then trailing my fingertips down the side of her neck. She's so velvet-soft. So warm and vibrant, her pulse ticking faster under her skin.

"Like you want me." Allegra wets her bottom lip, squirming closer on my lap. "Like you'd do anything to have me."

I nod. "That's true."

"And like… like I belong to you. Like if I really left, you'd follow me. You'd bring me back."

I lift my good shoulder, because I'm not proud of that fact, exactly. It's not very evolved. But it's true and I'm tired of hiding my feelings; tired of reining myself in. Tired of pretending that the way I crave this woman is normal or healthy or sane.

"Yes. Where you go, I follow. But not to bring you back to Santo, sweetheart. To keep you with *me*."

Allegra blows out a slow breath. "That's messed up."

"Yes. It is."

And if she still wants to leave, now is the time for her to do it: while I'm weakened and injured, trussed up in a sling, less ready to give chase. I couldn't even blame her, but Allegra makes no attempt to leave the bed. Instead she reaches between us, scratching her thumbnail against my bare nipple.

I hiss, hips bucking. The muscles on my torso go rigid, and my heart pounds faster. "Jesus. A single touch from you, Allegra, and I lose my fucking mind."

Her smile is catlike. "Good."

Our first kiss was a long, drawn out torment—an exercise in tortured restraint, swaying together in the light of the Christmas tree. We gave in just the tiniest bit, allowed ourselves the smallest taste of bliss.

This kiss is not about holding back. If that first time was a nibble, this is a feast. It's savage and hungry, all rough hands and the clack of teeth, as we devour each other in the silence.

The bed creaks. We're swapping breaths; nipping lips.

Stifling groans against each other's mouths, and I'm so hard I can't see straight.

Mine.

I nearly lost her. Nearly chased her away by dancing to her brother's tune.

Never again. I'll always be loyal to the De Rossis, but I'm Allegra's man now, down to the pit of my soul.

More than anything, I want to flip us over and cover her body with mine; to grind down against her and part her soft thighs. But this goddamn sling keeps me in check, and when Allegra wriggles forward, lining herself up with the hard shaft under my clothes, I screw my eyes shut and breathe out hard.

"Glasses on or off?" She's pinching the frames, hips rolling over my lap, watching me with wry satisfaction.

"On." I want to see her this time. Want to watch her lips part and her cheeks flush.

Allegra hums and leaves the frames perched on my nose, then strokes her palms down my heaving chest. "Agreed. I always liked your professor vibe."

The mattress creaks and teeters when she stands high above me on the bed, rolling down her leggings and panties and kicking off the tangle of her shoes and clothes in one go. They thump against the rug, and when she settles over my lap once again, sweatshirt pooling around her, there's only a single layer of fabric between us.

Fuck, I can *feel* her. The damp heat sears through my pants.

"If it hurts, tell me and we'll stop," Allegra says, pulling my waistband down.

I shift to help her free my rigid cock, my shoulder burning. "That's my line. Wait—" I catch her wrist as she lines us up, rising over where I'm leaned against the headboard. "I need

141

to get you ready first."

Because there is no way on this earth that I'm going to push in there without preparation; without making sure that my girl is slick and ready, her body aching with the need to be filled. I want her addicted to me, damn it. I want her to wake me up in the middle of the night because she can't wait until morning, slinging her leg over my hips.

Can't do that by barging in unprepared.

"I'm sure it will be... *oh*." Allegra's head tips back, eyelashes fluttering. She bites down on her lip as I stroke through her folds. Truthfully, she's already slick and warm, her body rolling eagerly against my palm, and as I press two fingers inside her, they slide in easily. Pumping in and out, I watch my fingers glisten in the lamplight.

A slender hand wraps around my cock.

I curse and circle her clit.

Everything with this woman is a competition. She's fierce and demanding; a force of nature. A lightning storm in human form. So I shouldn't be surprised that as I coax her body higher and higher, she twists her hand around my shaft; I shouldn't be shocked by the defiant spark in her eye.

Across the room, the door swings open, Santo already mid-sentence as he strides inside. The mob boss breaks off, cursing viciously, and as he leaves, he slams the door hard enough to shake the paintings on the walls.

"I told him he'd learn to knock," Allegra murmurs, completely unfazed as she rocks against my hand. I've gone rigid on the bed, a slideshow of possible gruesome deaths flashing before my eyes, but the teasing circle of her thumb over my cock-head brings me back.

"You're worth it," I tell her raggedly, drawing out my fingers and lining us up once again. "Whatever torture he dreams up for me, this was worth it."

"That's the spirit."

Allegra sinks down on me with a relieved sigh.

Allegra

There's always so much fuss made about sex, always so many people losing their damn minds over the act, that I always figured there was no way it could live up to the hype. Must be hormones or whatever, I thought, addling people's brains.

Well, consider me addled.

"Raul," I whisper, twisting my hips and working him deeper, my fingernails sunk into his good shoulder. My other hand scrabbles at the headboard, nails scratching over carved wood. "I… *god.*"

I've never been this close to another human being—and he's only halfway in. But I can feel the steady tick of his heartbeat through his shaft; can feel his life force thrumming inside my body. Holy shit.

Nearly lost him. Nearly ranted and raved, then lost my doctor forever.

I swear on my life, I will never pull something like that again. Next time I throw a tantrum, I'm taking Raul *with* me, not leaving him behind, even if he's gagged and slung in the car trunk.

When I tell him that, the doctor rumbles a laugh. "You couldn't lift me into a trunk, sweetheart."

"But you'd climb in if I asked you nicely."

"Probably."

As I sink down another inch or two, my eyelids flutter.

I want him closer. Want us sealed together so tight, there's no air between us; want us to blend together into one sweaty, gasping mess. Every time my hips rise and fall over his lap, delicious friction sparks between my legs, the pleasure thrumming up my spine.

Raul grips my ass with his uninjured hand, squeezing and kneading the flesh. Urging me on.

"Come on, Allegra. I know you're meaner than this."

My nails sink deeper into his shoulder, and the doctor lets out an approving hiss. He wants it harder? I can do that.

I may be the smallest of our inner circle, may not have Diego's bulk or Nico's strong arms, but I've grown up slamming trainers into crash mats, and there's power coiled in my slender frame. I grab a handful of dark blond hair and twist, then throw my ass down and take the last few inches of his cock inside.

The doctor grunts. His eyes are hazy behind their lenses, his cheeks flushed.

God, I love him so much.

"You're all rumpled," I murmur, riding him hard now, the headboard slamming into the wall. Santo's gonna kill us both for making this racket, but right now I don't care. "Your glasses are steaming over, Dr Ossani."

I want to ask how his shoulder is, to fuss over his wound,

but I bite the words back. He'll tell me if I take this too far.

We need to trust each other. We *do* trust each other when it counts the most.

Raul's palm cracks against my ass and I snarl, rolling my hips and fucking him deeper. My thighs burn with the effort, my knees digging into the screaming mattress springs, but all I can do is grit my teeth and keep going.

Feels so. Freaking. Good.

That thick shaft throbbing inside me… the rigid intrusion of Raul Ossani in my body… his hot breath against my cheek and the sting of his hand against my skin…

I whimper.

And I'd never whimper with anybody else. Would never let anyone else see me like this—needy and wild, unraveling on his cock. Desperate, with moisture brimming in my eyes, because I've wanted him for so freaking long.

Never thought it would happen. Thought I'd spend my whole life lonely and unheld.

"You're perfect." Raul's words press against the hot, damp skin of my throat, chased by his teeth against my pulse point. "Fuck, Allegra. Your goddamn body. You're so fucking perfect. When I get this sling off—"

"You'll do whatever you want to me. I'll let you do anything." I'm babbling now, making reckless promises, but if there's one man they're safe with, it's the doctor. "Oh *shit*, Raul. This feels…"

"Yeah." His breath is ragged against my neck. "It does."

"I love you."

The words leave me in a rush, just another strained confession as we rock together, the tension coiling tight, but Raul pauses for half a beat—then thrusts up harder beneath me, bouncing me in his lap.

Now *his* grip is mean, but I don't mind. I like it.

I want Raul Ossani's fingerprints all over my body.

"God, Allegra. Do you have any idea how much I love you?" He pulls my head back by my hair, then licks a stripe up my throat. I shiver. "Do you know how long I've wanted this? I'd fucking die without you. You're the air in the room."

He's good at these declarations. Very poetic.

"You're going to take this cock every day for the rest of your life. You're going to ride me like the queen you are."

"Well, I'd better not *always* do the work."

"Allegra." The doctor pinches my nipple through my sweatshirt, the pain hot and delicious. I gasp, working myself back down on his cock. "Don't fool yourself. I'll bend you over any piece of furniture I like."

And god, that's so messed up, but just the thought of it sends a blast of heat coursing through my body. I'm burning up so hot, there must be smoke rising off my skin.

"You like that." Raul's voice is darkly pleased. "Oh, we're going to enjoy each other, Allegra."

Enjoy each other. Love each other beyond all reason. Tomato, tomahto.

A harsh, breathless kiss seals the deal.

Then I'm rolling my hips, tension twisting in my belly, as Raul reaches between us to pinch my clit. And I freeze, my limbs seizing up as my muscles twitch, and I'm falling, toppling into an abyss.

I fall, and fall, and fall.

"You're beautiful when you come," Raul murmurs.

I close my mouth with a snap. But I'm helpless and groaning, pleasure wracking my body in waves, and as Raul swells and spills inside me, all I can do is let out a ragged wail.

"Good girl." He rubs my clit again and I toss my head back, ears ringing.

When I finally slump against the doctor's chest, I feel like I've run a marathon. Every muscle aches, and every inch of my skin is sweaty.

"Shoulder?" I mumble, my tongue thick in my mouth.

"I'm fine." A palm spreads over my back, stroking steady circles, as Raul presses his mouth against my temple. "Better than fine."

Yeah. Me too. This was the worst day of life, and now I'm floating on cloud nine. Think I aged five years in the space of a few hours, and now I'm so freaking tired.

"Can I sleep here tonight?"

Don't think I could move even if he told me to. I'm already breathing deeper, my eyes drifting closed as I sag against the doctor's muscled frame. Exhausted.

"Sleep here every night," Dr Raul Ossani tells me softly.

Well... if he insists.

I drop off with a smirk on my face.

* * *

Two days later

"There's a security breach." Santo stands at the head of the table, one hand resting on the back of his chair. With the other, he inspects his fingernails, but he's not fooling me. I'm his little sister, and I can see the tension in the mob boss's frame. "Someone is feeding information out of the De Rossi compound."

148

…Oh, shit.

"Who the *fuck*?" Nico asks, throwing himself back in his chair, as Diego snarls under his breath. Alongside Nico, his wife rests a soothing hand on his arm. She's wearing a red Christmas jumper with a snowman on it, her brown hair braided into two bunches, and her expression is worried.

I glance at my brother, waiting for him to accuse the obvious intruder in the room, but his pale eyes skate over Leah like she's already one of us.

Huh. We missed a lot in that safe house, then.

Interesting. I've always wanted more estrogen around here.

"How do you want to handle it?" Raul asks quietly, always the steady presence in the room. Together, he and Santo are like two icebergs, drifting calmly through the frozen wastes. Meanwhile, Nico and Diego are spitting fire.

"We're going to spill all our secrets." Santo's smile is as empty as an ocean trench. Whoever crossed this man has the worst kind of death wish, because he's my flesh and blood and even I'm shuffling further down the table, leaning closer to Raul. Those empty eyes make the hairs on my neck stand on end.

"Strategically," Santo goes on. "One secret in the earshot of each person on the grounds. Nothing truly vital, of course… then we'll see which piece of information gets used against me."

Yeesh.

I chew on the inside of my cheek, trying not to imagine the punishment my brother has in store. As the head of his empire, Santo rewards loyalty with protection and wealth—and punishes betrayal without a flicker of mercy. I stay away from those parts of the business, but I'm not an idiot. I know what goes on.

"We'll find them, boss." Diego leans forward, firelight flickering over the scar in his cheek where it disappears into his dark beard. "And they'll wish they were never born."

"Indeed." Santo finishes inspecting his nails and smooths a palm down his waistcoat. It's purple tonight, hugging his torso and bringing out the glacial blue of his eyes. "This is very boring for me."

I bet. That superhuman brain is happier when it's scouring the black markets for lost artworks, or reading the stock markets like an old mystic with tea leaves. Not digging up a mole in our own backyard.

"You know what would make you feel better?" Leah pipes up, and we all stiffen in our chairs. Santo has barely any patience at the best of times, but right now, he's hanging by a silken thread. His soldiers have been targeted, his castle is under siege, and Nico's strange little woman is talking to him like a buddy? Falasca slings an arm around her shoulders, protective and uneasy.

"What?" the mob boss asks, soft and deadly.

Leah beams. "Wanna play checkers?"

The silence makes my heart stutter. Then—

"Fine." We all blink, shocked into stillness as Santo pinches the bridge of his nose. "Lord knows you won't stop bothering me about it."

Only Leah seems unsurprised. She grins at the mob boss like this was inevitable, like she always knew they'd be best buddies, and god, my brother hasn't played board games since he was ten.

"Baby, maybe we should—" Nico begins.

"Your wife can make her own decisions," Santo snaps.

"Leave us, all of you. Falasca, you can stay, but only if you let her concentrate. I want a decent challenge."

Nico sinks back in his chair, equal parts relieved and confused.

Out in the hallway, Diego strides away, muttering under his breath. Raul takes my hand and leads me past several closed doors, then nudges one open and tugs me into a library. The walls are lined with bookshelves, tall enough to need ladders on special tracks to reach the highest books, but Bookworm Ossani leads me past all that to the balcony, pulling the glass door open.

The night sky is velvet black, glittering with stars, and snowflakes spiral down from the heavens. The grounds are already white, like they've been dusted with icing sugar, and hey. Maybe it'll stick this time.

"Nico's wife is... interesting."

Raul grunts in agreement, tugging me close and tucking my hair behind my ear. He's still wearing that sling, his suit jacket slung over both shoulders with one sleeve hanging empty. Underneath, his shirt is crisp and white.

God, he's sexy. I just want to rub myself all over him like a cat. Maybe I will once his wound has healed better.

The air is so cold, the tip of my nose is going numb. I press it against his throat as I say, "I guess she must be pretty special for Nico to marry her after a week."

Above me, Raul is quiet for a long time. Then: "I'm not waiting because I'm not sure. Is that what you think? I thought you'd want a big wedding with lots of guests and dancing and an orchestra."

My lips press together against a smile. I wasn't hinting, but I'll take this turn of events. "Yeah, I do."

"I *am* going to marry you, though, Allegra. Make no mistake. Once the time is right and we can have the day you always dreamed of, I'm going to make you mine."

"I'm already yours," I say, kissing his neck. "But you know there's this thing called an engagement, right?"

His laugh is breathless. Guess I'm working him up well, sucking bruises along the hollow of his jaw. "I planned to propose soon, but I thought that you'd want to pick your own ring."

Also true. Guess he really knows me.

"Well, in the meantime…" It's the simplest thing to slide the Ossani signet ring off the doctor's finger, and work it onto my own. "Hey, look! It fits."

I waggle my hand in front of Raul's face. His eyes gleam behind their glasses. "Of course it fits. I was meant for you, Allegra."

It's a freezing night, but our kiss warms me down to my toes. Just like the snow outside… we're settled.

III

Holly & The Henchman

Description

❧

I was blackmailed into spying on the kingpin.

Now I'm falling for his right hand man.

I'm a maid, not a secret agent. I don't belong in this world, and I *definitely* have no business snooping around the De Rossi compound. Each day could be my last, and I'll be lucky to make it through Christmas—especially with the way the kingpin's right hand man stares at me.

Because the enforcer is gruff. Brutal. He's scarred and brawny, and he watches me like a hawk. How will I ever survive this with his eyes on me all the time?

And… this is so messed up…

Why don't I want him to look away?

Holly

❧

One month ago

The Governor's office is stately. It's all polished wood, fine leather and the glint of brass, with rows of hardback books on high shelves, their spines never once cracked open since being put on display. An antique globe stands in one corner of the large room, and whenever I dust its surface on my rounds, I hear bottles clink inside.

I hate cleaning in here. This whole room feels… wrong. Like there's bad energy or malevolent spirits or something. I'm not a superstitious girl, but if I were, I'd refuse point blank to clean the Governor's office.

My plain black lace-up shoes sink into the rug. I clear my throat as I approach the desk. "You wanted to see me, sir?"

The Governor glances up from the newspaper spread over the desk, his eyes running down my body from head to toe.

I press my palms against my gray maid's dress, wishing it were baggier. Or floor length. Hell, made of burlap—anything

Holly

to keep those cold eyes off my body.

"Ah." My employer glances at a post-it note curling off the desk near his elbow. "Holly, is it? Yes, take a seat."

The visitor's chair is at least two inches lower than the Governor's own. I sink down onto it, mouth dry, and observe the man across from me.

Salt and pepper hair, artfully arranged to hide the way it's thinning on top, and a tailored three piece suit; expensive cuff links and a sour way of sucking in his cheeks. My employer looks like someone stuffed a bird of prey into fine tailoring. After his meteoric rise, he should be preening, but he's not.

The Governor has taken the political world by storm over the summer, has risen from relative obscurity to sudden power, and yet it's still not enough.

You can tell from the downward slash of his mouth, and the pinch of his graying eyebrows: this is not a man who knows how to be satisfied. 'Enough' is an foreign word to men like Governor Edwards.

I knit my clammy fingers together in my lap. "How can I be of assistance, sir?"

You know, this man may give me the heebie-jeebies, but I barely see him in my day-to-day work. And I *like* this job. When I applied for the maid position, I figured it'd be a stop gap on my way to something better; that it would be boring, horrible work. And okay, it does get dull for the last hour or so of my shift, but mostly it's meditative. A good workout, too. My arms have never been this toned.

Whatever I've done, I really hope I can fix it. Ruthie's relying on me to help make rent.

The Governor's chair creaks as he leans back, tugging open a desk drawer. He addresses its contents, his tone bored. "Your sister Ruth also works for the Edwards family, does she not?"

I nod, lips pressed together. Why is he asking about Ruth? Is he breaking the ice? We don't need to *chat*, he's my employer.

Whatever he wants me to do, he can just come out with it. No need to feign interest.

"Yes, she works as an aide to—"

"My son." Governor Edwards sucks on his teeth, pulling a paper file out of the drawer. He slaps it onto the desk surface and pushes it toward me, crinkling the newspaper beneath. "Take a look, Hannah."

"It's Holly." My fingers shake as I flip the file open.

The Governor grunts, and as a single syllable, it speaks volumes. It says, clear as day: *I don't care about your name, girl.*

That's fine. I'd rather he didn't notice me at all.

Inside the file are several sheets of paper, some scrawled with handwriting, some typed. There are restaurant receipts, a hotel room key, and...

I pinch the photograph between finger and thumb, my chest suddenly tight. Is it me, or is this room stuffy as hell? I can't— can't *breathe*.

"My son's, I believe. Ruth is too far along to change her mind now," the Governor says idly, flicking a speck of lint off his sleeve. "Hides it well, doesn't she?"

The image is black and white, grainy but easy to read. My sister's baby is sucking its thumb in the womb.

"Oh my god." I clatter back in my chair, my body damp with sweat under my uniform. This is—wonderful. Of course. We'll love this baby more than anyone in the whole world. But rents have been climbing higher, and we've already cut back every possible expense, and...

I blink up at the Governor. "Why are *you* showing me this?"

His smile makes my gut twist.

"Your sister Ruth is at a crossroads, Holly." My boss spreads one palm over the file and its contents, the receipts crinkling. "She's rather backed herself into a corner."

Well, it takes two to make a baby, I think furiously, but I swallow the words down and simmer in silence.

I can't make an enemy of this man. He's too powerful, holding all our futures in his gnarled grasp.

He starts tapping one finger on the file, drumming out a slow, agonizing rhythm. I can't look away from his manicured fingertip, not until he says, "Shall I tell you what lies down each fork in the road for your sister?"

I nod stiffly, shaking off wild daydreams of pushing him in front of a speeding car. "Yes, sir."

He clears his throat, settling in like he's telling a bedtime story. *Tap... tap... tap...*

"Down one road, Ruth is welcomed into the Edwards family. My son won't marry her of course—a simple dalliance can't ruin his life—but both child and mother receive full financial support and all the protection of the Edwards name. Things like college tuition and healthcare costs are not concerns that cross your sister's mind. She's free to pursue her own interests and raise her child as she sees fit—within reason, of course."

Within reason.

Right.

"And down the second path?"

Because there are worse things than struggling for money. Don't get me wrong, it sucks like hell, but it might still be a better trade than living under Governor Edwards' thumb forevermore.

Tap... tap... tap...

"Down the second path, Ruth is fired without references, her name dragged through the mud. Charges are brought against her for stealing from the Edwards property. For attempted blackmail, too."

I inhale sharply. "Ruth would *never*—"

"You would also be fired, without references, and left to support both mother and child. With all the extra shifts you'd have to work, I wonder if you would even find the time to visit her in prison?"

I grip the edge of the desk, dizzy with rage.

There's a paperweight in the corner of the table. It looks heavy. Like with enough force, it could dent an old politician's skull.

I *have* been scrubbing a lot lately. Bet I could do it.

"Which fork in the road will Ruth go down? The choice is yours, Holly."

I tear my eyes away from the paperweight and meet the Governor's cold gaze. His eyes are brown, but there's not a speck of warmth to them. It's like peering into a wintry pond. "Mine?"

"This could all end happily for Ruth. Her future depends on your cooperation."

I already scrub this man's toilets. What more can he want from me?

"I'm a maid," I say flatly. "All I do is clean."

"And listen." *Tap... tap... tap...* "I expect you hear things, too. Staff always do. The uniform makes you invisible, you see."

Straightening my back, I force the words between stiff lips. "I am discreet, Governor Edwards. If that is your concern, you needn't have threatened my sister. Whatever I hear or see under this roof is none of my business."

"I agree, of course," the Governor says, frowning slightly at the ultrasound, "but it's not me that I want you to clean for. And I don't want your discretion in this, Holly. I want to hear every sordid detail."

Ugh.

Spying.

He's talking about spying.

On a political opponent? If I get caught, they'll ruin my life just as easily as the man across from me—more easily, in fact, because their accusations will actually be true.

But Ruthie...

"Your opponents come here sometimes." Maybe I can reason my way out of this. "They might recognize me."

The Governor shakes his head, eyes gleaming. "It's not a political colleague I want you to clean for, Holly. Tell me: have you heard of the De Rossi crime family?"

My stomach sinks all the way to the wine cellar.

Of course I've heard of the De Rossis. I haven't been living under a rock.

And now I'm sure: there's no way I'll survive until Christmas.

Diego

ﾟ◦❀◦ﾟ

resent day

She's in the library. Holly. The little blonde maid that started work here last month; the number one suspect on my list of potential moles. God knows where a tiny scrap of a girl like that would find the bravado to spy on Santo De Rossi, but the timing lines up.

I hate that fact.

The library is dim, the ornate sconces casting golden pools of light, and Holly stretches up onto her toes to dust the higher bookshelves. As she reaches up, the hem of her black maid's dress rises up her thighs.

One inch. Maybe two.

Just enough to show an extra strip of soft, secret skin.

Tucked outside on the balcony, swallowed up by shadows, I watch her without blinking. There's a ladder attached to the bookshelves: one of those old-fashioned ones on rails meant to help readers reach the highest tomes, but either she hasn't noticed it, or she doesn't trust it to hold her. Well, Holly can't weigh more than her feather duster, can she? I could lift her in the palm of my hand.

Should I tell her? I could slide the glass doors open and poke my head inside, nodding at the ladder a few feet to her left. Would it scare her to learn I'm so near? I came out here for fresh air and some goddamn silence, but once she came into the library fifteen minutes ago, I should've made myself known. Instead, I moved closer and watched her, my breath fogging the glass.

I'm stupid over this girl. Something about her calls to me— maybe it's her small, slender frame, so delicate and... fuck, so breakable. Or maybe it's the swing of her icy blonde bob when she turns her head, the hair so soft-looking and pretty. Ever since she started working here, I've been walking around with a ball of tension in my gut, and it's not just suspicion.

I've been *wanting* her.

And losing sleep over it, too, tossing and turning every night until I give in and take myself in hand. Picturing her for just a few minutes, in that little maid's uniform or out of it. With or without the apron. Either way.

Inside, Holly grunts softly, straining to reach higher. I inhale, my heart pounding.

I want her to make that sound again. Want it so badly I can't think straight, and I need to be closer so I can hear it properly, nothing between us and no wind in my ears.

Because Holly doesn't *act* like a spy. There's no cunning to her; no calculating gleam in her gaze. The few times I spoke to her already, she flushed bright pink and stammered in response, tripping over her words... but maybe that's all an act. A rehearsed display.

If it *is* an act, it's fucking genius. I'm Santo De Rossi's scarred, brutal enforcer, and I've never been more disarmed than when that girl blinks up at me, lips parting. I want to lay my hands on her alright, but not to hurt her. Not for interrogation.

Only to coax out a certain kind of scream.

Inside the library, she rocks onto one foot, gripping a shelf for balance, straining and stretching to reach higher. Her feather duster quivers. Okay, time to move.

I slide the door open silently, padding across the rug with light steps. People don't expect it, what with the beard and the brawn, but I can move quietly when I want to—and when it comes to Holly, I'm *always* battling the urge to prowl after her in the shadows. Wrestling with my final scraps of nobility, trying not to descend completely into the darkness.

In here, without that pane of glass between us, I can hear everything. Her steady breaths; the rustle of her uniform; the silken slide of her hair against her collar. The creak of the floorboards beneath her shifting weight. She looks so small by those shelves, wobbling on one foot as she reaches up, and when she curses under her breath, I hear that too.

"Need a hand?"

Holly jolts, her feather duster clattering to the floor. She spins around, cheeks red and eyes wide.

"Oh! Mr Cedrone—"

She breaks off as I crouch down to pick up her feather duster. Down here, with my elbows resting on my knees, my face is level with her stomach, the taut planes of her belly pushing against the cotton of her dress with each breath. If I pressed my face against her stomach, would I feel her body heat? Would she let me rub my face on her and breathe her in?

See, it's thoughts like that that make me think I'm losing my grip. I push reluctantly to my feet. "Dusting the shelves?"

Holly pauses before she answers, and it's *this*, shit like this that makes her suspect number one. Why's she gotta think through her answer? It should be an immediate yes, no pause required.

"Um. Yes. But I couldn't reach high enough—"

"There's a ladder."

She follows my nod and blinks, cheeks flushing even brighter. "Oh. Wow, I guess I didn't look properly."

Not very spy-like. That's good. "It's safe if you want to use it."

"Thanks."

We stand there, awkward silence wrapping around us, and I curse myself for ever coming in here. I could've watched her for a while longer, maybe seen another glimpse of hidden thigh, and what do I care if Santo's top bookshelves don't get dusted? No skin off my nose.

Out there in the darkness, I could've looked my fill. Could've stared at Holly until my eyes ran dry, the wind howling all around.

The maid clears her throat, her pulse tapping out a fast rhythm beneath her jaw. "Is there anything I can do for you, Mr Cedrone?"

Oh, there are hundreds of things this girl could do for me, and they all flash before my eyes. Things on her back or on her knees; things with her dress rucked up around her waist. Things that end with my teeth on her throat and my seed spilling out of her, trickling down those creamy thighs.

And other things too, that somehow feel even more shameful. Things like her pressing a soft kiss against my beard,

165

or sitting in my lap for hours and telling me about her day. Smoothing down the creases in my shirt, or teasing me for the dusting of gray at my temples. *Sentimental* things.

Jesus.

"Yeah." I wrench my gaze away from her, feeling trapped. Feeling wild. "Yeah, do me a favor, okay? Don't linger in this room—in fact, don't linger in any room, Holly. Do your job, then get out. Okay? You don't want to draw attention to yourself, do you?"

Because if Holly's the spy... I don't know how I'll handle that. We've barely spoken, and already I think it might break something in me.

Her lips press together and she nods once. She's staring at the floor now, and won't look up, and I can't blame her, what with me barking orders like that. Was that really necessary?

Time to follow my own advice. I turn around and get the hell out of there.

Holly

᭰᭰᭰

He's on to me. De Rossi's enforcer: the man with a ragged scar on his cheek and swollen knuckles on his right hand, like he doled out one too many punches and the bones have never recovered. He knows I'm the spy.

Or he suspects, at least. Because if he knew for sure, I'd already be dead, right? Sinking down to the river bed with cement boots on my feet. But last night in the library, he dismissed me with this glare that saw right down to my soul. That told me he *sees* me, and he's furious about it.

Oh, god. How did I get into this mess?

Ruthie. Screwing my eyes shut, I force myself to picture my sister back at home in our apartment, knitting baby hats and wiping her eyes when she thinks I'm not looking. We have the same blonde hair but hers is longer, always braided to one side. Now that I know about her bump, it's impossible to miss, even with her baggy sweaters.

That's how I got here, and it's why I'll keep leaking information to the Governor. Because what's my alternative? Besides, it's not like these are good people, you know?

They're murderers. Criminals. Hell, the man with the scar, Diego Cedrone—he *oozes* violence. He bristles with it, and I shouldn't feel guilty.

So why do I feel so small and gross? Like a creepy little cockroach, sneaking around the mansion and listening at doors.

They're bad people. Bad people.

Bleurgh.

"Holly, you'll take the east wing today. Leave Dr Ossani's quarters, but clean the rest."

I nod, huddled in the kitchens with the rest of the staff. The head housekeeper keeps talking, doling out tasks, and I focus on breathing slowly, tamping down the constant anxiety that bubbles in my chest these days.

I'm not a good liar. Not a good sneak. Governor Edwards may not realize or care, but he's picked the absolute worst person to blackmail into doing his dirty work. I mean, I didn't even spot that stupid ladder, did I?

Will De Rossi kill me quickly when he finds out I'm the spy? Or will he drag it out and make me suffer? Will his enforcer be the one to do it?

Stainless steel pots and pans glitter on the wall above the huge ovens. I sway in my sensible black shoes, feeling woozy.

It's so hot in here. Must be a kitchen thing, the air always choked with steam and the scent of herbs, because everyone's cheeks are flushed and my hair is damp against the back of my neck. I'll sweat through my maid's uniform soon if they don't hurry this meeting along.

"No opening drawers. No lingering in doorways."

It's the same spiel we get every day now; the same unspoken warning that if we're suspected as the spy, life won't be worth living anymore.

I shift my weight from foot to foot, hands clasped tightly behind my back.

"Mr Cedrone will interview you all today. As soon as he's finished, return immediately to your duties and do not repeat a word that was said."

There's a flurry of nods, everyone wide-eyed and suddenly ashen, never mind the heat.

No one wants to speak to De Rossi's enforcer if they can help it. We all know the stories, all know what he's capable of, but who are we to refuse? I clench my fingers together, my chest so tight with anxiety that it could burst.

The way he stared at me last night in the library…

Cedrone already suspects me, I know it.

* * *

I'm pulled away from the laundry room in the early evening, with barely thirty minutes left of my shift. It's been a long, tense day of waiting for the tap on my shoulder, twisting myself into tighter and tighter knots as I clean, the nerves building the longer I work.

Now I've finally been summoned, and the windows are dark as I hurry along the mansion corridors to the allotted room. Snowflakes spiral past the glass, whipped away on the breeze.

I shiver.

Did he leave me until last on purpose? To make me squirm?

Did anyone else give my name? Do the other staff suspect me?

Oh, god. I'm getting an ulcer, I know I am.

The door creaks as I push it open, heavy wood swinging on its hinges. The room is dark, lit only by a single table lamp, and there are two armchairs facing one another in the center of the floor.

What *is* this room? There are some bookshelves and a drinks cart, plus a dartboard on the wall between two faded oil paintings of fruit, but it seems unused. The air is stale.

The door clicks shut behind me. I jump, spinning around to find Diego Cedrone watching me with those dark eyes.

"Oh." I smooth down my crisp, white apron with trembling fingers. "Hello again."

Cedrone nods at the armchairs. "Take a seat."

He's not a calming presence, not even after a month to get used to him. There's nothing reassuring about this man. With his scars and his beard and the brawny shoulders straining his black shirt, meeting him is like being tossed into a bear enclosure. Even when he throws himself down in the seat opposite mine, gusting out a sigh, there's something tense about him. Something ready to strike.

"Holly."

I nod, the ends of my hair swinging against my cheeks.

"You're new," Cedrone says, scratching his jaw, kicking one ankle up to rest on his knee. He's not reading from any staff file—just watching me from beneath lowered brows, sprawled and powerful. Everyone says that De Rossi's right hand men are all the same age, that they grew up together, but to my eyes, the enforcer looks years older. There are threads of silver at his temples that the others don't have.

Maybe it's hard living. All that violence and blood, adding to the lines around his eyes. Or maybe he doesn't handle stress as well as the others.

I can relate.

"Why did you become a maid, Holly?" he asks.

And even though it's insane, even though I should be tip-toeing around this man, my eyebrow ticks up. "I guess I just love to clean, sir."

I mean, what a question.

His mouth twitches beneath the beard, and for a crazy moment our eyes meet and hold. Sparks crackle through my whole body, simmering in my blood, and I'm clenching my knees together, suddenly breathless.

Why am I sassing the enforcer? Why do I feel so giddy? And why do I want nothing more than to crawl into his lap, settling my weight on those strong thighs? Gah.

Talk about no self preservation instincts. But the thing is, the enforcer and I... we've been orbiting each other for weeks. Always glancing up in time to catch the other's eye, always hyper aware of each other's presence. When he walks into a room, the nerves tingle under my skin—and whenever I meet his gaze head on, a muscle leaps in his bearded jaw.

I *know* him. I feel him on a level that I don't feel other people, and I know he feels me too.

Okay, that sounds nuts. So maybe I am just losing my mind from constant stress.

Cedrone tilts his head, watching me without blinking. In the lamplight, his eyes look almost black, but I know better. When he stared at me in the library last night, I saw the tawny flecks in his eyes and the mahogany rings around his pupils. He's got beautiful eyes—brown but so much warmer than the Governor's.

"You ever heard of Governor Edwards, Holly?"

Speak of the devil. Or think, anyway. I press my damp palms against my apron and say, "Yes. He's famous. Well, famous for a politician, anyway."

All true so far. Cedrone grunts, and the armchair creaks as he gets more comfortable. He's *lazing*, showing off how strong and at ease he is, and it's so messed up that it makes my belly tighten.

Those thighs really are big, even disguised by his fancy clothes. And those *hands*. They're like dinner plates. Is he huge all over?

Oh my god. What is wrong with me?

Here I am getting questioned by a man who'd wring my neck without a second thought, and all I can think is that I'd like to perch on his shoulder like a canary. Must be the nerves, making me hysterical.

"I didn't vote for him," I say. Maybe I can get through this by guiding the conversation, sticking only to the truth. "Governor Edwards gives me the creeps."

"He gives you the creeps through a TV screen?"

Shoot. "Yes?" But I don't sound sure. "Why are you asking about him?"

Do they know already? Am I a dead woman?

Cedrone shrugs, and it's like an earthquake of muscle and bone. Tectonic plates shifting under the fabric of his black button-down, and all I want to do is cling to his bulk and weep.

Because I've been dreading this all day. *Interrogation* is such a horrible word, but it's the one that everyone hissed under their breath in the kitchens. Makes me think of thumbscrews and fingernails being pulled out; groaning bodies hanging from chains in a damp stone basement. Drains in the center of tiled floors.

Does De Rossi have a torture chamber? I would not be surprised.

But Cedrone watches me, his expression neutral. The lamplight makes his tan face look golden, softening his scar, and I catch myself leaning forward like a flower tracking the sun. Desperate for an ounce of this man's warmth, even it means getting singed.

He watches me shifting closer then sighs.

"I don't enjoy this, you know," he says quietly. Almost like he's talking to himself. "I don't enjoy scaring women. Doesn't sit right with me."

"But you enjoy scaring the men?"

Cedrone's gaze is level. "Sometimes."

My mouth twitches, even though what he said really wasn't funny. "I bet you're good at it."

"You bet right. You see this?" He taps the ragged scar on his cheek. Jeez, the blade must've come so close to his eye. "Looking like an ugly motherfucker comes in handy sometimes. It's easy for people to believe I'm an animal, Holly, and they're right to think that. They know instinctively what I'm capable of."

My tongue gets stuck in my throat as I swallow. He's threatening me. Why does that hurt so badly? I cough, then say: "I don't think you're ugly. Mean-looking, maybe, but not ugly."

Cedrone huffs and leans back.

And what am I doing, trying to butter up the mobster? Sure, I meant every word, but that won't save me now. The truth is my only hope.

Selective truths.

173

"I'd have to be the biggest fool alive to spy on Mr De Rossi," I tell him, cutting to the chase as I crinkle my maid dress in damp fists. Cedrone can see that I'm nervous, but who cares? Only an idiot wouldn't be scared of this man. "I can't think of a worse idea. If I did that and got caught, I'd deserve everything that was coming to me—and I'd hate every second. I'd be the worst mole ever."

The enforcer grunts, watching me closely. Trying to sniff out the tiniest lie, but he won't find one here.

I push on, desperation making me chatty.

"One time, when we were teenagers, everyone in the neighborhood threw a surprise party for my sister Ruth, but they didn't tell me even though I'd have helped them out with it. Baked her a cake and found a good location and all that. I'd have been super helpful, but they knew I can't lie to save my life."

"Never?" the enforcer asks, dark eyes gleaming in the lamplight.

"Nope." Lord help me, it's true.

"Then tell me something, Holly. Are you afraid of me?"

Uh, *duh*. Diego Cedrone is a brutal mafia enforcer with blood on his hands. He could pick his teeth with my bones, and we both know it. There is only one correct answer here, but somehow, those aren't the words that come out.

"S-sometimes," I say.

If he stares at me any harder, he'll forget how to blink. "Only sometimes?"

"Um. Yes. Like—like right now, when you're questioning me and threatening me and scowling like that… yes. You're obviously very scary. I'm not an idiot. But other times…" I chew on my bottom lip, my belly squirming with nerves.

174

"Other times you seem… nice."

"Nice," Cedrone repeats flatly. Does he always fill the room like this? Does he always take up all the air?

"Safe," I say. "Like last night, when you helped me with the ladder. The other men here, I keep my distance and try to avoid their eyes. But with you, it's different, and I have this daydream of us where we're—"

Aaah!

I break off, face hot with embarrassment, and make a mental note to drown myself in whatever cheap alcohol I can find the second I get home to Ruth. *If* I get home.

I've been stressed for too long. I've finally snapped.

And it's this stale, warm room, and the overwhelming presence of this man. His spicy scent and the constant threat of death. It's all short-circuiting my brain and making me hazy, too ready to blurt out my secrets; too ready to do anything he says.

I can't believe I said that.

"Tell me," Cedrone commands, and his chair groans as he shoves to his feet. The enforcer prowls to the far corner of the room, raking a hand through his dark hair, then strides back. He stops right in front of me, looming over me with his face in shadow. "Finish your sentence, Holly."

His voice is so deep. I can *feel* it rumbling through me.

"I'm… we're…"

Am I really going to do this? Really going to blurt out my pathetic daydreams to my lethal crush? It's so humiliating, so desperate, and yet a tiny, mercenary voice in my brain whispers that maybe this confession will mean that when the time comes, my death will be quick. And isn't it better to talk about *this* than about the mole?

It's not like I'm lying. I really do think about this sometimes, especially when I'm bored dusting all the sculptures.

"Holly, I am not a patient man."

No kidding. The enforcer's practically vibrating with tension, a tendon standing taut in his neck. My shoulders ache from peering up at him.

"It's this daydream where... it's dumb." I shake my head, and god, even if this story saves my life, I can't confess it. "Please don't make me say this."

Cedrone's knees crack as he crouches in front of my chair, gripping both arms. The lamplight washes over his face again, and I can see his eyes. The tawny flecks; the warm mahogany rings. He's sort of beautiful once you look past the scars.

"Tell me," he orders, voice gruff.

Gah.

"We're in your suite," I say in a rush, like if I get this out quickly, it'll be less embarrassing. I'd prefer the thumbscrews at this point. "Out on the big stone balcony. You've dragged the leather armchair out there, and we're sitting in it together, covered in blankets and watching the snow fall. Feeling it melt against our cheeks."

Cedrone shakes his head slightly. He looks baffled. "You daydream about that? Sitting in a chair with me?"

"Sitting *on* you in a chair. With your arms around me, and—"

I cut off, because I *really* can't say the rest. The other things I imagine.

The enforcer's hard chest behind me, heaving with ragged breaths as he pulls the blankets aside. His scarred hand with its swollen knuckles, delving into the layers of fabric, seeking out my bare skin. His deep voice rumbling in my ear, his hot breath against my throat, saying: *"Is this all for me?"*

The room is pin-drop silent. I can hear the rush of blood through my own veins.

"And?" the mobster urges.

"And that's all! Just you and me. In that chair." My stomach hurts from all these nerves, and I've creased this apron beyond all hope of rescue. "I told you it was dumb, Mr Cedrone."

"Diego," he mutters, pushing to his feet. The room seems colder when he walks away. He scrubs a hand over his bearded jaw, watching me from beneath those thick eyebrows, and the pause stretches on until I've forgotten how to breathe. Then: "Run along now, Holly. And if you see anyone acting strangely…"

"I'll tell you, I swear."

So I'd better not look in any mirrors, I guess. The mobster turns away as I hurry for the door. He doesn't wish me goodnight, and I don't say another word either.

As my feet fly down the corridor, I'm lucky to be alive.

Even if I'm dying of embarrassment.

Diego

ꕥ

"**A**nything?"

The next morning, the boss summons me to his study. It's barely eight, but Santo's clearly been up for hours already, with an empty coffee mug by his elbow and dark shadows under his eyes. Though he's at home in his own mansion with nothing but his own people around, he's still dressed in a crimson waistcoat and shirtsleeves. Does he sleep in evening wear? Does he sleep at all?

"I've narrowed it down," I say.

The balcony door is open, the frosty morning breeze gusting through. It ruffles the papers on the desk and pierces through my clothes, goosebumps rippling across my bare forearms.

Shoving my hands deep in my pockets, I stroll to the bookshelves against the far wall. There are books in almost every room in the De Rossi mansion, and the ones in here are on every possible topic from history and economics to law and botany—though whatever order he's got them in makes sense in Santo's brain and Santo's alone.

"I want names."

Of course he does.

"The Merlotti kid." He's young, barely a foot soldier, but he's developed a taste for gambling. A hobby like that'll go south real fast.

The boss nods, lining up the pens on his desk to perfect parallel lines. "And?"

"Carlotta, the laundry lady? She's got debts. Medical."

Santo's mouth twists, but he says nothing. Stares into the middle distance, waiting for me to go on.

He wants to know if I'll say it—if I'll say Holly's name. Nothing gets past our boss, and he knows that I'm sweet on her; in fact, he doesn't care about the other names at all, because this is a test.

Really wish Santo would stop testing us all the fucking time.

"And Holly," I grind out, hating myself and Santo and even her a little bit. This whole situation is so messed up. "The new maid. She's... slippery. Kept changing the subject when I questioned her."

Changed it to the one topic with the power to distract me. Played me like a beat-up old fiddle. That little picture she painted of the two of us, curled up together in a snowy wonderland? I couldn't sleep last night, I fixated on it so badly.

Not that I'm sour about it.

"Any of them have ties to the Governor?" I ask, because of course Santo will have already thought of this. He's always three steps ahead.

"We're looking into it. It won't take long." The boss rolls his stiff neck, but there's a pleased smile tugging at his mouth. The sort of smile that sets off alarm bells ringing in your head. "And we've leaked different secrets to each staff member.

Held conversations where they could overhear, so one way or another, they'll reveal themselves soon enough. We've got the spy, Diego, I can feel it."

If Santo squeezes that fountain pen any harder, he'll have an ink explosion on his fancy clothes.

"And then what?" I ask, throat dry.

I've never asked that question before. Never much cared about the fate of Santo's enemies, beyond how much it cost me in dry cleaning.

Holly's different. Maybe that was the whole point of her daydream confession, but in any case, it worked. I don't want her in pain.

But… maybe it's not her. Maybe it's Carlotta or the Merlotti boy, and Holly's just a sweet little thing who blushes when I get near. Who crinkles her maid outfit when she gets nervous. Who wants me closer, and who might let me steal a taste.

Fuck. I need to get her alone again.

"Then I'll remind everyone of who I am." The boss's tone is almost pleasant, his hand steady as it draws a file across his desk. "That will be all."

My footsteps to the door are muffled by a thick Turkish rug.

I leave Santo alone in the frozen air. Just how he likes it.

* * *

As evening falls, a few rounds with Nico in the boxing ring get my head on straight. Heavy bags hang from chains all around the edges of the basement, all available for me to pound out my frustrations, but there's nothing like wiping the smirk off Falasca's face to put me in a better mood. By the time we're unwrapping our hands, breathing hard together over by the bench, I'm practically whistling.

"Jesus." Nico prods at his jaw, glaring at me out of the corner of his eye. "I think you knocked a tooth loose."

I shrug, happy as a clam. "Shoulda ducked."

It's been a long day. Hell, a long *month*, and December's only half done. Hit men and spies; shoot outs and rushed weddings. It's like living in a goddamn soap opera around here.

There have been lots of changes lately. I miss simpler times.

Nico's voice bounces off the concrete, even as he speaks quietly. "Santo says he knows. Says he's already sure, but waiting on some final details."

I sniff and take a long drink of water. It's not over until we're one hundred percent sure.

But Nico's watching me, eyes weirdly bright. "He says it's your favorite maid. How about that, huh?"

My grip tightens on the water bottle, denting five finger-prints into the metal. I lower it and swallow. "We don't know until we know."

And suddenly, I don't want to be here anymore. My good mood has fled, and I'm back to sour and stressed and so damn worried about Holly. Will he order me to kill her? How did she get herself in this mess?

Does she hate us? Is that it? Lord knows we've made plenty of enemies over the years; turned plenty of souls against us. Maybe Holly got caught up in old drama, and now she's taking her revenge. It wouldn't be the first time angry ghosts have come back to haunt the De Rossis, and it won't be the last.

"You want me to handle her if Santo's right?" Nico says it lightly, but he's squinting at the far wall. It's a kind offer, such as it is, especially since I just loosened his tooth. He'd go easy on her, that's what he's saying, and he'd spare me the nightmare of doing it myself. Seems that every fucker in this building knows I'm far gone for Holly.

"No." I flex my throbbing fingers. "I'll do it."

Don't want anyone else laying a single finger on her. Don't want them within half a mile of that maid.

Holly

Diego finds me on the top floor of the mansion, pushing a vacuum along the cream carpet of a guest suite in neat rows. Like a farmer tilling her fields or something.

I dunno. Cleaning gets pretty boring.

He watches me from the doorway, dark eyes glittering. I chew on my bottom lip and keep vacuuming, pretending I don't see.

Then: "We're doing this right now." His gruff voice makes my insides fizz to life. "Tonight, okay? Shut that off."

"I'm busy," I say, just to be contrary, but even as the words come out, I toe the vacuum off and turn to face him. As if I could keep away.

The mobster nods at the glass balcony doors. "Will it work up here?"

Um. What?

He huffs at my bemused expression. "The daydream you told me about yesterday. The armchair in the snow. Will it work up here, or does it have to be in my suite?"

I blink at the brawny man in the doorway, my thoughts spinning wild. If I insist it has to be in his rooms, will he take me there? I could see his bed. Take greedy lungfuls of his scent. But what if his suite is off limits and this is my only chance?

"Here's good," I mumble.

Diego marches into the room, crossing my perfectly tilled cream field with agitated steps. He yanks the balcony door open, a gust of wind fluttering the drapes, then casts around for a suitable armchair.

I point at a chintzy number in the corner. One of De Rossi's vintage rescues.

"Will that fit us?"

"It had better," Diego mutters, striding over and lifting it like it weighs less than a bag of sugar. Muscles bulge and flex under his black button-down shirt, the sleeves rolled up to display his corded forearms, and oh god, my face is already on fire.

"Blankets?" he calls from outside, the armchair scraping against the stone balcony. I stumble to the ottoman at the foot of the guest bed.

Is this really happening? I pinch my thigh through my maid's dress.

No, I—I think it is.

Oh wow.

I've dreamed about this scenario before, obviously, but in my dreams, there are fewer... logistics. I just blink and find myself in Diego Cedrone's lap, his hands roaming greedily over my body, and then I dive into kissing him like my life depends on it.

Of course, my life may *actually* depend on it, but that's not a fun thought. I push it away.

Even up here, in a guest suite that barely anyone uses, the blankets inside the ottoman are luxurious. The finest taste. They're dark velvets and pale wools, fuzzy and quilted and sleek, and I plunge my hands into the ottoman, relishing the softness against my bare arms.

"What are you doing?" The low voice comes from behind me and I jump, my breath catching.

"Nothing." I pick the top three blankets, scuttling past him for the door.

There is no way I'm going to tell Diego Cedrone, brutal mafia enforcer, that I am a tactile little princess who likes to rub soft things on her skin. Nuh-uh. Not gonna happen.

But what would his beard feel like against my thighs?

Nope. Doesn't matter.

It's dark already, though it's not even that late, and thick clouds block out the stars. Snowflakes spiral on the breeze, whipped against the mansion walls, and down below us, the lawns and hedge maze are caked in white.

Holiday lights glow from the balcony railing, wrapped around the stone. They're out on the trees in the grounds too, twined around the branches.

It's beautiful. Then I glance over at the enforcer and my heart gives a lurch, because *he's* beautiful. Primal and deadly, yet with something vulnerable about the way he looks at me.

"C'mon." Diego sits in the armchair, grimacing when it creaks, then gets the blankets ready. He pats his thigh. "Before you freeze to death in your little maid's dress."

Yessir.

A thin layer of snow crunches under my shoes as I cross to

185

him, heart pounding like I've run ten miles, not walked three steps.

"Um." It's so awkward climbing onto his lap. We've barely spoken before, have hardly exchanged more than loaded glances, and now I'm putting my whole weight on him? Crawling onto him and trying not to knee him in the family jewels? "Is this—?"

"Yeah." Diego shifts me on his lap. He wraps me up in all three blankets, then cradles me against his chest. "Yeah. This is it, right? Like this."

A bubble of manic laughter crowds up my throat, because how the hell should I know? I've never sat on a man before—unless you count Santa's lap at the mall when I was a little girl.

"Holly? What are you giggling about?"

"Well, you have the beard, I guess," I wheeze, reaching up and petting his furry jaw. "But I can't picture you sliding down a chimney."

The enforcer huffs a laugh. "You're calling me old."

"No, I—"

"You're calling *me* old. De Rossi's vicious henchman; the man with blood on his hands and no soul in his eyes. And now this pesky maid is sassing me, and I oughtta—"

His fingers dig through the blankets, tickling my sides, and I shriek and squirm in his lap, grinning so wide. And I haven't laughed like this in months, haven't felt the knot of terror in my chest ease in so long, and he's perfect.

So perfect. I never imagined he would be like this.

We fall still, both breathing hard, our breath forming white plumes in the night air. Diego's only in his shirtsleeves, and meanwhile here *I* am bundled up like a fleecy burrito. I pluck at his collar. "Are you cold?"

"No. I run hot." His dark eyes bore into mine. "Always have."

Let me test that statement. Diego hisses when my icy fingers slide against his neck, exploring his warm skin, but he doesn't flinch away. If anything, he presses into my touch.

"Believe me yet?"

"Maybe." Biting my lip, I flick his shirt button undone. Then another, and another, and I can't believe my own freaking daring. Apparently spying on a brutal crime family has turned me wild. "Let me try in here."

Diego's big head tips back with a grunt when I slide my hand inside his shirt, smoothing over the muscled planes on his chest. His eyes are half-lidded, watching me, and even in the dark, I can feel the scars on his bare skin.

Chest hair, too. God, he's so *manly*. I squeeze my thighs together and try to level out my breathing.

"You like what you find, Holly?"

I wet my lips. My voice is hoarse. "Yes."

"Well, you can touch me wherever you want, baby. Tonight, this scarred old body is all for you."

Tonight.

Right. I bite my lip and stare at the hollow of his throat. It's dim out here, but we're lit by the string lights and the guest suite and the glow of the snow, and I see his throat bob. My fever's cooling and he knows it. My fire's been banked by a big dose of harsh reality, because tonight is all we have. Tonight is all we'll *ever* have.

Diego's hands tighten on me. One on my waist, one on my thigh, gripping me possessively through the blankets.

"You're not going in yet," he warns, his voice gruff. "You're not running away from me. Don't be scared of me, Holly. Not yet."

No, I'm not scared of him—yet. But I will be soon, won't I? And we both know it, so that's what this is about. This dreamy interlude. These stolen moments together out under the snow, where neither Santo De Rossi nor the Governor nor anyone else can reach us.

How long has he known I'm the spy? Has he already told his boss?

And why am I still alive? Why does he want me at all, knowing what he does?

"You've turned to stone in my lap," Diego mutters. When he speaks, I feel the words rumble through his chest. "Is that all we'll get, then? Ten minutes of teasing, and then it's done?"

I blow out a long breath. And maybe he's asking too much of me, or maybe he's giving me more than I deserve, but I can't tell anymore. Everything's jumbled up. All I know is that I don't want this to be over yet either.

The armchair creaks as I move against him, shuffling around on his hard thighs, rearranging myself so I'm sitting on his legs and facing him head on. His dark eyes gleam as I wind my arms around his neck.

"You don't trust me," I point out. "So why would you come out here with me all alone?"

Diego's grin is slow and warm. It spreads through me like hot toffee sauce. It makes my toes curl in my sensible shoes.

"Holly. I think I can take you."

My laugh is pained. "Jerk."

And then we're meeting in the middle, both lunging forward at the same time, inhaling sharply as our mouths join. *Yes*, my brain goes. *Finally*.

Don't stop. Don't ever stop.

And his hands are in my hair and I'm yanking on his shirt front, and it's so hot and dark and blurry. He tastes like peppermint and brandy, and his beard scrapes against my cheeks, and he really is burning hot.

My heart is so raw.

I'm frowning into our kiss, slanting our mouths together harder, and my world tilts on to its side. I'm surprised the mansion doesn't topple over; surprised trees wrapped in holiday lights don't fly past our balcony.

Surely the earth just moved for everyone. Right?

Diego's tongue swipes along the seam of my mouth, knockin' on the door. I let him in, groaning. Of course I do.

Because this man could ask me for anything tonight, and I'd give it. He could touch the parts of me that no one has ever touched before; he could plunder my body like the merciless criminal he is. I don't care. I want it all.

And as he kisses me back, harsh and desperate, all I can think is: *I'm sorry.* Over and over I think it, with each frantic beat of my heart.

Sorry that I'm lying to him.

Sorry that I'm such a crappy spy.

Sorry that tonight is all we'll have.

And sorry that whatever happens to me, he'll have to be the one to do it. It's nuts, but my heart breaks for him just thinking about that, because hurting me? It will destroy Diego Cedrone. I know it down to my soul.

"Don't come back tomorrow," Diego grates out, pressing whiskery kisses along my throat. "Don't come back, you hear? You stay away where it's safe."

Safe from him, maybe.

But not safe from Governor Edwards, nor from De Rossi. The mob boss won't let me spy on him then quit and Diego knows it, even if he's fooling himself right now. I'm screwed. There's nowhere on this earth that I could run to get far enough away—and besides, what would happen to Ruthie and the baby?

I made a deal with Governor Edwards. My only hope is seeing it through, and maybe, just maybe, he'll take care of her like he promised once I'm gone.

"Holly?" The mobster gives me a little shake, then sucks a bruise on my neck. He's marking me, but I don't care, because if I'm going down tomorrow, I want to be wearing the proof of tonight. A bittersweet memento. "Are you listening to me? You stay away from now on. You don't come back, and you run. Okay? You run far."

I pet his bearded cheek. "Okay," I lie.

His deep sigh is pure relief. And what would it cost him if I did what he said? Would he take my place, drawing De Rossi's rage?

He's such a good man.

Well. With me, anyway.

"It's nice out here, right?" I jerk my chin up at the snowflakes tumbling all around. "I know it was a weird daydream, but it's pretty good when you're in it."

"The best," Diego says, and his throat sounds like it's been scraped raw.

An icy breeze sweeps over our balcony and I shiver, burying my face in his warm throat. His arms wrap around me, holding tight.

One kiss will never be enough, but this is all we have.

And he's right. It's the best.

Diego

The next morning, Santo finds me out on the grounds, doing a lap of the compound through the snow. Usually, I'd leave grunt work like this to the security team, but with prices on all our heads and one gunfight already this month, I'm not taking any chances.

Besides, I can't sit still. Not today.

"I've already doubled up patrols," the boss says, falling into step by my side. He's wearing a long, dark coat, hands tucked in the pockets, and his pale cheeks are pink from the cold.

"Just making sure." I walk faster, but he matches me easily. The bastard's not even breathing hard, despite the knee-deep drifts of snow.

"There are more cameras, too." He points one black leather glove at the nearest tree, where a red light glows between the branches. It might be obvious, except for the string lights wrapped around the tree, camouflaging the camera's watchful eye.

Hiding something vicious under the holiday cheer.

Typical Santo.

"Any news?" I ask.

The boss hums, non-committal, and anger flashes through me, hot and bitter. Though I've been loyal to him my whole life, though we grew up together, there's a part of me right now that wants to snap Santo's neck and bury him in the nearest snowbank.

I could do it, probably. He's faster than me, but I'm heavier.

And it'd be signing my own death warrant, especially with these cameras all around, but maybe Holly could get away. Maybe they'd forget all about her after my betrayal.

"Don't do anything reckless, Diego." Santo speaks softly, our steps crunching through the snow. It's as though he can read my mind, and he knows exactly how tempted I am, and if anything, it amuses him. "I know you're fond of the maid—"

"Holly," I interrupt. The least this asshole could do is say her name. "Her name is Holly, and I'm not fucking *fond* of her. That's like saying the Sahara Desert is a bit warm."

Santo sighs, like I'm being ridiculous. All these pesky feelings are so tiresome to him.

When he stops walking, I grind to a halt too. Old habits die hard, and I've been Santo De Rossi's attack dog for most of my life. We both stare at the mansion, squinting against the cold wind, coat collars flapping.

"There's something I want to show you," Santo says at last.

My gut sinks all the way down to bedrock.

* * *

They've got her in a concrete room in the basement—the one with a drain in the floor. Holly's tied to a chair, her wrists and ankles wrapped with duct tape, and her black maid's dress is rumpled.

Her head hangs low, and her breathing is shallow. Have they hurt her already? I'll burn this whole fucking mansion to the ground if they have.

"We spoke to the PI." Santo follows me into the room, in shirtsleeves and a forest green waistcoat now. He nods at a paper file on a table near the wall. "Got some background on her. But I thought you might like to do the honors."

Like to? I'd rather jump off the roof. But if it means no one else touches her...

"You're sure, then?"

Holly's blonde hair hangs across her cheeks, and she looks so tiny in that chair. I scan her bare limbs for cuts and bruises, my heart hammering, because the little maid can hear every word we're saying crystal clear, but she doesn't look up. She's defeated.

I hate this so much.

"Yes." Santo leans against the back wall, folding his arms and watching her. "We found ties to the Governor, and our warehouse in the garment district got raided last night. That's the piece of information we fed her."

Twice damned. Ah, Christ.

Well, Santo never does anything by half measures. If he was gonna catch my girl in a lie, he was gonna do it thoroughly.

"I want to know why she did it." The boss inspects one thumbnail, looking bored. "I want to know the exact information she passed along. All of it."

So far, so obvious.

"And then I want her cooperation with a special task."

My gut twists. "But we can't trust her," I say, desperate to spare her from whatever this is—and over in her chair, Holly's shoulders droop another inch. But I've hurt her for no reason, because Santo shrugs, unfazed.

"We don't need to trust her for this."

One minute later, Holly and I are alone in the cold, concrete room. How is it drafty without any goddamn windows? I cross to her, throat tight, and crouch in front of her chair. The drain beside my knee is dark, and I try not to look at it.

"Baby." She's sniffling, lips pressed together in a tight line. Trying not to cry. "Did anyone hurt you? Are you hurt?"

There's an agonizing pause, but then Holly jerks her chin from side to side.

No, they haven't hurt her. Fine. Everyone in this compound can live a few minutes longer.

"You need to tell me everything," I say urgently, checking her fingertips for circulation. Did they wrap the duct tape too tight? "Just tell me everything and we'll go from there. You don't need to protect the Governor, do you? Not that old asshole? So whatever bind you're in, you just tell me all about it and I'll fix it for you. Okay?"

Between the ends of her hair, Holly's chin wobbles. "S-so nice to me," she whispers.

Nice to her? *Nice?*

No one has ever called me nice in my whole goddamn life— no one except this girl. But she's already sucking in a shaky breath; already raising her chin. Her eyes swim with tears, but she spills it all in one garbled rush.

Her employer, the Governor.

His threats against her sister.

The baby.

"W-we've been making baby clothes," she hiccups, crying

outright now, wild eyes bouncing around all the walls. "But if he sends Ruth to prison—please, you have to help her—"

"I will." It's the easiest promise I've ever made, whatever it might cost me. My palms stroke up and down her arms. "I'll take care of Ruth, I promise. And I'll take care of *you*."

Her laugh is strangled. "After I complete De Rossi's task."

Dread twists in my gut. And my mind's already whirring, trying to figure a way out of this for her, but Holly straightens suddenly and looks me dead in the eye.

"Forget it. I want to do whatever it is. I bet it's spying on the Governor, right? Turning double agent?" Her jaw firms at my shrug, because yeah, it's probably that. It's the only thing Holly can offer the boss at this point. "Then I'm happy to do it. I *want* that horrible old creep to pay for what he's done to me. But..."

Her courage drains away as fast as it came, and Holly's smile is wobbly.

"I'm still a terrible spy."

Ah, shit. I rub my chest, and I'm so fucking worried about her. Is this what love feels like? Watching your heart wander around outside your body, getting into scrape after scrape?

"You need to tell me everything you passed along. Everything, baby."

She nods. "It's all on a burner phone on the top floor. I hid it in one of those fancy vases in the alcoves."

I breathe out a laugh. "Smart."

And that should be it, but there's one more thing I can't help asking. One more thing eating away at my insides. "Why didn't you come to me with this, Holly? Why didn't you confess? I could've helped you weeks ago."

Her gaze shutters, dropping away to the floor, and already

I wish I hadn't asked. "I wasn't sure."

"Whether I'd help you?" My words have turned harsh, but I can't help it. I'm wound too tight, my insides knotted with fear, and this room is somehow cold and stuffy at the same time. And my knees ache against the concrete and that drain keeps drawing my eye and that duct tape's cutting into her wrists and I hate this.

Hate all of it.

"We have a connection." So why do I sound so angry about it? "I know you feel it too. You could have come to me anytime."

"We barely spoke before yesterday!" Her chin's up again, eyes flashing, and even as my insides lurch, it's a relief to see her fighting back. Holly grips the arms of her chair, glaring at me as she yells: "You're a mobster, Diego! I'd be the world's biggest idiot to spill everything to you just because I have a crush!"

Well. Yeah. Okay, maybe.

"But I'd have kept you safe," I insist.

"I know that *now*." Holly rolls her eyes, glaring at the ceiling. "God. You are such a…"

I wait, our yelled words still bouncing off the concrete walls. Nothing.

"Such a…?"

The maid's eyes narrow on me. "Such a doofus."

My cheeks ache when I grin. "A doofus? Jesus, Holly. Hold something back."

Cold seeps through the floor into my knees as I lean forward. I go eighty percent of the way, and I wait for her there. Not gonna kiss her by force while she's tied to a goddamn chair, that's for sure.

But my girl puffs out a little breath, and then she's craning forward too, chair creaking. Her hair tickles my cheeks as she kisses me, soft and slow and sweet.

"I'm sorry," she whispers against my mouth.

"Don't be," I tell her, and my words are gruff but my hands on her arms are gentle. My chest aches like a motherfucker, though. "Not like any of this is your fault."

I kiss her again, stealing some of that sweetness. That warmth. Her lips part against mine with a sigh.

And we're alone—for now. In this room that doesn't lock, where every sound echoes off the walls, and it's the worst possible timing but I can't help kissing her again. And again. And again. I kiss her until heat crackles through my veins, my heart drumming against my ribs, and every part of the outside world is hazy.

"Your wrists—" I start to say, breaking away and breathing hard, but Holly shakes her head and strains against the chair to reach me again.

"Leave them."

Her muffled moan when our mouths slant together—that's my new favorite sound. Holly's hands clench and flex, tied helplessly to the chair, but I know from last night that she'd be touching me everywhere right now if she could. Tugging on my hair and slipping those cool hands inside my shirt, mapping my chest with greedy little sounds. Petting my beard and grabbing my shoulders for balance.

But she can't. She's at my mercy.

"You know, there's something about having you tied up, Holly. In other circumstances, I've gotta say…"

She laughs, shaking her head, but her cheeks flush a darker pink. Interesting.

198

I lean in, pressing the words against her fevered throat, and she shivers under my hot breath. "I think you like it too. Maybe you've even thought about this before. Shall we test my theory?"

Holly's breath catches… and then she nods once, quick and sure.

I fucking knew it.

Throwing a glance over my shoulder at the closed door, I slide both hands up her thighs. Up, up, under her maid's dress, her bare skin so warm and soft, and in an ideal world I'd drag this out—but we don't have much time.

Already, I'm crawling out of my skin with how badly I need her. And Santo could come back at any second.

The boss would not be amused, but it'd be easier to hold back the ocean than to stop this now.

"You're gonna cry out for me, Holly." I'm kneading her thigh muscles, sucking harsh kisses down her throat. She's so small and soft and perfect. "Those are the only screams you'll ever make in this room, but it going to be quick, okay? Quick and rough, just this once."

"O-okay." She's nodding again, flushed and bright-eyed. Her knees inch farther apart—as far as the chair will allow. "Okay, hurry then. Touch me."

My thumbs dip to her center, and god. Her panties are soaked. We've only exchanged a few kisses and some heated words, and she's already wound so tight she's panting, hands tied so she can't ease her own ache.

My shaft swells behind my fly, thick and urgent. I ignore it, and Holly's hips shift as I rub her through the cotton, her back arching. Two hard points dig into her dress, and I spare one hand to tease her nipples, then twist and pinch.

She hisses through her teeth. Her head lolls, eyelids fluttering.

So goddamn responsive.

My thumb rubs her through the fabric.

"You said quick and rough," Holly huffs, hips twitching up again. "Quick and rough, Mr Cedrone. And now you're teasing."

"So impatient," I mutter, but she's right. We don't have time, and I grip the crotch of her panties in my fist, then tear it out in one go. She yelps, fabric ripping and chair shrieking against the concrete, but then my fingers are on her, petting and soothing. Sliding through her wetness, coasting between her folds.

What I wouldn't give to rub my length along that.

"You're soaked, baby. Can you hear how wet you are?" We both pause, breathing hard, and the only other sounds are the slick little noises between her legs and the echo of her shout still fading away. Holly whimpers. "That's the sound of a needy girl. One who needs her man's fingers inside her. Don't you think?"

"Yessss," she hisses, trailing off when I lean forward again and mouth at her jaw. There's no flair to the way I kiss her; nothing but scraping teeth and the rasp of my beard and my tongue lashing greedily over the salt-sweet taste of her skin. I could swallow this girl whole. "*Oh.*"

My thumb finds her clit beneath the dress, and I'm flying blind but it doesn't matter. She's giving me all the direction I need, choking out those little moans and gasps and wriggling in the chair, her body betraying every single thing that feels good.

She feels good. Like a goddamn miracle.

And I can't believe she wants this, after everything. Can't believe she wants *me*, but the scars and calluses on my hands don't seem to put her off. If anything, she bucks against them, moaning louder.

"The boss will hear you," I warn, pressing one fingertip inside her.

Holly laughs, burying her face in the crook of my neck. "I don't care. We'll tell him you whipped out the thumbscrews."

I'm close to whipping out something, alright, but thumb-screws ain't it. "Santo won't believe that."

"I don't care," she pants. "I don't care."

And she's close already, I can feel it. Body tensed and pulse thrumming faster in her throat, and it's definitely quick but I promised her rough, too, didn't I?

Jaw hard, I shove my finger deep inside her, her channel so snug and hot around my knuckles. She's... new to this. Fuck.

But there's no turning back, and it's not like I'll let her go after this. Won't let her go back to her normal life and date around before she settles down with some other asshole. Holly is *mine*.

So I'm glad she's new to this. Just the thought of her with another man makes my head pound, and I bare my teeth as my finger saws in and out of her.

And the lack of experience hasn't stopped Holly from groaning, hips rising and falling as she tries to hump my hand. Hasn't stopped her from sucking bruises on my throat, claiming me like I claimed her, her breath coming in hot puffs against my skin. She's a little wildcat.

"Diego," she says, her voice kinda slurred. "*Please.*"

I smirk at the far wall, then add a second finger. And with my thumb on her clit and two thick fingers inside her, Holly stiffens up in her chair, gripping the arms until the metal creaks.

I graze a fingertip over the pucker of her ass. Just the tiniest touch.

"Oh my *god*." My maid jerks and thrashes in her chair, wailing loud enough to bring down the mansion, her cheeks red hot. She comes and comes and comes, body pulsing around my fingers, and the thought of my length wedged in there instead—it makes my throat dry.

The thud of footsteps is our only warning. I draw my fingers out and tug her dress down, moving to block her from view as the door slams open.

Santo glares down at me, lip curled in disgust. "For fuck's sake."

Holly

~~~

Turns out De Rossi doesn't just want me to turn on the Governor. He wants a private tour around the politician's mansion, and he wants it tonight.

"Are you sure?" I squeak, swaying on the back seat of one of his fancy cars hours later as we're swept through the dark countryside. Diego's wedged right beside me, his thigh flush against mine, and the mob boss watches us coolly from the seat opposite.

I'm in my gray maid's uniform. The one from my job before. Feels like a thousand years ago.

"This is so risky," I say, pleading with De Rossi to believe me. "Governor Edwards has tons of security, and if anyone recognizes you—"

"No one will recognize me."

"But if they *do*, his security detail are all armed—"

"Governor Edwards has a private function this evening." De Rossi smiles, and my heart beats faster, but not like how it does for Diego. This must be how little furry rodents feel when they get cornered by a snake. "He's been hoping for a dinner invitation at the admiral's home for months, and then tonight he received one out of the blue. His security team will attend as a matter of course. Isn't that convenient?"

The car lurches around a bend. I feel sick.

"My sister…"

"Is safe and settling into her new room at the compound as we speak." De Rossi picks an invisible fleck of dust off his fancy suit pants. Even when breaking and entering, he dresses like he's attending a gala. Ice blue eyes flick up to me as he says, "You really don't have a choice, you know."

Diego shifts beside me, his mouth turned down behind his beard. He doesn't like this. Doesn't like the way I'm risking myself tonight, going back into the lion's den—or the *other* lion's den, I suppose. But the mob boss is right: what's my alternative? Frankly, I'm surprised to still be alive.

If this is the penance De Rossi wants from me, I'll pay it and be thankful, because something tells me that if Diego weren't so freaking attached, I wouldn't be nearly so lucky.

Even if this *is* a terrible idea.

"Well, there will still be the regular security guards. So we should go in through the staff entrance and stick to the service corridors, and if anyone catches us… we'll need a cover story."

"We'll say I'm your lover. There for an illicit tryst."

I snort, just as Diego bristles beside me, my brawny mobster suddenly puffing up and filling two thirds of the car. An illicit tryst? Who talks like that?

"Fine," I agree, because it's the most believable explanation, even if in reality I much prefer scars and swollen knuckles to fancy waistcoats. "Let's hope we don't get caught then."

De Rossi's mouth flattens as he glances over me. "Indeed."

Diego's still grumbling under his breath when we pull to a stop on a dirt path near Governor Edwards' grounds, our vehicle hidden by thick woodland. It's the closest we can get without using the driveway and drawing attention, and I'm feeling pretty smug that I thought of it.

The night is freezing when we step out into the darkness, doors shutting quietly. I shiver in my maid's dress and blink at the second vehicle idling behind us.

"Why do we need two cars?"

De Rossi sniffs, his features extra sharp in the headlights. "We'll leave separately. The reasons are none of your concern."

Whatever. This is the weirdest night of my life, and we've barely started yet. "Come on, then."

I turn and start trudging in the direction of the mansion, snow crunching underfoot, but a big hand grips my elbow before I make it three steps. Diego spins me around and flattens me to his chest, his breath hot on my ear.

"You're not his fucking *lover*."

Hands roam over my back, my ribs, and plunge into my hair. Mapping his territory. I laugh weakly, gripping two handfuls of his shirt. "No kidding."

"Don't get caught, baby. I'm serious. I don't want that shit spoken out loud, not another single time."

Ah. How to soothe a jealous, bristling mobster? I reach up and pet Diego's cheeks, his beard soft against my palms. He glowers down at me, dark eyes glittering in the moonlight.

"We won't get caught."

He puffs out a breath. "Good."

"And I'll be back with you soon, and we'll pick up where we left off."

Diego rumbles out a pleased sound, and behind us De Rossi

205

mutters, "Good grief."

The snow glistens on Governor Edwards' grounds, white and ghostly, and in the distance, the windows of his mansion burn with light.

"Let's get this over with," the mob boss mutters, and tugs me away by the back of my dress.

* * *

We're not the only ones who slip through the staff entrance. Two surly men in suits and earpieces follow us inside, then melt into the darkness with a jerk of De Rossi's chin.

"What are they…?"

"They're running an errand for me. Come on."

Governor Edwards' mansion is dim, cloaked in shadows. Pools of light spread beneath sconces across the rugs and floorboards, but it's not enough to make the rooms feel warm or welcoming. Everything is austere.

"Charming," De Rossi mutters as we pass an oil painting framed on the wall. It's of an old timey town square, with three men standing on the gallows as they wait to hang. "Of course he has terrible art."

And it's funny, because the mob boss seems more offended by the Governor's taste in paintings than by anything else so far. He glares at the scene, his nose wrinkled in distaste.

"At least it's an original?" I whisper, leading him into a side corridor that only the staff use.

De Rossi scoffs quietly. "An original piece of shit. Not everything is worth collecting, you know. Some things aren't worth the canvas they're painted on."

I hum as we slip through the corridors, fighting a smile.

Why is this suddenly fun? I'm losing my mind.

Focus, Holly. Focus.

My pulse spikes with each distant thump and rumble of voices, but it's nothing out of the ordinary. Just the normal sounds of the Governor's mansion at night. And when I wheel around a corner and slam to a halt, sucking in a sharp breath, there's nothing but velvet silence behind me.

Guess the mob boss is better at sneaking than I am. Figures.

"Oh! Holly, isn't it?" The night-time housekeeper smiles at me, confused, from where she's marking off some kind of checklist on a clipboard. She's standing to one side in the corridor, but it doesn't matter. Our path is blocked. "I didn't realize they called in extra hands tonight. Did they send you to help with inventory?"

My palms are damp where they press into my hips. "Um," I manage. What are words? What do humans say to each other? "No, I... I mean, maybe I could help you once I'm done with this, but first I need to..."

"No problem." The housekeeper waves a hand, and her smile at me is kind. She turns back to her clipboard. "I shouldn't try to poach other staff. Carry on."

I clear my throat. "Okay."

I hover as she turns to face the wall, engrossed in her work, and weigh our options. I could make an excuse and head back the way we came, then find another route—or we could test our luck, and hope that whatever's on that clipboard is truly fascinating.

Well. Color me crazy, but I'm feeling bolder by the minute. All these mobsters must be a bad influence on me.

"Goodnight!" I chirp, bustling past, and the housekeeper raises a hand without even glancing over. I don't dare turn back, don't falter in my steps, but when I round the next corner, Santo De Rossi is by my side, keeping pace.

"You're like a cat burglar," I breathe. "Or a magician."

The kingpin inhales sharply. "Never," he states, "*ever* say anything like that to me again. I've killed men for much less."

But was Diego in love with those men? I think not, and I'm just starting to realize that my man gives me a certain kind of armor in this world. His protection extends around me, even when he's not here.

I beam at the corridor stretching ahead, and I probably have cartoon hearts floating in my eyes.

"The Governor's study is around that corner. I'll poke my head in first, then you follow. Oh wait, what if it's locked?"

De Rossi's strides quicken, and there's a tinkle of keys. "That will not be a problem."

* * *

In the end, I don't know what I expected. Pigs' blood splashed over the walls and a dagger taken to all the paintings? That was obviously never going to happen, though the mob boss looks sorely tempted on that last point.

Instead, Santo De Rossi is controlled. Almost bored in his perusal. He strolls around the bookshelves, huffing at the titles and the way the spines have never been cracked. He glances at the framed photo of the Governor's son on his wall, and carefully selects the right key on his stolen ring to open the desk drawers.

"Where did you get those?" I ask as the top drawer slides open. We're working in the dark, not willing to attract attention with any light beneath the study door. Instead, De

Rossi settles into the leather chair, then scans the Governor's private letters by the light of the moon spilling through the windows.

"I had them cut weeks ago. Be quiet now, please."

I purse my lips and wander to gaze out over the grounds, wrapping my arms around my waist. My stomach hurts.

Even with the Governor gone, this room feels... off. Malevolent. His bad energy clings to the furniture like a foul smell.

"When he called me in here to blackmail me, I thought about braining the old creep with that paperweight."

De Rossi grunts, his black leather gloves whispering over pages and pages of private documents. "You would have saved me a lot of time."

I spin and watch the mob boss examine every single artifact locked away in the Governor's drawers. He's like an archaeologist, picking over ruins to find something of interest. "But you're not going to kill him, are you?"

Because *that* doesn't fit. All this fuss for the story to end with a stray bullet?

De Rossi's smile is humorless. He draws a phone out of his pocket and snaps photos of some kind of legal contract. "Not immediately."

"And tonight is about..."

I trail off, hoping for an answer. And somewhere deep down, De Rossi must be warming to me, because I actually get one.

"Tonight is about saying hello." The mob boss closes the drawers with a soft *thunk* and locks them all, then pulls an envelope from his pocket.

I squint at the red paper. "A holiday card?"

"'Tis the season." De Rossi places the square in the center of the desk. "Do you think he'll display it?"

Ha. I shake my head, baffled and amused and still kinda thrilled by this little nighttime escapade. "I think he'll freak the hell out."

The mobster stands. "Good. Shall we be on our way?"

I wander to the door, then check both ways in the corridor. As we sneak back through the shadowy mansion, something prods at the back of my mind.

"What about those other two men you let in? What about their errand?"

There's a long pause, and my flash of fear tastes sour.

"Don't trouble yourself with that," De Rossi says softly.

Diego

⁓꩜⁓

I've worn a trench through the snow by the time they get back, pacing up and down between the trees for what feels like hours. A snapping twig is the only sign of their arrival, and I wheel around in time to see Holly and Santo slipping between the ghostly tree trunks, two thieves in the night.

"Did you do it?" I call softly, already striding to meet them. Santo nods just as Holly flings herself into my arms. She's shivering in her thin maid's uniform, her teeth chattering in my ear, and I put her down long enough to shrug off my coat and wrap it around her shoulders.

"The others are following behind," Santo says, strolling to the lead car and popping the trunk. A small electric light glows inside, washing over his sharp features and making his cheeks look gaunt. The air smells like pine. "You should leave before she sees."

"Before I s-see what?" Holly says, the cold slurring her words. She glances between us, her blonde hair almost silver in the moonlight. "Before I see *what?*"

"Come on, baby." I draw her away by the elbow, leading her through the snow to the second vehicle. "We've had the heaters on, getting it good and ready for you."

"Diego Cedrone, if I've been the accessory to a crime, I should know about it!"

Holly's so easy to lift in a squirming bundle. So easy to deposit in the back seat of the car, her outraged curses ringing in my ears as I belt her in. Gotta go, gotta go.

The car door slams shut. My footsteps crunch through the snow as I round the vehicle.

In the distance, a pair of Santo's soldiers appear between the trees, one carrying a pale shape slung over his shoulder. Both men are stoic and silent, their suits whispering as they walk.

"Excellent." Santo straightens as they get near, rapping on the side of the open trunk. "In here, please."

I shake my head, and my heart sinks down to my belly, because there's no way my girl hasn't seen.

Sure enough, Holly's rolled her window down when I slide into the car, and she's leaning halfway out to watch the scene in front of us. "Oh my god," she says, as the pale shape stirs against the man's shoulder, making dazed noises. "Oh my god! That's a woman!"

Santo spares us an evil smile. Ass.

"It's the Governor's daughter." I tug Holly back inside as Santo's captive lands in the trunk with an *oof.* They must have her bound and gagged. "Don't worry, he won't hurt her—the boss doesn't hurt innocents. He's just borrowing her for a while."

The window hums up as I speak, and I jab the button like

it might make it go faster. Like it might magically stop Holly from asking questions, and from looking at me with that doubt in her eyes.

Fuck.

"He's kidnapping her," she says. It's a statement, not a question.

"Yes." I settle back against the leather and nod for the driver to take us away. The car jerks backward, lurching over the uneven snow, and my girl sways in her seat, looking queasy. "This is the mob, Holly. You knew that already."

"He's *kidnapping* her. And we're letting him do it!"

A harsh breath gusts out of me, along with the last of my hope. Because who was I kidding, thinking she'd want to stick around? Thinking that she'd want anything to do with us and our world? With *me*?

Holly is good. She's innocent and sweet, and when she came on my fingers earlier, she gazed up at me like I'd given her the moon on a platter.

It was too good to be true, and this car is stiflingly hot, the air scented with burning dust from the heaters. Up front, the driver's partition inches toward the roof, and he's a smart man because he's avoiding my eyes. Pretending not to hear this.

"Listen to me." The leather creaks as I shift to face her head on, my gaze hard even though my insides are knotted with misery. The partition thumps softly against the roof, and then we're alone, rocking over the snow, leaving Santo and the Governor's daughter in our exhaust. "Edwards is a prime time fucker. He started this war with Santo out of the blue, and he blackmailed you and threatened Ruth. He's gotten one of us stabbed and one shot already, and there's *still* a price on all our heads. Do you hear what I'm saying?"

The breath shudders in and out of my lungs. Holly blinks up at me from the depths of my coat, her eyes so huge, and she's like one of those little anime things, especially in her maid's dress. Damn it. Should have known this could never be real.

"The Governor won't stop until Santo's ruined and we're all dead. *Or* until the boss reminds him who he's dealing with. Which option do you prefer?"

The car lurches around a bend. I spread one palm over the ceiling, determined not to flatten her.

"There's a price on your head?" Holly mumbles, her fingers hooking onto my shirtsleeve. "Yours too?"

Is that strain in her voice from worry? Or is she still horrified with me?

"He won't hurt her." I *need* Holly to get this. "Santo's a cold motherfucker, but he won't hurt an innocent woman. She'll get a nice cushy stay at the mansion for a few weeks, complete with room service and all the movies she can watch, then once the Governor agrees to our demands, she'll be dropped back on her daddy's doorstep without a scratch on her. I swear it."

Holly's chin wobbles. Her lips press together, and she looks so damn overwhelmed. Well, Jesus, who can blame her? Her life has been nothing but danger and mayhem for weeks, the poor thing.

I risk stroking one fingertip over her cheek, and wait for her to meet my eyes. "I promise," I tell her. "Trust me."

And I will never renege on my promises to this woman. My word has always been gold, but with Holly? I'd rather slit my own throat than lie or disappoint her. I'd rather never speak another word in my life than lead her wrong.

As she stares up at me, eyes flitting between mine, trying

desperately to read me—I gaze back, laying myself bare to her. Showing her my whole crooked soul.

What's left of it, anyway.

When Holly finally nods, I'm too wrung out to feel triumphant. I lean back in my seat and stare blindly at the world whipping past outside.

* * *

A soft knock drifts through the pounding of my headache. I scowl at the door to my suite, spinning a glass of whiskey in my hands, my limbs sprawled in the leather armchair that Holly told me once she daydreamed about.

That was so long ago. Decades, it feels like, not days.

"What?" I grunt.

I'm not in the mood to debrief with Santo. Not tonight. Yeah, he's the boss, but his antics have cost me *everything*—and though I know on some level that it's not fair to blame him, that I'm a grown man who makes his own choices…

Fuck, I'm just not in the mood.

I tip back my glass, the whiskey burning my throat.

"Um." A hesitant voice floats through the door. A *female* voice, and Christ knows Allegra and Leah don't ever tiptoe around or sound unsure. "Diego?"

"Yeah." I've already launched out of my chair, tossing back the last of my drink and flinging the glass at the bed. It hits the covers and rolls onto the rug with a muffled thump, and my legs are like jelly as I lunge for the door. "Yeah, I'm coming."

When I wrench it open, she's there. Blonde hair damp and a little darker from a shower, her little body wrapped up in a soft-looking white robe and blue pajama pants.

Holly. My Holly. Something deep inside my chest settles down, purring like a soothed house cat just from having her near.

Does she need something? Is she hungry?

"You can snack whenever you want," I say, like an idiot. "The kitchens are always open, so take whatever. That goes for Ruth, too."

"Um," Holly says. "Thank you?"

She tilts her head, her expression bemused, and now we're just standing in this plush corridor together in strained silence. Waiting for the other shoe to drop.

"So…" I scratch my beard, frowning down at the maid. Because why is she here? Seriously? The way Holly looked at me in the back of that car, you'd think she'd never want to lay eyes on me again. "Did you and Ruth get settled in okay?"

I guess if she needs a pair of hands to lump the furniture around or whatever, I'm game. I only had a few mouthfuls of that whiskey before I threw it at the bed.

So glad no one saw that. What is wrong with me?

"Yes. I mean, it's way nicer here than our crappy little apartment. The heating works, for a start, and there's no damp on the walls. So that's an upgrade, and way better for the baby."

Holly fiddles with the belt of her robe as she speaks, watching me carefully. I swallow hard and listen, leaning against the door frame, soaking up every word.

Every sentence, every tidbit, every glance from her is precious. And this is all I have now. This is all I'll ever have.

"Diego?"

I grunt a reply, my temples pounding as I stare down at the love of my life. How long will they stay with us? Will I get to see her with Ruth's baby? I bet she'll look like an angel when she holds the little mite. Like one of Santo's fancy paintings of goddesses or whatever.

"Are you..." Holly sighs, her shoulders drooping. "Have you changed your mind about me?"

...What?

Have I changed my mind?

Have *I* changed *my* mind?

Jesus Christ.

Holly's slung over my shoulder before her next breath, just like Santo's captive back in the woodland earlier tonight. I slam the door behind us, marching her over to the bed, then wheel away at the last second and aim for the armchair instead.

"Hey!" Holly pounds on my back with her little fists, but she's laughing too. Kicking and wriggling. "What the hell, Diego!"

When I collapse back into the armchair with her in my lap, she's red cheeked and grinning. Those arms slip around my neck like the world's sweetest collar.

"You're still not scared of me, huh?" I jiggle her on my lap, suddenly enjoying myself way too much. Headache? What headache? "You're gonna let the mean old mobster put his rough hands on you again?"

"Maybe." Her saucy little smile—god, it kills me. Makes me want to kiss her and spank her and pet her hair all at once, and I need more goddamn hands. "But I'll be checking in on the Governor's daughter, Mr Cedrone. Don't think I won't."

Holly punctuates her words with a stern tap on my nose, and Christ, she's perfect when she's bossy. Sitting up all righteous in my lap, back straight and eyes determined.

"Fine by me." Her pajama pants are brushed cotton, so soft

as I stroke my palms up her thighs. She smells like laundry powder and shampoo, and it's so domestic it warms my aching heart. "I won't ever lie to you, baby. Not about anything, but especially not something like that."

Her smile is softer this time. "I know."

The room is warm, the lighting dim. Glancing around, I'm almost embarrassed by my sparse existence, because there are barely any signs of life in here. It could be mistaken for one of the guest suites—if it weren't for my wallet, phone and keys on the dresser, and the fallen whiskey glass on the rug.

That's okay. All the more space for Holly's stuff to spread, brightening up every corner of my world.

Will she wear this little white robe every night? What about *just* the robe, with nothing under it? I tease the belt undone, watching her steadily.

And Holly lets me.

Jesus, she doesn't just let me. She leans back and shrugs her arms out of the sleeves, then tugs her pajama shirt over her head. Baring her body.

The shirt lands somewhere over by the wall. Her nipples are hard already, dusky pink and delicious, and the minx arches her back, showing off for me.

"Perfect," I rasp, cupping her. Weighing and squeezing. "Ah, Holly. You're perfect all over. I knew you would be."

The room was warm before she came in, but now it feels hotter than a sauna. Or maybe that's just the way she's got my heart pounding, my blood rushing through my veins. I'm not stopping to crack a window, that's for sure; wouldn't stop if the mansion burned to ash all around us, not now that I've got her.

Finally.

"I'm new to this," Holly murmurs, shifting in my lap. Rubbing her ass over the lead pipe currently trying to burst its way through my boxers, and nibbling on her bottom lip like the world's biggest tease. "So you'll have to be patient with me, Diego. I might not be any good."

"Impossible," I say immediately, ducking my head to lick her nipple. Sure enough, my girl gasps and squirms against the rasp of my beard, gripping my shoulders for balance, and my mouth curves into a smile against her heated skin. "You feel that, baby? You feel how you respond to me? We were built for this, you and me."

She's hot and damp between her legs, scorching through those pajama pants with how badly she wants this. Thank god. I stroke her there for a few minutes, up and down, up and down, until Holly huffs and scrambles off my lap to stand in front of the armchair.

"Not *that* patient," she grumbles, shoving her pajamas down to her ankles. "I want to know what you feel like inside me before I die of old age."

"So grouchy," I tease, already working my belt open. "I'll have to fuck that temper out of you."

Her reluctant huff of laughter makes me grin. "Promises, promises."

It takes some fumbling, in the end. We're both nervous; both breathless; both panting with how badly we need to feel our bodies sink into each other. And the armchair is cramped and the leather keeps squeaking, but it's still the best moment of my long, lonely life when Holly positions my cock at her entrance, her thighs trembling.

"Ready?"

Hell yes, I'm ready. I take her hips and squeeze.

"Don't go easy on me, Holly. I may be an old man, but I can take it."

"Oh, please. You're not old." She rolls her eyes as she sinks down, eyelids fluttering when she feels the stretch of my shaft pushing inside her. "Not... oh, god..."

"Take your time." My thumb circles her clit, my calluses against her slick flesh. "I'll fit, baby, you just take your time."

"Uh-huh." Her eyes are hazy; her nod is slow. Holly bites her lip as she circles her hips, feeling me press against every part of her. "You're so..."

She trails off, chin dropping, and grips my shoulders for balance. I open my mouth to coax the rest of that sentence out of her, but Holly sinks down another few inches and steals my breath.

I'm still squeezing her hip with one hand. Circling her clit with my free thumb. Counting backward from one hundred and trying desperately not to notice the wet heat of her; the snug fit of her channel; the little puffs of breath against my neck.

"Baby," I croak, then Holly sucks in a deep breath and sinks all the way down.

I tilt my head up at the ceiling, blinking away stars.

Holly

~❦~

Diego Cedrone is a very big man. He's muscled and strong, with thick, long fingers and hairy knuckles. When I played with his arm in the back of De Rossi's car earlier, I worked out I'd need both hands to wrap around his wrist. So I figured the enforcer must be large all over; that I'd be setting myself a challenge by taking him to bed.

Or to armchair, anyway.

Point is, I knew what I was getting myself in for.

At least: rationally, I knew. Intellectually, I knew. But there's a whole world between knowing something theoretically in the back of your mind, and working that hard, throbbing truth into your pussy.

Because Diego is *huge*. Thick and veined, with a ruddy head and big balls to match. It takes me lots of pauses and short gasps, takes several stops to regroup, and once I'm fully seated on the mobster's lap, I feel like I deserve some applause. The backs of my knees are sweating.

"You're doing so well, baby." Diego squeezes and releases my

221

hip, staring up at the ceiling. He's frowning in concentration, and I'm going to take that as a compliment. Diego's throat bobs as he swallows. "Everything okay down there? You're not in any pain, are you?"

I press my lips together, my chest suddenly so warm inside. Because as a mobster, this man's whole life has been about doling out pain: drawing out confessions and giving warnings; meting out Santo De Rossi's judgment. Yet with me stretched around his shaft, Diego's eyes are tight with strain, and concern is etched on every single gruff feature. He swallows again, hard.

I pet his dark beard. "I'm good."

"We can stop whenever you like. Or I could lick you instead, how about that? I've been wondering how you taste, baby, wondering it for weeks now—"

"I'm good," I tell him again, wrapping my arms around his neck, trying to figure out how to soothe him. Men are visual creatures, right? "You wanna see what it looks like?"

Diego blows out a hard breath. Then he screws his eyes shut and drops his bristly chin. Peeks one eye open, then stares avidly at the sight between my thighs.

And listen: I'm no expert, but I think we look *good*. His shaft is slick and shining, my body stretching to let him in, and as I lean back on his lap, the head of his cock prods against my stomach.

"Jesus," Diego grates out, spreading one hand over the sight of his length inside me. "*Jesus*."

"Uh-huh." I roll my hips, nerves sparking with each new brush of contact. "Can we keep going now?"

"*Yes*."

And he's everything I thought he would be. Strong and

222

sturdy, his skin salty to the taste. Brutal and demanding, surging up beneath me to spear me on his shaft. But there's also reverence in his eyes, and when he smooths his scarred hands along my body, petting and squeezing, I've never felt so treasured in my whole life.

"Holly. My Holly."

Our bodies rock together, heat building between us. My cheeks are on fire, and the slick sounds of our bodies joining are so loud in the room.

"Never gonna let you go after this. You hear me? There's nowhere you can run, baby. You're mine now."

The words are uttered like a threat, pressed against my mussed hair, but my heart beats brighter with each dark promise.

I don't want to run from this man; don't want to spend a single day apart. Why the hell would I ever want that? And his obsession with me? The possessive glint in his eye when he looks my way?

I love it. I can't get enough.

"You've picked your man now, Holly, and I hope you like this cock, because it's the only one you'll ever take. But I'll make it good for you, baby. I'll make you cry out every day for the rest of our lives, you'll see."

I bury my smile in his throat, ears ringing with these filthy declarations.

Who knew the enforcer would be so chatty?

"Gonna put a ring on your finger and my seed in your belly. Is that what you want? Huh? A little baby of your own?"

Rough teeth scrape along my shoulder, and I let out a blissful sigh.

Yes, it's what I want. *He's* what I want. My scarred mobster.

The man from my daydreams.

"Holly. You listening to this?"

I choke out a laugh, nodding my head, and his shaft is so thick, sliding in and out me as I roll my hips. It's so intimate, I can feel his heartbeat down there.

"Yeah, I'm listening. I want it all, Diego." Everything he's offering me and more: I want it all.

His breath gusts past my ear. "Good. That's settled, then."

And it's such a funny thing to say, such a weird way to settle things between us, but it's perfect too. I wouldn't change a single thing. And as Diego's thumb finds my clit again, rubbing steady circles, my mouth drops open on a silent scream.

Blood rushes in my ears. I stiffen on his lap, muscles twitching. My whole body flashes boiling hot, nerves throwing off sparks, and I come and come and come until I crash against his chest with a ragged groan.

Yeesh.

His shirt buttons dig into my cheek. Definitely need to get him naked next time.

"Holly," Diego says. "Fuck, Holly."

He swells inside me, throbbing. Pulses once, twice, three times, both hands gripping my hips and holding us sealed tight together as if I might try and pull away. As if I don't love his wet warmth spilling inside me.

Ha. He'll learn.

"Mmph," I say into his shoulder, leaving a drool patch on his shirt. "Oh my god. That felt good. That was good, right?"

"Yeah." His breaths are ragged, his chest heaving against my cheek. "Yeah. Better than good. That was the best thing I've felt in my whole fucking life."

And we sit there together, hot and sticky and rumpled in

our chair, swapping breaths back and forth and trading sweet kisses.

Next time, I tell him, we'll try the bed. Or maybe the shower.

"Whatever you want, baby." Diego's beard tickles the top of my head as he kisses me there. "From now on, it's whatever you want."

* * *

Three days later

I scoop up another handful of snow, my fingers numb inside the pair of leather gloves I borrowed from Diego this morning. The wind nips at my cheeks, and the midday sun is bright as I pat my handful against the snowman's belly.

"The shape is all wrong," Ruth murmurs, working on the lopsided white head. "His shoulders are quite wide, have you noticed? And his waist is trim. It's too bad he hates everyone and everything or he'd be a real catch."

I snort, bending down for another handful. We're out on the De Rossi grounds, half-hidden by the hedge maze, and I'm so glad to see my sister relaxed and pink-cheeked that I could skip around the whole mansion.

I was so worried that Ruth would hate it here. That she'd be scared and on edge and it wouldn't be good for the baby, and we'd have to find somewhere else to live, far away from Diego. My heart crumbled at the mere thought, but Ruth has settled in like one of the family.

Could I even bear being apart from him at this point? I don't think so.

And: "We've got it!" Allegra calls, jogging across the grounds with Leah at her shoulder. Both women are dark-haired and grinning, and there's a lump hidden under Allegra's sweater.

As the kingpin's sister, she was the only one brave enough for this mission. Frankly, I still can't believe she's got one, but that lump is incriminating as hell.

"We need sticks," Leah declares when she reaches us, hunting around on the ground. Ruth points her to the two we already fetched. "Ah, perfect."

Leah's married to another mobster—and though Nico and Diego aren't blood relations, she's already declared me her future sister-in-law. I smiled so hard that evening, my cheeks ached all the next day.

Can this be real? Can Ruth and I really slot in here so easily, welcomed into the warm arms of the mob?

"Oh, I love that one," I say as Allegra pulls the embroidered silk waistcoat from under her sweater. It's midnight blue, the fabric slippery and fine. Leah jabs both sticks into the snowman's body, and Allegra slings the waistcoat over his makeshift shoulders.

We all stand back, gazing at our work.

The snow-Santo is lumpy and lopsided, one stick-arm twice the size of the other. He's short, too, way shorter than the real deal, his squat body listing in the snow. Sometime while I was busy with the belly, Ruth stuck two pine needles above his pebble eyes, like grumpy little eyebrows.

Allegra cackles. "He's perfect. Wait, I need a photo of this."

And we're too busy giggling and posing with our Franken-Santo to notice our men until they're standing beside us, staring down in horror.

"Is that...?" Raul asks, glancing up at the mansion windows. The doctor looks paler than usual, his expression grim.

"Shit," Nico says, and then he's yanking the waistcoat away and kicking the snowman down, pelted with snowballs by his enraged wife. "Shit!"

"Bullies!" Leah yells. "Schoolyard bullies!"

"Give me that phone, Allegra. Delete that photo right now—"

Diego takes my arm and steers me away from the yells and peals of laughter. Ruth watches them all from one side, smiling calmly and stroking her belly.

"What were you thinking, baby?" Diego tucks a lock of hair behind my ear, shaking his head. His fingers are chilled from the cold, what with the borrowed gloves on my hands, and his scar is ghostly on his cheek. At least his beard's keeping his chin warm. "Santo's a kingpin, not a kindergarten teacher. If he caught you all with his waistcoat—"

"We were going to put it back!"

"Giggling and posing like that—"

"Oh, please." I yank on Diego's sleeve, just wanting to touch him. "We all know he's locked away with the Edwards girl again. His *captive*. A meteor could hit and Santo wouldn't notice."

Diego's mouth twitches, but he frowns down at me, all mock-stern. "Well, I had other plans for us this afternoon, but if you're too busy trying your luck with the boss..."

"What plans?" I'm already bouncing on my heels in the snow. We've only been together for a few days, but I've learned that Diego has the *best* surprises, and it's Christmas Eve. A time for miracles. "What are we doing?"

"Oh? You're not too busy then?"

I tackle the mobster with all my weight, but we both know he only falls back into the white drifts 'cause he's humoring

227

me. Still, any excuse to crawl on top of him and stuff snow down his collar. "Where are we *going*, huh?"

"To pick out a ring!" Diego yells, his deep rumbly laugh vibrating right through me. Then he catches my eye and goes all solemn. "If you want to, I mean. We can wait a while longer if you prefer." Those big hands squeeze my waist through my winter coat, possessive and greedy, and he adds, "Not *too* long, though. Don't leave me hanging. I'm not a patient man, remember?"

Me neither. I'm not patient when it comes to this, when it comes to *us*, and I want this man's ring on my finger right this second. My cheeks are hot as I launch to my feet, bending down to yank on his coat sleeve. "Up. Up, up, up. Let's go."

It's a perfect day. Cold and crisp, the grounds echoing with laughter, and I haven't touched a damn vacuum in nearly a week.

I'm ready for this. For our next chapter.

Ready for anything, as long as it's with him.

IV

Kingpin All The Way

Description

∽ജ∾

I kidnapped the Governor's daughter for revenge.

Now I'm fussing like a goddamn mother hen.

I'm a mob boss, not a nanny, but one look at Erin Edwards crowds my brain with constant worry. Is she eating enough? Resting well? Is she warm? Is she safe?

I need to focus, damn it—need to ruin her father's life, then send her back to the smoking rubble, not get *attached*. What is wrong with me?

But against all the odds, my captive doesn't hate me like she should. She *trusts* me, crowding closer for comfort, and I…

I can't think. This is a disaster.

Because when she blinks up at me like that, there's nothing I wouldn't give her. She can have my kingdom, my crown...

My whole lonely life.

Santo

S he takes far too long to wake up. Under normal circumstances, patience is my forte: I will happily wait weeks, months or even years to ruin a man if it means my victory will taste all the sweeter. But Erin Edwards takes *hours* to wake up after being kidnapped last night, and by the time she stirs against the pillows, my temper is frayed.

I've already worn a track along the guest suite rug with my pacing. Already irritated myself with the constant need to check her pulse, her temperature, her rolled-back eyes.

"Mmph," she slurs, shoving her freckled face deeper into the pillows. Finally. There's a patch of drool beneath her chin, and I scowl at the damp fabric. Those cases are Egyptian cotton. "Wha'timesit?"

I suppose being drugged and abducted would be a blow to anyone's dignity. Still, I wrinkle my nose at her bedside, leaning back in the armchair and checking my watch.

"It is seven minutes past eight."

I stifle a smirk when she jolts against the bed. The Gover-

233

nor's daughter scrambles upright, blinking around the room with bleary eyes, and it's clear that last night's sedative is still making her thoughts soupy. She hadn't even noticed I was here.

Amateur.

"Wha's... where am I? Who are *you*?"

Erin Edwards sways on the mattress, one arm pulled at an awkward angle behind her. Chocolate brown curls are wild around her shoulders, and those freckles spread over the bridge of her nose, blurring together like a permanent blush. We took her from her bed last night, and she's wearing a matching pajama set—a cream pinstripe shirt and tiny shorts.

The shorts are... compelling.

"I am Santo De Rossi, and you are at my home. As an honored guest," I add with a cold smile.

Has she noticed the silk tie leashing her wrist to the bed frame yet? I don't think so. Good lord, how has this woman survived to adulthood?

Miss Edwards shivers, her eyes growing wide. "De... De Rossi? *The* De Rossi?"

I wait for an actual question, the fire popping in its grate across the room. It's hot in here—uncomfortably warm, really, but I had an odd flash of panic after bringing her in here that she might have gotten chilled outside in the snow. There were goosebumps on her bare legs.

I've only just kidnapped her, after all. Failing to take good care of her would be terribly wasteful. She's no use to me struck down by the flu.

"Oh!" My captive finally gapes at her wrist, wrapped tightly in blue silk, and yanks hard on the leash. The bronze bed frame doesn't even creak.

Solid. Every object in this mansion is well made—I pride myself on that fact.

"The more you pull, the tighter it gets." The muscles in my back twinge as I stand, crossing to a side table with a jug of lemon water and two glasses. "I suggest you stop for the sake of your circulation."

Cool water splashes into the first glass as I roll my stiff shoulders. Seems I'm getting too old to stand vigil all night without back strain. How troubling.

"I don't understand," she mumbles.

No, she wouldn't. Why would this sheltered society girl ever expect to meet a mob boss? When would our paths ever cross without my divine intervention?

Erin Edwards is kept far from her father's shady political dealings. Far from everything important in her family, in fact. Apparently Edwards daughters are mere decoration.

Bizarre. When I held my own baby sister for the first time, I knew immediately that I'd burn the whole world down for her—and I am not a sentimental man. Governor Edwards is a dinosaur.

"Here. I expect you're thirsty."

Raul told me the sedative would dehydrate her, but my captive eyes the glass of lemon water in my hand like I'm holding out a hissing cobra. I suppose that's fair. I *have* drugged her once already in the last twelve hours.

"Watch," I command, then take a small mouthful from her glass, swallowing it down. There's less water now, but at least she accepts the glass, sipping cautiously and peering up at me with wide eyes. Unexpected warmth spreads through my chest at the sight, chased swiftly by irritation.

Does this girl always look so guileless? Innocent and

freckled and fucking *sweet*? Have I kidnapped a milkmaid? Good grief.

"Your father has made an error in judgment, Miss Edwards." The armchair creaks as I sink back into it, my own glass in hand. I don't *need* to explain myself, of course, but I'd prefer she stopped trembling. "Several errors, in fact, and I've taken you as insurance that he won't make any more."

"Me?" She blinks, her eyebrows pinching together.

I roll my eyes. Did she hit her head on that car trunk? "Yes. Obviously you."

"But he won't…" Erin trails off, biting her bottom lip, and I stare at the small gap between her front teeth for a moment before shaking my head.

Focus.

It has been a very long night.

"Won't care?" That's what she stopped herself from saying. From admitting out loud—either to herself or to me. "Not privately, perhaps, but your father cares greatly about his public image and you are part of that, Erin. There are plenty of ways to pressure him with you, believe me."

"Oh."

I wait, knuckles working against each other, but the Governor's daughter doesn't say any more. Just that one dejected syllable, then her chin drops and she stares at her wrist again. Tugs feebly on her tie.

"Stop pulling on it," I snap. "I told you, you'll hurt yourself."

She mutters something under her breath, and it's probably better that I didn't hear it. There's a headache brewing behind my left eye.

"You won't be here long." Who exactly am I trying to reassure now? I push the rest of my water into her hand, swapping it out for her empty glass, then stride across the guest suite. "You are a tool for me to use against your father, and once you are no longer useful, I will return you home. You have my word."

"Your word," Erin murmurs. She's still staring around the room, dazed by last night's sedative, and I have the bizarre urge to bundle her up in a blanket. Maybe check her temperature one last time before I go.

Will she remember any of this? Is the girl even lucid?

Fuck. I need to catch up on sleep.

"Don't try to escape," I warn, my grip tight on the door knob. "And don't irritate me. If you cooperate, I assure you the time will fly."

"Fly," she repeats again numbly, and her hand is shaky as she sips from the water glass.

There's a burning sensation behind my ribs. I wrench the door open and get the hell out of there.

* * *

One wretched hour of troubled sleep later, I'm back behind my desk. My fortress walls. The winter sunlight is pale and watery, barely warming the windows it shines through, though it makes the stained glass panel sparkle and cast jewel-toned light across my study floor.

The mansion hums with activity. Steps drum along corridors; doors open and close. The scents of fresh baking drift through the floors from the kitchens, and there's a distant burst of laughter somewhere out on the grounds.

"Well?" I snap, at the head poked around my doorway, my voice harsh with irritation. It's uncalled for but Raul doesn't flinch, stepping quickly inside. It may be morning, but he's dressed in a tailored suit and crisp white shirt, one sleeve of his jacket hanging empty off his shoulder. A sling crosses his chest, holding his arm in place.

A healing bullet wound, courtesy of Governor Edwards. Not directly, of course, but by a hired hand.

So messy. I'm surrounded by amateurs.

"She's fine. The drug will take a few more hours to leave her system, but she's already clearer." The door closes with a thump behind him, and our doctor turns to eye me closely. "*You*, on the other hand..."

I pinch the bridge of my nose, a headache squeezing my temples. "I'm fine."

He scoffs softly. That noise would have been unthinkable mere weeks ago, but apparently bedding my younger sister has made Raul bold.

A crucial error.

"She seemed... surprisingly calm. Did you check her head for bumps?"

"Hardly." Raul frowns behind his glasses. His dark blonde hair is ruffled above his forehead. Did Allegra accost him on his way here?

Probably. I suppress a shudder.

"You say she was calm? She wouldn't let me get within arm's reach of her. Kept kicking out and trying to scratch me with her free hand."

"Really?" I fall back in my chair, trying and failing to match this new image with the shy milkmaid from earlier. Must have been the sedative after all.

Pity.

The doctor hums and strolls to the nearest bookcase. "What

has the Governor said?"

"Nothing yet." Snatching up a pen, I tap the end on my desk. I've been waiting for his response, for threats, for anything. Instead, there's been radio silence.

"If he gets the police involved," Raul begins, "or the FBI—"

"He won't." Governor Edwards is as dirty as they come, and I made sure to express that knowledge in the holiday card I left in his home. He won't risk his precious reputation—not for anyone, and for Erin least of all. "But he'll do *something*. Step up security, especially around the girls."

"Done."

"And tell the kitchens to send me up a bathtub of coffee."

Raul's mouth twitches and he nods. "Alright. Or you could try this newfangled thing called sleep…"

As if it is truly that easy for everyone. Head meets pillow. Off to slumber land. For fuck's sake.

"Raul, if you say one more stupid thing to me this morning, I will shoot you myself."

Another nod, brisker this time. The humor's gone from the doctor's eyes, and I feel another flash of that burning sensation in my chest. Am I getting ill?

"I'll nudge him along through the day. Ruin a few investments, halt his supply chains, etc. Maybe trouble his donors. Poke him until he responds."

"Then I'll send up that coffee." The doctor turns to go. I'm scowling at his back when he pauses with one hand on the door knob and looks back. "You'll need to assign someone to her personal care. Don't forget you've tied her to the bed frame, Santo. She'll need the bathroom, the same as any other human."

"Yes, obviously," I say, though I had not in fact thought of that. God, this is why I don't keep animals. Too much fucking caretaking. "I'll see to it."

Raul leaves without another word, and I'm left in the muted silence of my office. My shirt collar feels too tight, and I tug at the fabric.

Who do I trust with Erin Edwards' personal care?

I tug harder. There must be someone.

Erin

Well, chalk this up as the worst Christmas ever. Sure, the big event is still a few days away, but something tells me I'll either still be tied to this bed frame by then, or worse. Hopefully not buried beneath those snow-heaped rose bushes I can see through the window, but there are no guarantees.

How did I get here? I *know* my father is shady as hell, though I've never learned any details, obviously. God forbid anyone keep me in the loop. But less than twenty four hours ago, I was planning my secret escape from this life, my working VISA to Australia already confirmed and my passport renewed. Instead...

"Come on," I growl, tugging on the blue silk that lashes me to the bed frame. "Come *on*." Every time I pull on it, the knot around my wrist grows a little tighter, just like the kingpin warned, my fingertips tingling. But I can't *not* fight. That'd be like giving up before we've even begun.

I need to get away from all this bullshit. Crime bosses and

politicians and my horrible family. Gala events and polo matches. All of it.

I will survive this, and then I'm going to disappear down under as planned. Start a new life as a whole new Erin. Unsheltered and free.

Just as soon as I escape this pickle I'm in.

A brain wave makes me sit up straight, and I can't believe I didn't think of it before. Blame whatever drug they gave me, I guess, or the panic of waking up to an icy mob boss watching me sleep, because this is so freaking obvious.

I rearrange myself on the bed, cross legged on the pillows, then bring the silk tie between my teeth—and start gnawing.

It's… less effective than I hoped. I scowl and keep chewing, grinding the slippery fabric between my teeth, eyes fixed on the door. My throat is dry, my jaw aching, but I keep going, ignoring the drool soaking into the fabric. Gross.

That watchful gaze is the only reason I see the door knob turn in time. I yank the tie out from my mouth and hide my wrist behind my back, trying to look innocent as the door swings open.

De Rossi. The man who sat by my bedside as I snored into strange pillows; the man who stole me away from my bedroom last night. The mob boss prowls into the room like he owns it, which—duh. He definitely does. But then he strides over and stares like he owns *me*.

"Thirsty?" he snaps. I stifle a flinch, but he definitely sees it, some unreadable emotion flickering behind his pale eyes.

"Y-yes." I'm not faking this stammer for effect. This man makes me nervous as hell, though weirdly not as panicked as the other people who've been in and out. "Water, please."

De Rossi gusts out a sigh, like I'm *so* inconvenient, and

crosses to the jug and glasses on the side table. It's been refreshed recently, ice cubes and slices of lemon bobbing on the clear water, and I steal a moment to examine my captor as he pours two glasses. He's... not what I expected.

I've seen pictures of Santo De Rossi before, of course. He's an international crime boss; there are plenty of photos of him floating around, although only at public events when he *allowed* those photographs. And I always thought he dressed so fancy because of the events he attended, but here he is in his own home before noon, clad in rolled white shirtsleeves and an embroidered forest green waistcoat.

I press my lips together against the sudden urge to smile.

So weird. Must be some kind of captive's hysteria.

When De Rossi turns with two full glasses, returning to my side, I take in his dark, wavy hair, pushed back from his forehead; his sharp cheekbones; his stubbled jaw and the shadows under his eyes. This man looks like he needs the world's longest nap, but I have enough survival instincts not to mention that fact.

"Here." He holds out one glass, but I wait, expectant. Just because the one earlier was fine...

De Rossi rolls his eyes, then takes a small mouthful. I watch the column of his throat shift, the water sliding down as he swallows, then accept the glass without argument.

God, I'm thirsty. I tip the glass back, emptying it in three desperate gulps. The mob boss watches my display, nose slightly wrinkled, then sips from his own glass and hands that over too.

My stomach lurches, sloshing with too much liquid, but I keep drinking greedily, even when the mob boss brings the jug over and sits at my bedside, pouring me glass after glass.

By the time we've emptied it, I'm squirming on the bedspread, my bladder about to burst.

"Oh, look." De Rossi's voice is deep but soft. He tilts his head, watching my leg jiggle. "The consequences of your actions."

I snort, but my cheeks are flaming hot. I do *not* want to pee myself in front of this man. "Dude, it's your mattress."

"Dude?" De Rossi straightens, affronted. "I am not a dude."

"Okay." I yank on my wrist pointedly. "Can you not be one while you untie me?" Or hell, while he brings me a bowl. Not picky at this point.

A big part of me thinks he won't do it. That he'll let me sit here in my own filth or whatever, because this man is famously cruel and I am officially his enemy's daughter. I'm at his mercy, with no one here to rein in his worst impulses, and if this were truly the Santo De Rossi of the newspapers, then I'd for sure be left to mess myself. I'd be kept in a cage in a dank basement, too.

Instead, my captor sighs and pushes to his feet, producing a small knife from somewhere among his tailored clothes.

I splutter, scrambling back on the bed as he leans over me. Broad shoulders block out the windows, and his shirt collar is open enough to see the edges of his collar bone. "You just carry that around?"

"Evidently. Stop squirming, Erin."

I grit my teeth, chest heaving as he looms over me, the faint scent of his cologne filling my nose. He smells *fresh*, like sea spray and cold wind and the crackle of lightning.

"There." My wrist sags suddenly, dropping to my thigh. I roll the aching joint, wincing at the tight tie, and De Rossi plucks up my forearm before slicing away the fabric with a single motion.

My numb fingers flex. Pins and needles swarm through my hand, hot and prickly, and my captor holds up the half-chewed silk, sodden with my drool.

"This," he says, shaking the tie in front of my nose like a bad puppy, "is disgusting."

I take his offered hand without even thinking about it, stumbling down off the bed on shaky legs. "Shouldn't have tied me up with it if you liked it. Anything you leave in arm's reach, that's fair game."

"Noted."

There's a door in the corner of the suite, and he leads me there across the plush overlapping rugs before nudging it open. My hand is tucked tight in his, and I remind myself furiously that it's to keep me from running away, not—not for any other reason.

"I'm going to let you go in there alone."

My laugh is strangled, and I bounce off the bathroom doorway as I stumble through. The tiles are warm beneath my bare feet. "Very gracious of you."

"There are supplies to shower and brush your teeth. Take as long as you need, but do *not* abuse this show of trust, Erin. I am not in the mood to deal with you."

Deal with me? Like… punish me? Kill me? I bite my lip against a full-body shiver, and paste a bright smile on my face as the door swings closed. "Gotcha. No funny business."

The last thing I see before I'm left alone is a pair of scowling icy blue eyes.

Erin

I wait until nightfall—then a few hours longer. I wait until the constant sounds of activity in this mansion fade away, replaced by sleepy silence.

There will still be people awake. Staff and security and whatever. I'm not a complete dumbass, but my chances of escape are a thousand percent better in the dead of night. Guaranteed.

Weird that De Rossi didn't tie me to the bed frame again. I fully expected to come out of the bathroom in a cloud of minty steam and find him waiting, harsh and impatient, ready to drag me back to my assigned spot and lash me there. A tiny, ridiculous part of me was looking forward to it.

Instead, I came out of the bathroom, bundled in a fluffy robe, to find a fresh pair of silk pajamas on the suite's coffee table—and a whole load of new freedom. An empty room, and nothing but fancy furniture and my own company.

And hours and hours to plan.

The door's locked. Obviously. But that's not the only way

out of this room, is it? I hold my breath as I peel the sheets off the bed, ears straining for the sound of footsteps coming nearer. There's nothing but quiet and the rustle of fine cotton. A pipe gurgles in the wall.

This is how people always escape in stories. Knotting their bed sheets together and climbing out of a window. Has Santo De Rossi never seen a movie?

The night air is brutally cold as I ease the balcony door open, gusting inside and chilling me through the thin layer of my pajamas. They're the same style as my own pair, a silk shirt and little shorts, but they're dark blue instead of cream.

They fit me perfectly, too. Better not wonder too much about that.

"Easy," I whisper to myself as the balcony door creaks, swinging open on its hinges. I pause again, but there are no approaching footsteps.

If anything's gonna give me away, it's my damn stomach, growling louder than a pack of wolves as I gather up my sheets and tiptoe outside. A layer of snow covers the balcony, freezing my bare toes, and I try to work quickly, tying my makeshift rope to the rail with clumsy fingers.

How far down is the ground?

I lean out to check, then regret my life choices when my head goes woozy. Far. Pretty far. But there's a balcony on the floor beneath mine, so maybe I can hopscotch down somehow, or get back into the mansion and sneak away from there...

I don't know, okay? But I have to try.

"Spider Erin, Spider Erin..."

Singing to myself softly as I swing myself over the rail, there's a real chance that I've gone mad. That whatever drug they gave me, or the experience of being held captive by a sexy, mean mobster with zero food all day, has cracked something in my mind. Why else am I wishing I could say goodbye?

The rail is so cold the metal hums, and my grip on the sheets is clumsy. By the time I'm a few feet down, arms wobbling and snowflakes churning all around, I can't freaking breathe, I'm so scared.

Bad idea. Bad idea. Really, really bad idea. Daring escapes down makeshift ropes are for girls who did well in gym, not reedy bookworms who haven't eaten all day.

The wind buffets me until I shriek, snowflakes gusting up my pajamas and melting on my bare skin, and as I slide in jerky spurts down to the balcony below, I'm praying under my breath for a miracle, for mercy, for a second chance at life—

My toes meet the snowy balcony, and I sag with relief… then glance up and turn to stone.

Santo De Rossi stands at the glass door, arms folded over his chest and jaw clenched. How much of that did he see? Did it look as lame as it felt?

"Erin." He says my name, his mouth forming the word even though no sound comes through the glass. He's pale with fury, every line of his body taut, and dread is a hard knot in my belly.

Maybe I could stay out here. Dying in the snow is supposedly a peaceful death, right? Don't people go all warm and happy right before it's over?

The balcony door wrenches open, and his single command cracks like a whip. "Get in."

I stumble past the mob boss on frozen feet.

Judgment time.

* * *

"That was very dangerous."

I'm bundled up in three blankets, curled obediently in the armchair next to the fireplace. Apparently I made my great escape directly into the path of De Rossi's personal study. He saw everything. Awesome.

"And so stupid, I cannot fathom it. Truly, your awful logic is giving me a migraine."

Is it so surprising that a captive would try to escape? I don't think so, but the mob boss is agitated as he coaxes the fire higher, stabbing the logs harder than necessary with an iron poker. Firelight dances over his features. It softens him up for a moment, despite the scowl.

That hot poker's not for me, is it?

"Um." I glance at the clock on the nearest bookcase. It's past three. "I thought you'd be asleep."

The scathing look he throws me makes my belly flip. "You thought wrong. But I'm sure that's a comfortable experience for you, Erin."

Ass. "You can't seriously take a girl captive and not expect any escape attempts. You left me the bed sheets and an unlocked balcony! You practically begged me to try this!"

De Rossi rolls his eyes, pushing to his feet. And he's so close suddenly, close enough that I could reach out and spread my palm on his stomach. Could feel that fancy waistcoat against my fingertips, and the hard muscles beneath...

The loud gurgle of my stomach makes my cheeks flame red.

"You didn't eat?" De Rossi clips out. "I had food sent to you. Several options for each meal."

I shrug, burrowing down like I could hide my blush in the

blankets. My reply is surly. "Didn't want to get drugged again."

The clock ticks on the bookcase. The mob boss stares into the fire, a muscle leaping in his jaw, and after a while I think maybe he's forgotten I'm here. Then: "Fine."

He strides across the study and jabs a button on the phone on his desk. Mutters a series of clipped orders, too quiet for me to hear, his frown on me the whole time.

I sink down to my nose in the blankets. Have I pushed him too far? This is an international crime boss, after all, not someone I should rankle. It's so easy to forget that when he's chiding me, my body relaxing whenever he gets nearer. He's like one of those poisonous flowers, beautiful but deadly, luring in the poor, stupid butterfly to her death.

De Rossi leans against his desk, folding his arms and watching me. "My doctor will check you over after that little stunt."

I shake my head quickly. "I'm not hurt."

"And then you *will* eat a full meal, even if I have to feed you myself. You are not going on some ridiculous hunger strike."

Um. What?

The mob boss rolls his neck and glares up at the ceiling. He stays like that even when there's a soft knock on the door, another man slipping inside. "This is more trouble than it's worth," he tells the newcomer, ignoring me completely now.

I recognize the man who approaches me, running a clinical gaze over my face and bundled form—though he's swapped his earlier suit for a black t-shirt and gray sweatpants. Sleep-rumpled dark blond hair and glasses; one arm in a sling. He tried to examine me earlier too, but I wouldn't let him.

Something tells me this time it's not optional. There are two of them and one of me, and they are both tall, strong men.

Yeesh.

I hold both hands out of the blankets, palms out. "I'll cooperate."

"Yes, you will," De Rossi mutters, though he still won't look at me.

"Did she fall? Knock herself against anything?" The doctor is all business, bending over me in the armchair with a frown. I ball my hands in the folds of the blanket, fighting the urge to kick him in the chin.

"No," my captor mutters. "But she might have hurt herself on that ridiculous rope. Or on the balcony rail above. The metal will have been cold."

The doctor grunts, flipping back the top blanket. "Hey!" I yell, flipping it closed again. I'm in my pajamas under here! Just those stupid tiny shorts!

"So much for cooperation," De Rossi snarls. I flatten myself back against the armchair as he prowls closer, anger curling his top lip, and he's terrifying like this—but I know who I still prefer.

"Can't..." I glance between the two men, palms sweaty where I grip the blanket. "Can't *you* check me over? Not him?"

The doctor's eyebrows bounce up his forehead, and De Rossi stares at me for a long moment. The fire pops in the grate, and my pulse thumps in my ears. God, why did I ask that?

"...Alright."

I'm not the only one who's shocked by his agreement: the doctor blinks behind his glasses, and even De Rossi looks discomfited for a moment before waving the doctor away from the armchair and crouching in front of me. "What do I

251

need to look for?"

"Grazing." The other man falls back a few steps, watching me with renewed interest. There's no heat to his gaze, just pure calculation. "Cuts or swelling. Any sign of forming bruises. Check her fingers and toes for early signs of frostbite, too."

"Foolish girl," De Rossi mutters, plucking my hands up one by one and examining each finger. My palms are slightly red from gripping the rope, and he scowls at me before dropping each wrist. "Hands are fine."

"Good," the doctor says.

I swallow hard.

It's strange seeing this man's hands on my bare feet. I slide them one by one out of the blankets before he needs to go looking, and he cups my ankle in one strong hand then examines me quickly with the other. He turns my foot this way and that, masculine thumb smoothing almost absentmindedly over the arch of my foot, and I hide a shiver in the blankets.

"Feet are cold but fine."

"Excellent." The doctor's leaning against the desk, and he's enjoying this way too much. His mouth keeps curling up on one side, and his eyes sparkle behind those glasses. "Check her legs, Santo."

"Do we need him here?" I whisper.

De Rossi ignores me, flipping open the blankets. The cool air from the room makes me shiver, goosebumps prickling over my bare skin, and the mobster's hand feels like a red-hot brand where it touches my left knee, tilting my leg both ways. He doesn't touch me anywhere except my knees, and yet I can *feel* his gaze wandering over me like a caress.

"Some bruising." De Rossi glares at a spot inside my right

252

thigh. "Come and check this."

I squeak in dismay, but settle down after one of his looks. I guess the other man *is* a doctor, so… whatever.

"That's fine." The doctor stands over us both, frowning at my leg in the dim light. "The bruising will come through overnight, and she won't even feel it in a few days."

"Good." De Rossi waves him back, and we both seem to breathe better with the other man a few steps away. I chew on my bottom lip as my captor finishes checking me over, running his gaze over my arms and making me lift my shirt to bare my stomach briefly. The backs of his fingers are cool against my cheek when he checks my temperature. "She's a little flushed."

"You don't say," the doctor murmurs, then straightens when De Rossi turns with a glare. "She's fine, Santo. She's been under a lot of stress, and she just climbed down a rope in the freezing cold, that's all. She needs food and sleep, in that order."

"I already told the kitchens."

The doctor nods. "So make sure she eats, then have someone take her up to bed."

I grimace at that statement, but De Rossi doesn't seem to like it either. He jerks his head at the door, and his shoulders don't relax until the other man is gone.

"Don't make one of your goons take me up to bed," I say quietly. "I'll go, but just… just don't."

The mob boss pushes to his feet with a sigh. "Fine. You are a very troublesome captive, Erin."

I squint up at him, but I'm fighting a smile. "Is there any other kind?"

Santo

～～～

Governor Edwards doubles the price on my sister's head shortly before dawn. So predictable. I lean back in my desk chair, scowling at my laptop screen, and press a button on my phone.

Allegra answers after the second ring. "Hm? What's up?" She sounds groggy, her voice thick with sleep, and there's a low, masculine murmur in the background. Fucking Raul.

"He increased the bid on you," I say shortly, my words calm even as my heart races. "Stay inside today. Keep where people can see you."

She scoffs, but already Raul's murmuring something to her, soothing the flare of temper. At least their bond is useful for something. "Fine," Allegra bites out, "but I'm not hiding away forever, Santo. Wrap this shit up quickly, will you?"

A freckled face drifts across my mind, hazel eyes beseeching, and my chest feels even tighter as I respond. "Of course."

It's an obvious play for the Governor to make: I took his daughter, so he threatens my younger sister. An eye for a twisted eye. Except Allegra is here, tucked safely in my stronghold, and since the attack that left Raul's arm in a sling, our security has been impenetrable.

Meanwhile, the Governor's daughter is entirely at my mercy. He didn't make a single peep for the first twenty four hours she was gone—no panicked threats, no attempts to get her back. Was probably more concerned about the investments I've been ruining. For all he knows, I've been torturing her this whole time.

He really doesn't care about her at all, does he? I suspected as much, but to see the evidence for myself... I push to my feet, feeling queasy.

The inevitable path of this conflict plays out in my mind as I stroll through the mansion hallways, barely seeing the paintings and sculptures I pass.

I take the Governor's daughter as insurance.

I ruin his finances.

Expose his son for embezzling that charity last year, and threaten his donors away.

I take apart his platform, wealth and reputation, piece by sordid piece, until Governor Edwards is a broken man who will never pose any threat to me again.

And then, once we're both absolutely certain that I've won, I'll kill him. Obviously.

It's a bit drawn out this way, perhaps, but it's smart to make an example of him. God forbid any more upstart politicians get the wrong idea.

"Boss?" Nico falls into step beside me, and I inhale sharply and glance around. Seems we're on the second floor, prowling through the east wing. "Leah's working late at the bookshop tonight. With everything escalating, I want to send extra security while she's there."

"Fine," I agree absently, turning into a room at random. It's a barely used sitting room, with armchairs and a drinks trolley and a piano in one corner. "Send whoever you need. Go with her too, and report back to me every hour."

Nico's shoulders drop, tension falling away. "I was gonna ask that next. Thanks, boss."

As if I'd make him guard me instead of his wife. Allegra regularly accuses me of being emotionally constipated, but even I know where Nico's priorities should lie while we're under threat. And though he asked nicely, we both know he'd have gone to that bookshop either way. He can't keep away.

No one fears me anymore. Not the people close to me, anyway. It's fucking annoying.

Hazel eyes, peering up at me, wide and trusting...

"How long until Christmas?" I ask abruptly, marching toward the drinks trolley then veering away when I remember that it's early morning.

"Tomorrow's Christmas Eve." Nico's grin stretches across his face, and he scratches his stubbled chin. His dark hair is still damp from the shower. "Why? You gonna hang stockings for all of us on the mantel? Have we been good this year?"

My fingers itch for my gun. I pinch the bridge of my nose instead. "No. So everything's alright with Leah? She got the bookshop open again?"

"Yeah," Nico says, and he's more subdued now. Peering closer. "Another headache? They're coming thick and fast these days. Maybe you should talk to Raul."

"I'm fine," I mutter, but then find myself waving at my chest, the words spilling out. "But I keep getting this... this burning sensation..."

Nico frowns, and his obvious worry is almost moving. I drop both hands, shaking off the moment with a sigh. "It's fine. Too much time around imbeciles gives me indigestion."

He snorts. "Guilty as charged."

Nico doesn't ask me why I'm wandering the halls aimlessly, still dressed in yesterday's clothes, and I don't tell him. And once his footsteps drum away down the corridor, I allow myself a rare moment of weakness, dropping into the nearest armchair with a groan.

Is it worth all this just to make a point? To maintain my ruthless reputation?

And what will Erin think of her father's death? It might hurt her, certainly—but she might also be relieved.

Will she ever forgive me?

I scoff and bury my face in my hands while I'm safely alone. I've been the ruthless De Rossi kingpin for so long now, impenetrable and cold, that I've mastered the art of falling apart quickly in stolen moments of silence.

This is how it needs to be. I'm a criminal and her captor. I've worked too hard, fought too long, spilled too much blood to build this empire to risk it now—and too many people rely on me to keep them safe. Allegra and Raul and Nico and Leah, even Diego and the maid he's in love with.

The weight of it all crushes me from above; squeezes the air from my lungs and makes my bones creak. My eyes fall closed.

I allow myself one minute of sheer exhaustion.

One idle thought about how things could have been different. Another life entirely, with a certain freckled face smiling by my side. A life of sleep and laughter and petty concerns about things like whose turn it is to do the dishes. Maybe I'd have been something boring. A professor or a writer. An art dealer, perhaps.

Then I push to my feet and smooth the front of my waistcoat, soothed by the familiar silk against my palm.

This is how it needs to be. And only children pine after fairy tales.

* * *

"Feeling cooperative?"

I rap against the guest suite door as I open it, peering around Erin's deluxe makeshift cell. The lights are all off and soft breaths drift from the bed.

Ah. My captive is snoozing.

I should leave. Should close the door and let her catch up on sleep after her antics last night, not walk further into the room and flick on a table lamp, but as everyone knows, I am not a good man.

Golden light spills across the rugs. Erin's breaths are slow. Steady.

Even as a kidnap victim, she gets more sleep than I do.

The door falls shut behind me as I stroll across the suite, hands tucked in my pockets, and now we're truly alone. Erin is a small lump in the bed, piled high with blankets, and a rejected pillow lies tossed on the floor.

She snuffles, burrowing deeper into her pile of bedding. I stand at her bedside and observe, ignoring the dull ache in my chest.

"Mmph?" Erin says after several minutes, her hindbrain finally realizing that she's not alone. "Whazzat?"

"Erin." I sink down into the armchair. "I have a proposition for you."

She's frozen under her blankets, not breathing since she heard my voice. And though I scowl at the wall, a headache flaring in my temples, I know it's not an unreasonable reaction.

I took her captive.

I watched her sleep... again.

I—

"*Gawd*, you people hate sleep, I swear. What time is—it's not even seven thirty, Santo! We were up most of the night!"

It's an effort to keep my face blank as she fights her way out of her tangled bedding, red-faced and rumpled, her silk pajama shirt twisting around her body. Erin harrumphs her way to a cross-legged seat, glaring at me from the center of the mattress, and she clearly does *not* fear me right now.

So the milkmaid has a temper under those freckles? Interesting.

"What can you possibly have on my schedule today that couldn't wait for a reasonable hour?" she asks, so scathing. But her hazel eyes track over my chest and arms, that flush deepening as her gaze wanders.

It's incriminating, the blush staining her cheeks. She doesn't hate finding me here, no matter her bluster.

"A proposition," I repeat. She'd know that if she paid an ounce of attention. "And seven thirty *is* a reasonable hour, Erin. Such a spoiled little princess."

Her fingers twitch, like she might actually lunge for me, and her tiny growl sends a pleased ripple down my spine. "Are all mob bosses huge jerks?"

I fight a smile. "Exclusively."

"Well I am not a morning person, so if you want a biddable

259

captive, come back in an hour or two."

"I want photographs," I say, ignoring her rant and leaning back in the armchair. "Of the two of us. Photographs that will ruin your father's career. I can do it in other ways, obviously, but this process is dragging and I'd like to speed it along. Will you cooperate?"

Erin plucks at a sheet corner in her lap. "Why would I do that?"

"An exchange." I tilt my head, heart drumming. "Ask me for something in return."

"A plane ticket to Australia," she says immediately, and something inside me ices over. She's fleeing to Australia? That's—that's as far away from me as she could possibly go.

But what did I expect when I set out to ruin her family? And a trade is a trade. I'm a man of my word, though not much honor besides.

"Alright," I agree, the words stiff. "But not right away. Not until this is all over."

"By January," she fires back. "Or there's no deal."

So soon. But... maybe it's better this way. I'm already far more attached than is wise, and it's not like I could ever keep her. Not like she'd stay here willingly with me.

"By January." I put out my hand and she shakes it, her fingers so small in mine. "I'll have food and clothes sent up to you. Be ready in an hour, and for god's sake, drink some coffee."

Erin

~~~oⱥoꝺ~~~

I will never admit this to Santo De Rossi, but I feel like crap after climbing down that stupid rope last night. I've strained muscles in my back that I didn't even know I had, and the bruise on my right thigh is tender when I poke it.

"Relax," he mutters as I walk by his side through the mansion, but he's not the reason I'm holding myself so stiffly. My back aches like hell, and I'm tired and grouchy and...

And like I said. Not a morning person. But the last thing I want to do is ruin the fragile peace between us, so I gust out a long breath and force my shoulders to drop.

"Sorry." He's startled by my cautious smile, ice blue eyes bouncing over my features. "I drank, like, a gallon of coffee but it didn't touch the sides."

Santo frowns as he holds another door open for me. "I'll let you sleep in next time."

Aw. Well now I'm all warm and fuzzy.

The De Rossi mansion is all fancy oil paintings and chandeliers, like my father's house but grander. I follow my captor through the hallways, peering around with mild interest, but nothing truly steals my breath until the conservatory.

A wall of humid air hits us the second we walk inside. It's muggy in here, with glass walls and ceilings high above, and tropical plants cover almost every surface. Vines dangle and trees loom, sunshine sparkling through the glass, and the faint sound of trickling water cuts through the quiet.

"Oh my god." I point stupidly at a flash of red high above. "There are birds in here."

Santo's mouth twitches. "So there are."

You'd never guess it was snowy outside. That we're in the depths of winter. For the first time in months, I'm warm to the marrow of my bones.

"Well, I don't know why you made me wear *this*, you weirdo." I pluck at the woolen Christmas sweater I found left on the coffee table after my shower: black with a sequin reindeer. Paired with jeans and sneakers, the backs of my knees are already sweaty. "It's an elaborate torture, I'll give you that. Death by heat rash."

He rolls his eyes, but the mob boss seems almost cheerful as he leads me over cobbled paving stones, weaving between garden furniture and trestle tables. "So dramatic."

My grin falters when I realize we've got company: one of Santo's henchmen is setting up a camera on a tripod. There's a bench swing dangling from an overhead beam, already wound with tinsel and string lights, and the display is professionally lit with a warm glow.

"Oh shit," I mumble, my brain finally catching up. This looks like...

"Our holiday card," Santo confirms with an evil smirk. He takes an offered bundle from the stranger and sets it on the bench, then flicks open the buttons of his waistcoat. It's dove gray today. "Trust me, the idea that the Governor's daughter is dating a mob boss will kill his political career in ten seconds flat."

I've never thought of myself as a vicious person, but that statement gives me a mean little thrill. Over the years, my father has made an art form out of putting me down and making me miserable. Controlling my life and trapping me under his thumb. Payback time.

"When you told me the plan, I thought you meant sexy photos."

The man fiddling with the camera chokes quietly at my confession. He's brawny and bearded, with a scar running down his cheek, and he stares at the screen like he's trying to burn a hole through it.

Santo peels off his shirt, folding it carefully and setting it to one side. Those *muscles*. There are faded scars too, white lines criss-crossing his ribs where old blades slashed his skin. Knife fights with the mob boss?

I want to lick him. So not fair.

"And yet you agreed," he says lightly, and my cheeks burn hot. Yeah, well. It wasn't the worst idea I'd ever heard. "Photos like that would be too easy for your father to spin. He could paint you as a victim and himself as a hero, and turn the situation to his advantage. A holiday card, on the other hand, sent to all the power players in the city…"

"It makes us seem serious about each other. Domestic."

"Exactly." His approving glance makes my tummy flip, and then he's shrugging on a matching black sweater, complete with a slightly bigger reindeer.

"And this won't damage your scary mob boss vibe?"

"No." There's a flash of teeth as he grins, settling onto the bench swing. "Even the underworld has a sense of humor. And they'll know it's not real."

…Right.

Only an idiot would forget that detail.

"Try to look more natural," the henchman rumbles two minutes later, waving a giant hand in our direction. I slide an inch closer to Santo on the bench swing, already sweating under my clothes.

The *heat* in here, jeez. No wonder I'm bright red and all… jittery.

The man frowns but he snaps a few photos, then shakes his head. I tilt my head toward Santo, thrilling at his sea spray and lightning scent as I whisper in his ear.

"Are you sure your goon is the best photographer around?"

"Diego's fine." Pale eyes narrow on me. "And you can't keep calling my men goons."

"Santo's little helpers?"

He pinches my side, and I snort. When we look up, the g—Diego is staring at us, nonplussed. Has he never seen his boss joke around before?

"What if I sit on his lap?" I suggest, feeling bold. And I aimed my question at the photographer, but Santo's already drawing me onto his strong thighs. The bench swing wobbles as we rearrange, but Santo slides closer to the middle and it settles.

"You're enjoying this," he murmurs in my ear. His breath wafts over my curls, tickling the strands against my neck. "You could have cuddled up to me at any time, Erin."

Somehow, I don't think that's true. This man is cold and distant and work-obsessed—usually, anyway. Absolutely not the cuddling type. This interlude, with his strong arms

264

wrapped around me and his lips grazing over the curve of my neck, this is just make believe.

"Bullshit," I wheeze, wriggling closer until my sore back is plastered against his chest. I'm blocking his reindeer from the shot, but I don't care. My head tips back against the mobster's shoulder, and my gaze is fuzzy as I stare up into the canopy of tropical leaves. "As if you'd let me climb all over you in real life."

Santo's arms tighten around me, and his words are soft. Just for me, buried in the curtain of my hair. "Try me, Erin."

Woof.

"Domestic," the photographer calls gruffly. "Not R-rated, remember? Simmer down, both of you."

Santo's chest rumbles with a laugh as I cackle. And this is *fun*, this is the lightest I've felt in... well, maybe ever. Has anyone ever held me this tightly before? I don't think so.

Not sure anyone's ever held me at all, now that I think of it. Not since I was a little girl with a nanny. Well, that's pathetic.

"You've gone wooden." A thumb strokes over my ribs, steady and comforting. "Have you had enough?"

Ha. It's the opposite problem. "Dude, we could do this all day and I wouldn't get enough."

And I don't know what it is about this man that makes me spill my secrets so readily—that makes me open and trusting and so freaking vulnerable, to a mob boss of all people. But Santo De Rossi hums, low and pleased, and when he whispers, "Not a dude," my toes curl in my borrowed sneakers.

I mean it, you know. I want this moment to last forever.

"Say cheese," the photographer says, and I swear he's hiding a smile.

I beam at the camera and refuse point blank to think about

the future.

* * *

Santo walks me back to my room, touching me the whole way. There's always a palm resting on my lower back, or fingers playing in my hair, or knuckles smoothing down my upper arm, and everywhere he touches me—everywhere he's touched me already—burns hot and sensitive, nerves prickling under the skin. I bite my lip against a whimper, but I don't think he even realizes the effect on me.

"You were excellent."

His smoky praise makes my heart pound. What other nice things could I get him to say?

"You certainly earned that plane ticket, Erin."

Just like that, my happy bubble pops. Because oh yeah, I'm leaving in a few days, and this wasn't some adorable first date—this was a trade, cold and calculated like everything else with this man. He needed that holiday card photo, nothing more.

So why's he still tracing my wrist as we walk?

"I aim to please," I say, but Santo must hear the bitter tone to my voice, because he draws his hand back and doesn't touch me again the whole way back to my door.

I stomp inside, all grouchy and flustered again. Does he really need to leave so soon? Surely even mobsters take time off over the holidays. Can't we, like... go for a walk or something? Maybe watch a movie together?

"I'm going to leave this door unlocked," my captor says, frowning down at me. He's back in his waistcoat and shirtsleeves, and it really shows off his broad shoulders and trim waist. And those freaking forearms—

"Are you listening, Erin?" Nope, I was not. What was he saying? Something about staying indoors and security guards patrolling the grounds.

"I'm not going to make a run for it, Santo. You're my ticket out of here, remember?" Not just the De Rossi mansion and my current predicament, but *here*. My family, the society pressures, my *life*. "Before January, that's what we agreed." Then I'll become the new Erin, complete with one of those dorky hats with corks dangling from the brim.

"Yes."

His mouth twists, and he looks so unhappy up there. Always so cold and stiff and severe. I rock up onto my toes before I can think better of it, spreading my palms over his perfect chest.

"Erin—" Santo cuts off with a groan as my mouth meets his. And I've pictured what this might be like a gazillion times since meeting this man, but I always figured it'd be like making out with one of the marble statues in the alcoves. I never imagined that he'd be so *unruly*.

But Santo spins us both, flattening me against the door frame. He presses one thigh between my legs; tips my head back and kisses me hungrily. And this is not the cool, controlled press of lips I expected, this is... this is...

I'm being eaten alive.

His hands are everywhere, squeezing my hips and waist and tits then tugging on my hair, and he snarls against my mouth before kissing me harder. What happened to the ice cold kingpin? Where's the pinnacle of restraint?

"Fuck," Santo mutters before plunging his tongue into my mouth. It strokes against mine, hot and teasing, and when I suck on his tongue, he thumps a fist against the door frame over my head, then crowds closer. He's hard against my stomach, his body prodding me with unspoken demands. "*Fuck*, Erin."

I hum in agreement, tugging on his dark hair and rolling my hips against his body. He's all I can smell, taste, touch. "Come inside. Blow off kingpin duties for the day."

His laugh is strained. "I'm your captor."

"Mhm." Hooking one finger in his waistcoat, I tow him into the guest suite. Santo's eyes are dark as he prowls inside. "I'm completely at your mercy, De Rossi. Got any suggestions?"

He kicks the door closed without looking back. "So many. You have no fucking idea."

Santo

⚜

I make her watch a movie with me. Not because I'm so desperate to waste two hours of my life on some brainless comedy, but because Erin's worked up and bright eyed, blushing behind those freckles, and I don't want to rush this. I need to break the heat of the moment so she can think this through.

She truly is at my mercy here. Before I touch her, I need her to be sure—and if I don't distract myself in the meantime, I'm liable to tackle her to the rug and tear that sweater down the middle.

"You're not even watching," she gripes after an hour, poking me between the ribs. I'm leaning against her headboard, Erin curled against my side, and no, despite insisting on this activity, I'm not watching. I have far better things to focus on.

"Because it's inane."

She huffs, her breath warm against my throat. "This was your idea, jerk."

"And I stand by it." Whenever I stroke my thumb over her

hip, she shivers and squirms closer. Where else is she ticklish? Her leg's tossed over mine, and she's practically lying on top of me, her breaths coming quicker against my skin as time wears on. It's maddening—and perfect. "This movie is ridiculous. A green, hairy man who hates Christmas? Who cares? The company, on the other hand…"

I stroke a fingertip down the back of her neck, and I'm rewarded with a full-body shiver. Erin scoffs and bats me away, scrambling up to straddle my lap, and then those hazel eyes are fixed on mine.

The movie drones on in the background, the bright swirl of color completely abandoned. Forget distractions. I gave her an hour to think it through, didn't I?

And Erin has decided. "If you wanted to have your wicked way, Mr De Rossi, you should have just said so." She grinds her ass down against my lap to illustrate her point, and I grab her hips and squeeze.

"Careful," I warn. She shouldn't push me right now. I'm on edge, overheated with a racing pulse, and I want her so badly my teeth ache.

Erin flicks my nose. I catch her wrist, heart drumming.

"We could have done this earlier," she points out, curls bouncing as she jerks her chin. "Right there in the doorway."

My growl cuts through the quiet as I flip her over, straddling her with my knees on either side of her waist. She blinks up at me, shocked and helpless and so flushed. After one heartbeat, her mouth curves up.

She likes this.

Fuck, *I* like this. Since when do I like this?

Since you stuffed her in that car trunk, I tell myself, the pinch of guilt chased away by her body rolling up against mine. Erin has the right idea. What's one tiny abduction between friends?

"So many fucking freckles." I sound angry about it, my voice harsh, but she grins. "You're such a fucking milkmaid, Erin. And that gap in your front teeth, I can't—can't think when you bite your lip like that."

Plucking up both wrists, I check her palms again for redness before wrapping both hands around the bed frame. She's spread out beneath me, eyes wide and chest heaving, and the sight of her makes my head pound.

"Couldn't do this in the doorway," I say. I've never heard my own voice like this—ragged and strained. "I'd tie you properly, but you chewed through it like a little wild animal."

Better to not push it, too. Better to calm this down. And maybe we should dial this back, go back to the movie—

Erin rocks up without warning, hands still gripping the frame, and rubs her cheek against my thigh. I go still, and I can't—can't breathe.

Is she…?

Does she want to…?

"Closer," she says, so breathless, and I move without thinking until my knees bracket her shoulders, sinking into the mattress. She cranes up again, mouthing at my cock through my pants, and I choke back a shout. When I grab hold of the bed frame, I squeeze so hard the metal creaks.

This was not the plan.

I was going to take *her* to pieces, not the other way around.

"Let me," Erin murmurs, like she's reading the frantic thoughts bouncing around my mind. "Come on, you big, scary kingpin. Just a little taste."

It's an effort, but I roll my eyes. "This is a very elaborate escape plan." My belt buckle clinks as she tugs it open one-handed, the other still fixed to the frame, and I'm not stopping her. Why am I not stopping her? "Surely there's a better way to lower my guard."

"Do you see me trying to run?" Those hazel eyes bore through me, seeing far too much. Seeing the doubt gnawing at my insides, the bottomless desire. The longing for this to be real. They crinkle as she smiles, and her hand is warm as it wraps around my cock, drawing it out into the air. "Come on, live a little. All work and no play makes Santo a dull mobster."

Dull? I hiss through my teeth as she leans up, flicking her tongue over the head. She thinks I'm dull? We need more explosions around here.

"People will think I forced you." The words taste sour, and I grimace down at my captive as she runs the flat of her tongue up my shaft. My hips twitch forward, fucking gently past her lips. And hell, maybe it makes me the worst kind of villain, but I can't stop this now. Can't bring myself to push her mouth away: it's too hot, too sweet, too mischievous.

Her tongue dances over me as she gazes up, so beseeching, and if someone walked through that door right now, I know exactly what they'd see. A cold, vicious criminal, hunkered over his innocent captive, pinning her to the bed and fucking into her mouth.

I squeeze the bed frame until my knuckles sing. Don't care. Can't stop.

Sweat beads my spine under my shirt and waistcoat.

When Erin pulls her mouth away with a pop, her chin is slick. She beams up at me, and that fucking gap tooth—I'm losing my mind.

"You're not forcing anything. And no one who really knows you would ever think that, Santo."

Well, does anyone really know me except for this woman I stole? Anyone at all?

She has far too much faith in me. Far too much trust, but she *sees* me. I can't deny it.

"Enough chat." I gather up a fistful of soft hair, guiding her head back to my cock. "Put that pretty mouth to good use."

Erin's delighted laugh blurs into a moan, and then she's slurping. Bobbing. *Sucking.*

I need her. Australia is too fucking far away, and I'd need to keep her with me even if we never did anything like *this.* Even if all I had from her was an occasional conversation; a smile on a rough day. Doesn't she realize that no one else is like her? That no one else helps me relax? Doesn't she understand?

Heat crawls up my chest, and my pulse is deafening in my ears.

So fucking good.

"Going to keep you, Erin." She moans and sucks harder, cheeks hollowing, but this isn't part of the game. I mean every damn word. "Fuck that plane ticket. Do you hear me? You're *mine.*"

Her eyelids flutter, and I grit my teeth. It takes every ounce of my self control not to thrust into her throat, but I hold back. Just.

And the heat of her mouth; the lash of her tongue; the vibration of her moans tingling through my balls—it builds and builds until I forget to breathe and I'm tugging on her hair, giving a last-ditch warning.

She pulls off just in time, flopping back on the mattress with a pleased sigh.

I come on her chest, splattering the sequin reindeer.

"Hey!" She peers down at herself, blinking at the mess I've

made of her Christmas sweater. For a moment, we stare at each other in silence, both breathing hard.

Then Erin buries her face in her hands and howls with laughter, and I'm already crawling down her body, lip curled back from my teeth, yanking at the button on her jeans.

"Your turn," I snarl, half embarrassed and so turned on, and she grabs my hair and twists, still giggling.

Jesus Christ. Her thighs drape over my shoulders and I settle in.

We're going to bring down the mansion.

Santo

~~~

The next morning, I lean back in my desk chair and watch the headlines with a smirk. My jaw aches from bringing Erin off until she wept with exhaustion yesterday, but that's not the only reason this is a good day.

It's Christmas Eve.

It's snowing outside.

And Governor Edwards' life is ruined.

The media are having a feeding frenzy, showing the story of his downfall on a loop. His son's arrest for embezzlement, with the grainy footage of a shocked man in his thirties being pushed into a police car; the Governor's sudden bankruptcy, with shots of priceless (yet tasteless) artwork carried from his home; and best of all, his confirmed links with known criminals.

The image of our fake holiday card hovers on the screen, two reporters debating its implications. Did Santo De Rossi rig the election? Who else has the big, bad kingpin bought? Do the politicians need to clean house? Etc, etc.

Delicious.

"Causing chaos?" Allegra elbows her way into my study with a vicious grin, a bowl of granola held two inches below her chin. She strolls to the desk, then watches my laptop screen for a few moments. "Idiots," my baby sister declares.

Everyone says we look similar. Well, those who are brave enough to comment on our appearance do, anyway. Allegra and I have the same haughty chin, the same sharp features and dark hair. The same shadows under our eyes.

Though since she and Raul got together, she seems less exhausted all the time. *Happy.* It's the only reason he's kept all his limbs.

I rub my chest, frowning at the wall. That burning feeling again.

"You okay?" She eyes me closely, chewing a spoonful of granola. There's a bead of milk on her top lip. "Want me to get the doc?"

They're engaged, so why does she still call him that? Oh god, I bet it's some role play thing. Does my baby sister have a medical kink? For fuck's sake.

"You don't have to kill him, you know." Allegra nods at the screen. "If it'll scare away your girl. Just make him miserable for life and let that be enough."

I roll my eyes, pressing the button on my phone to call for coffee. Obviously that's an option. I'm not a wild animal, ruled by impulses alone, though my skull won't stop buzzing with them. "I realize that."

Allegra takes another huge bite of granola, chewing thoughtfully. She always sees too much when she looks at me.

And I can't stand it, so I lash out. "You're disgusting when you eat, did you know that? Take smaller bites."

Why am I being such a dick? Two minutes ago, I was smirking serenely, but now I've got hot snakes wrestling inside me. I want to peel off my own skin. I want to claw at the walls until my fingers are bloody. I want—

If I spare her father's life, will Erin stay with me willingly?

Allegra hops up onto my desk, nearly spilling milk everywhere. She ignores my outburst completely, though I suppose she's used to my moods. And why on earth would Erin want to sign on for *this*?

"That warehouse is still standing—the one the Bulgarians used to hide all their shit. You said we could have fun with it, remember?"

She waggles her eyebrows, and just like that, I exhale. I did say that. And it *is* Christmas Eve.

"Alright. I'll bring Erin."

Allegra's eyes gleam.

"Don't scare her," I warn. "Or I'll send Raul away for a month on some fucked up mission."

A scoff. "Fine. But you'll have to trust us with her eventually."

Maybe. Hopefully. Can't think about that right now; can't get my hopes any higher. My chest burns.

"She's green. So go easy on her, or you'll all walk home in the snow." Hey, since the Governor withdrew the hits on my inner circle, running with his tail between his legs, I can order their drivers to leave them on any highway I like. Harmony is restored.

"Meet across the water at twelve?" Allegra slides off my desk, slurping from her spoon.

"Tell the others." I rap on my desk, already picturing Erin's face. Maybe this will do the trick. "Family fireworks."

277

* * *

Erin rocks back on her heels, wiping a pearly white bead of my release from the corner of her mouth. She's kneeling between my spread thighs in the back of the car, and she grins up at me like she loves this as much as I do. Not possible.

We've already kept the car idling for twenty minutes at the side of the empty street. I've brought her off with my hands and mouth until the tinted windows steamed over from her panting. The driver's probably napping behind that partition, snoozing against his steering wheel.

There's no more stalling. She's going to meet the others— properly. An official introduction. Will this convince her to stay?

I restore my clothing to order and open the car door. Unfold myself into the street, then lean down to help her out.

"Once upon a time, a mouthy captive named Erin called her abductor dull."

She snorts, her boots crunching against the snow as she wobbles out to my side. Is she warm enough? I had boots and more sweaters and a winter coat sent to her room, along with a hat, scarf and gloves. I'm still fretting over her pink little nose.

She sniffs against the cold, peering out at the river. The water glitters past the stone walls, gunmetal gray and icy cold. "And then he killed her and dismembered her on a river bank?"

I bark out a laugh. "This is a collaborative story. Is that really how you want this to go?"

"Nope." Her gloved hand slips into mine. "Dismember me another day."

"If you insist." Her breath forms little white clouds, and I can't stop staring at her. Is she in love with me yet? How can I hurry this along? "The others are joining us for this. My, ah—my favored goons."

It's worth making the effort to joke when she rewards me with that laugh. Her fingers squeeze mine, and I practically float over the snow to the edge of the river. The warehouse is squat and ugly, hunkered on the opposite bank.

"See that building?" I point at the boarded over windows, the spray painted walls, the shadowed doorways like missing teeth. We already sent a crew to check it's empty. "Do you like it? Do you think it's pretty?"

"Um." Erin looks at me like I've gone insane. "It's—ugh. No, it's horrible. Why, is this some kind of passion project? Are you trying to flip it?"

Ha. "Wait for it." I draw her in front of me and squeeze her shoulders. My chin grazes against her gray woolen hat, and I count under my breath from ten.

The explosion shakes the earth. Waves rush across the river surface, splashing against the bank, and smoke rises in a blackened pillar toward the sky. Everything is red hot, the heat washing over our cheeks, and the air sizzles.

"Holy—"

"Yeeeees!" Allegra and Leah whoop together, running toward us along the bank. Raul, Nico and Diego follow behind, Diego's new girl tucked under his arm. Were they all hiding together, trying to glimpse Erin and I? I'll punish them for that.

"Oh my god." Erin's staring at the burning warehouse, her body rigid, but when I lean around to check her expression, her eyes are bright. "Oh my *god*. You just blow stuff up? Whole buildings? You can do that when you're a kingpin?"

"And when you're a kingpin's girl."

She flushes bright red at that, and I could kick myself. Too much, too soon.

"Who wants mulled wine?" Leah reaches us first, eyeing my captive with blatant curiosity. She draws a giant thermos and a stack of paper cups from the depths of her coat, and her dark hair dances on the wind.

"Baby," Nico calls, his voice echoing over the disturbed water. "You've been hiding those this whole time? What the hell?"

His wife ignores him, still peering at Erin. She pours the first cup, then holds it out like a ceremonial offering. She's wearing mittens with penguins on them.

"You don't have to," I mutter, rubbing my girl's shoulders through her coat. "She's a bookshop owner, not the chieftain of a distant land."

But: "Thanks," Erin whispers, taking the cup of warm wine, and my shy milkmaid is back. I rub my cheek on her head, ignoring the shocked gazes all around.

What? I have feelings. I'm perfectly capable of getting attached.

For instance: Raul has informed me that these burning sensations in my chest are most likely *emotions.*

"Next time, we roast marshmallows," Diego declares as the others reach us, and his girl Holly elbows him in the gut.

"Don't you dare. I like you with eyebrows."

They burst into a loud debate, everyone weighing in, but I tune it all out, focusing on my grip on Erin's shoulders.

It's… uncomfortable, at first. Being here with them. Their stares make my neck itch, and I keep wanting to drag Erin away and keep her all to myself. Flatten her against the nearest brick wall and rut. Every time one of the men glance at her I choke back a snarl, even though I *know* they're all head over heels for their own partners, and I'm jealous of every minute we spend here, Erin's focus on someone else.

She's mine.

She *will* be mine.

Does she want me yet? Permanently? What else could I blow up to convince her I'm not dull?

Whatever it takes, I'll do it. I'll pay whatever cost.

I cannot let this woman go.

Erin

Christmas Day dawns bright and snowy, and with the puff of warm breath against my stomach. Santo De Rossi, feared mob boss and notorious villain, scrapes his teeth against my hip bone, crawling slowly down my body.

"Open up, Erin."

His voice is low, gravelly with sleep. After our little outing yesterday and an hours-long poker game with the others, he crashed in my bed and slept like the dead.

He looks cute when he sleeps. More innocent, somehow.

Never going to tell him that.

Muscles shift in his bare back, the sheets pooling around his waist, and Santo's stubble grazes my inner thigh. Strong hands grip my ass, lifting me easily, rearranging me on the bed, and I choke back a sigh.

God, I love it when he does that—treats me like a toy. Arranges me to his liking. So messed up, but it makes my whole body flush hot.

"Merry Christmas," he growls against my clit.

"Hap-Happy Christmas," I squeak, eyes already screwed shut. I'm grabbing fistfuls of the bed sheets, tugging and twisting, because the mob boss is *good* at this. And I guess it's no surprise—he's eaten me out so many times in the last two days that he could probably do it blindfolded. But even as I peek down at him past my own flushed chest, there's no sign of him getting bored down there.

He scowls at my pussy like he's annoyed at how much he likes it. And when he licks me, dark and possessive and so freaking *hungry*, something whispers in the back of my brain that he'll never stop.

If I stayed here, Santo De Rossi would kiss me down there every single day. He'd spread me over that fancy desk in his study and feast. He'd *possess* me. That's what the voice says.

Wishful thinking, obviously.

"You can—you can fuck me," I gasp, blushing at my own daring. As if I'd even know what I'm doing. But why hasn't he tried yet? "If you want to, I mean."

Because I've been thinking about it non-stop, weighing his heavy, hard shaft in my palm every time I go to my knees. Wondering how it would feel pushing inside me.

Whether it would hurt. Whether he'd roll his hips like he does sometimes, laying on top of me, like he's trying to grind me into the mattress, and how *that* would feel.

God, I want it.

"Please," I whisper, but Santo's dark hair brushes my thighs as he shakes his head.

"Later," he says, and it's that tone he uses. The one that brooks no argument. My nipples tighten, even as I huff at the ceiling.

"We don't *have* much longer—"

283

He spanks my slit without warning, the hot sting rushing through my flesh, and I arch off the mattress with a strangled moan. Holy shit. How do I make him do that again?

"Later, Erin. Now behave."

Oh. My. God.

I never thought I'd be into this: being bossed around by a man, being *owned*, being punished and praised. All those years of being lonely in my father's house, I always pictured my ideal love story, and my fantasy husband was someone sweet. Safe and nonthreatening; the sort of man who'd wear cargo shorts at a barbecue. A math teacher, maybe.

Santo De Rossi is no math teacher. He slides his tongue inside me, grip bruising on my hips, and his growls vibrate through my nerve endings until I can't breathe.

"Shit! Santo!"

He grunts in approval, pushing two fingers past my entrance and sucking on my folds. Wet noises fill the air, and it's so crude, so shameless, and I'd die of embarrassment if he weren't licking me like that, teasing and nibbling until my brain is filled with white static and my body goes rigid and—

"Good girl." The kingpin watches me fall apart, darkly pleased. His fingers are slick and shiny as they pump inside me. "That's right. Cry for me."

Tears have gathered in the corners of my eyes. I blink them away, sniffling and fuzzy.

So good. I'm limp as he crawls back up my body: a spent rag doll. I should offer to return the favor, but I can't move an inch.

"I think I like you ruined," Santo tells me, pulling the sheet back over my chest. He frowns at the sight for a moment, then tugs it back down so my hard nipples poke into the cool air. "It's certainly quieter."

I lift one wobbly arm long enough to thump his shoulder. "Ass." And I'm still floating somewhere above the ceiling, lost in the glow, so I risk the question. "So how does a girl get your cock, Mr De Rossi?"

"She earns it," Santo says mildly, but he won't meet my eye. He's teasing, but neither of us is laughing.

I chew on my bottom lip, staring at the rumpled bed sheets. Haven't I earned it yet? Doesn't he trust me? Maybe he doesn't want me that badly after all.

"I have something for you." The gruff words interrupt my downward spiral, and Santo's back flexes as he leans over the side of the bed, rummaging in the pile of his clothes. When he comes back up, he hands me a cream envelope and I sit up too.

A Christmas gift? For me?

The fancy paper scrapes as I peel it open. Inside, there's a glossy black card with the photo of the two of us in matching reindeer sweaters. *Season's Greetings*, it says, and my cheeks ache from grinning.

"Half the city got one yesterday. It ruined your father's career in one blow."

"They should've seen the after shot," I say, thinking about the pearly beads of release clinging to poor Rudolph.

Santo winds one of my curls around his knuckle. "Indeed. Keep going."

I flip the card open, fully expecting a first class ticket to Oz, but there's only a short message from Santo, complete with an angry little kiss mark. I tip the envelope upside down, and a key drops onto the bed sheets.

"I bought your father's house," Santo explains, quiet but

clear. "Rushed the sale through. It's in your name, and you can do what you like with it. Sell it or redecorate it. Donate it or level it to the ground. You know we're always happy to blow buildings up."

I blink hard, staring at the key like it might not be real. That house was my de facto prison for most of my life, and now it's mine? I get to decide what becomes of it? My nose is itchy. Think I'm gonna cry.

"No one's ever…"

"Bought you a mansion?" Santo's smile is crooked, and I'm still not used to seeing him like this. Happy and warm and open. I kiss the ever-present scrunch between his eyebrows. "Well, be fair, Erin. That is a high bar."

"Shut up." I bury my face in his neck and breathe him in. His pre-shower morning smell, when he's still sea spray but with the faint tang of sex and sweat. I love him like this.

"I have also decided to let your father live. I've already ground him into the dirt; I don't *need* to do more to prove my point. You would prefer if he lived, correct?"

My laugh is strangled. "Correct. Thank you. This is all… wow. I thought it was gonna be a plane ticket, I had no idea…"

I trail off when Santo goes rigid.

"You still want that, then?" His words are clipped. Angry. I lean back and though I laugh, my stomach hurts. Why is he glaring at me like that? Why is he moving away? The bed is so cold when there's distance between us.

"Well, yeah." Don't I? I mean, what's the alternative?

I need to be smart. Santo *stole* me, he literally stuffed me in the trunk of a car, and maybe he finds me entertaining for the time being, but soon enough he'll lose interest.

Believe me, I get old real fast. My father and brother could barely stand to have me in the same room, and they were my family. How likely is it that the kingpin will like me any better after a few months?

"You want me," he says, and it's an accusation. "You just begged me to fuck you, Erin."

My cheeks burn and I tug the sheet up, covering myself. Does he really need to throw that back in my face? "Yeah, well. Maybe it's Stockholm Syndrome."

A muscle twitches below Santo's eye. "I see. So what if it is?"

That's his answer? So what?

"So then it's not *real*," I say, hating the words even as I hear them, because nothing about this feels fake. My hands tremble where they grip the bed sheets. "And even if it is—"

"What?" Santo snaps. "What then?" He's glaring at me with such disdain, and it's like my first hours here all over again. Back when we were strangers, before we ever touched. Before we felt this kinship. Can't believe his tongue was inside me only minutes ago.

It's freezing in this room. I shiver, yanking the covers higher.

"Well, then you still have all the power! You could get tired of me. You could change your mind and I'd be left with nothing, completely screwed, with no family and no one left in the world, and meanwhile you have *everything*. Come on, Santo. You like strategy. How exactly do I play a hand like that?"

I break off, chest heaving, and he stares at me. Those glacial eyes withdraw from me slowly, until it's like he's not even here. So distant.

"Th-thank you for the gift."

It's no use. He's rolling out of bed, dressing in sharp, jerky motions. He pulls on just enough to protect his dignity, shirt hanging open and waistcoat scrunched in one hand, then strides from the guest suite, the door closing behind him with a snap.

I'm left alone. Wheezing for breath, arms wrapped tight around my stomach.

I gaze around the room. The sofas and coffee table and closet door all blur as my eyes swim, but he doesn't come back.

Crap.

That did not go well.

* * *

Someone knocks on my door in the late afternoon. I'm out on my balcony, bundled in the winter clothes that keep appearing like magic while I'm in the shower, staring at the red sun as it sinks over the grounds. Everything is white and snowy. Pristine and ice cold.

This weather suits him. Can't imagine Santo in a heat wave.

I don't respond to the knock, but the door to my suite cracks open. A blonde head pokes in, and a private smile flits over the stranger's face when she sees me outside. "I like the balconies here too."

This girl's familiar somehow with her light blonde bob, and it's not just from yesterday. She picks her way through the guest suite furniture and joins me outside, already bundled in a thick green sweater, and it's not until she turns to gaze at the grounds that I recognize her.

"Did you…?"

"I worked for your father, yeah." She shoots me a wry smile.

"As a maid. Then he made me spy on De Rossi, and surprise! I got caught. I, um. I actually helped Santo." Those cheeks burn red, and I raise an eyebrow, waiting. "I broke him into the Edwards mansion the night you were kidnapped."

Huh. An accessory to the crime. What do you even say to that?

"The sedative was a bit much."

The maid winces. "Sorry. I had no idea until it was too late, and then Diego promised you'd be okay, and... are you? Are you okay?"

My mouth twists, and I chew that question over. Am I okay?

As kidnap victims go, I've been treated like royalty. At this point, I'm not even being kept here against my will, I'm just being... kept. Treasured.

"Yeah," I admit, and the woman sighs with relief. Holly, I think everyone called her earlier. "Why, are you gonna break me out?"

Those shoulders go back, and Holly's pointed chin raises. "If you ask me to."

Shit. Okay, I like this girl. And I don't know why I'm suddenly confessing my whole soul, but I slump over the railing like a loser. "Actually, I'm not sure Santo would even care at this point. He'd probably thank you for clearing the guest suite."

Especially after the things I said to him this morning. The way I thanked him for the incredible gift.

God, why did I make such a big deal about that freaking plane ticket? It's not like I even *want* to go, not if he feels the same way, but the things I mentioned are all true. The power imbalance. The captor thing. One of us needed to say it.

There's no manual for relationships like this. Is it so awful

289

for me to feel nervous?

"You didn't see him before, so I get that you won't realize this." Holly draws a shape in the snow heaped on the railing— a love heart. "But Santo De Rossi smiled exactly once in the whole month I worked here before you arrived, and that was at the moment they laid you in his trunk."

I snort, and Holly shoots me a grin.

"He never sleeps. Never smiles. Definitely never laughs or takes days off. Or he didn't, anyway, before you came. I'm sure there are other things too, other differences I don't see, but hey. I was just the maid."

Holly flicks a lump of snow off the railing, then winks at me before walking back inside. "Dinner's in an hour," she calls as she crosses the room, "and I know you're hungry. We can hear your stomach growling from downstairs."

I cough out a laugh. "I'll be there."

"Good."

The door thumps shut again, and the wind is fresh on my cheeks, but I'm toasty warm, glowing from the inside.

Why do I need a plane ticket? I'm home.

Santo

I'm staring out at the grounds, arms folded, when my study door creaks open. It's dark out there, overcast and stormy, heavy clouds blocking out the stars.

"Leave me," I mutter, not bothering to turn around. The wind moans past the glass balcony doors, rattling them in their panes.

A soft voice says, "Screw that."

I spin around, heart leaping. "Erin."

She's pale and tired, those freckles standing out extra stark on her skin, but she gives me a wobbly smile as she comes inside. Her curls are braided over one shoulder, and she's twined tinsel around the end. The door thumps closed behind her, and she holds up a plate covered with tin foil.

"You missed Christmas dinner, you giant scrooge."

I did? My stomach twists, and I realize far too late that I'm hungry. How long have I been working in here non-stop? What time is it?

"I was busy." Busy licking my wounds, anyway. Busy

291

scheming and plotting and trying to find a way to make this impossible woman *choose* me. Trying to be the man she deserves. "Is Allegra furious?"

"Spitting feathers," Erin assures me, setting the plate on my desk.

"Well. Every cloud, I suppose."

My captive snorts, and I stare at her. Maybe if I stop blinking altogether, I'll catch something: a twitch or a sigh. Some kind of signal; a clue to her mood. But Erin's a cipher in that green long-sleeved dress, her face unreadable as she sets a fork by the plate.

"She wanted you there," she says slowly, choosing her words with care. I don't think we're talking about Allegra. "Does work always come first?"

"This does." I stroll over to meet her at the desk. "Want to see what I've been doing?"

Erin shrugs. "Sure. I won't understand half of your mob stuff, though."

Maybe not right away, but she's brighter than anyone else in this building. If she wants to, she'll pick it all up.

But: "It's not 'mob stuff'. Come here." Sinking into the desk chair, I pat one thigh—and I don't exhale until she shuffles around the desk and settles onto my lap, the skirt of her dress spreading over my legs.

God. The relief of having her near again is a physical thing, a knot loosening in my gut. I press my face against her hair and *breathe*, all the jagged pieces inside me settling back into place.

I hated this day apart. Too many miserable hours without her.

"I'm sorry about earlier," Erin whispers, and she's clinging to my forearms. When did I grab hold of her like this? I'm squeezing her tightly, like someone might snatch her away.

Not likely. They'd lose an arm if they tried.

"Santo," she says again. Her fingers play at the edges of my rolled sleeves, slipping underneath like she's greedy for bare skin. Secret skin. "What did you want to show me?"

Right. Focus.

Jesus.

Clearing my throat, I tap at my keyboard, the laptop humming back to life. The screen brightens, and Erin leans forward, squinting at the columns of numbers.

"Ooookay. What is…?"

"Those are your investments. I've put them in your name. There's a couple million there, but if you want more to feel comfortable, you can have it. And my wealth is also your wealth, of course, but this money is specifically yours."

Erin squawks, and I rub my cheek on her head as I keep talking.

"Then you already have your father's mansion, but there's also this." I hit a key and a real estate listing pops up, covered with pictures of a penthouse apartment in the city. It's eclectic and colorful, filled with plants and bright artworks and bare brick walls. Very Erin. "You'll have the keys by Monday."

"Oh my god." She grips the edge of the desk, wheezing faintly. I rub gentle circles between her shoulder blades. "You can't—*Santo*. This is way too much. You can't do this."

"I can do what I like. That is literally the whole point of being a kingpin."

"But—"

"You were concerned about your independence. About what would happen if we parted."

"Yes, but—"

"And about the power imbalance. This way, you have your own money. You have your own property if you ever need somewhere to go."

"But I don't want to live apart!" Erin wails, and I smirk and tug her earlobe between my teeth before replying. Her warm weight is perfect on my lap.

"Rent it out, then. Or use it for overpriced storage—I don't care, because the point is you have it. It's there if you need it, so you can stop second guessing this."

"Oh my god." Erin folds forward over the desk, face buried in her arms. "My stomach hurts. This is way too much. Way, way too much."

My mouth twists, and for a moment I think that perhaps I've misjudged; pushed her too far. But I didn't build a criminal empire by being a coward, and the way she's shifting on my lap... she's squirming. Turned on and trying to hide it. I go for broke: "There's more."

Erin hiccups a broken laugh, grinding down harder, and I grin before brushing a kiss to the back of her neck. I've got her. Triumph riots in my chest.

"This is Rocco." I whistle sharply, and the study door opens. Erin sits bolt upright as a brawny man in his fifties shuffles inside, dressed in a dark suit and earpiece. His head is shaved and his expression is placid. "He answers to you. *Only* to you. Right, Rocco?"

"Yes, boss."

My withering stare makes him swallow.

"I mean—yes, Mr De Rossi. I work for you now, Miss Erin."

She pinches my wrist and hisses, "My very own goon?" She's jiggling in my lap, fizzing with excitement.

294

"Exactly. Leave us, Rocco."

Erin waits until the door snaps closed before she scrambles around in my lap, throwing her arms around my neck and pressing hot kisses down my throat.

"This is way too much." She yanks at my shirt, buttons flying. "I was going to stay anyway—you know that, right?"

I do know that. At least, on some level, I did. But this makes her happy, so I'm going to do it. Call me a tyrant; I don't care.

I catch her wrists, waiting until she leans back and meets my eye. My captive is bright pink, breathing hard, and my words are strained, but I need to get them out. She needs to understand.

"There is one thing I will never, ever give you, Erin. Do you know what it is?"

"If you say your cock, I'm gonna scream—"

I squeeze her wrists gently and she clams up. "It's a plane ticket away from me. Never. Going. To happen. You're *mine*, do you understand?"

She tugs her wrists free, unbuttoning my clothes at lightning speed. "Oh god. Oh my god. I swear, if you don't fuck me in the next ten minutes—"

"You're *mine*," I snarl, leaning back as she spreads my shirt and waistcoat open, chair creaking. My thighs widen; her nails score red lines down my bare chest. "Say it, Erin."

"I'm yours." My belt buckle clinks as she fumbles it open. "Of course I'm yours, you asshat."

We both exhale as she draws out my length, hard and throbbing in her palm. The head is flushed, a bead of moisture clinging to the tip, and her fingers are maddeningly gentle.

"Get up. Take off your clothes."

"So bossy," Erin grumbles, but her eyes gleam as she hops

up and complies.

"All of them. The underwear too."

"Yeah, yeah." Her outfit lands in a pile of fabric on my rug. "On the desk or on your lap?"

"The desk." I snatch up the plate covered in tinfoil, leaning back to set it on a nearby bookcase, because I do not want unexpected gravy to interrupt this moment. When I turn back, she's naked, kicking her heels as she sits on my desk.

The air empties out of my chest. "Erin," I croak.

Want her so badly. Is this real? Is she finally mine?

"Come here," she murmurs, and her smile is so soft as she crooks a finger. It sharpens, though, when I stand and my cock points between her legs. "Ah, there it is. My favorite Christmas gift of all. Hey, I didn't get you anything!"

I kiss away her pout. "You could not be more wrong."

She pushes the open shirt off my shoulders. I step closer, bare skin pebbling under her palms, and as I notch at her entrance, my heartbeat slams in my ears.

What if she doesn't like it? What if I scare her off somehow?

"Come on, baby," she coos, nudging my ass with her heels, and if anyone else called me that, I'd set them on fire. But it's Erin, so I grit my teeth against a pleased groan, pressing forward into her tight, wet heat.

Jesus.

I sink inside. She sucks me deeper.

Heaven.

"That's it," she says on a blissful sigh, legs parting wider. "Holy crap. That is it."

Yes, it is. I rock into her with shallow thrusts, sparks crackling down my spine, and watch every flicker of emotion on her beautiful face. The initial pinch of discomfort; the decadent sigh of pleasure. The greedy way she bites her bottom lip, urging me on as a blush climbs her throat.

She's perfect.

So perfect.

She's the ultimate work of art, my only possible partner, and she's *mine*.

"Erin," I rasp, sucking a bruise on her neck as I fuck her harder, the desk rattling beneath us.

We'll need to rejoin the others soon. I'll need to make up for missing dinner, and there will be one crisis or another demanding my attention. There's always something, but for right now, the outside world does not exist.

It's just me and my milkmaid. Her little tits bounce as I thrust between her legs, and her hazel eyes crinkle when she catches me staring.

"You're mine too," Erin murmurs, and it's embarrassing how much those words affect me, my thrusts getting sloppy and wild. I grip her thighs so tight there'll be fingerprint bruises there tomorrow, and I'm so hard inside her that it hurts. "Come inside me," she whispers.

Fuck.

I get her there first, one thumb rubbing her clit, tendons standing out on my neck from the strain. I rub and thrust and lick at her throat, and when she tightens around me, muscles squeezing and fluttering, the study echoing with her breathless cries—I lose it.

I press my face against her hair, and I empty my whole tarnished soul inside her. On and on, I fill her up, until it drips onto the desk beneath her and I surely need some kind of sports drink to recover.

"Erin."

She rubs both palms over my heaving chest. "I know. Love you," she mumbles, and she sounds as dazed as I feel.

She loves me? I'd turn the whole useless world to rubble for her. "Love you too," I mutter instead. "Marry me tomorrow."

"Mmkay."

Erin

❧◦◦❧

ive years later

"Leah and Nico have got the kids in a snowman competition," Holly says, nudging the door open. She slips into the den where we've gathered after lunch—one of the rooms on the top floor of the mansion, scattered with squashy armchairs and a fire dancing in the hearth. Torn wrapping paper lies in piles on the floor. "You okay, baby?"

Diego groans from where he's stretched out on one sofa, a cool washcloth draped over his scarred face. He ran interference with the kids all morning, absorbing the holiday mania like a champ, and the brutal mobster is ruined.

"Poor thing," Holly coos, crossing to sit on her husband's chest. "Such a hero."

"Vom," Allegra says from her position in Raul's lap. She narrows her eyes. "Falasca doesn't complain, and he's got twins."

Diego flips her off, still buried under his washcloth.

The room is warm, and my eyelids keep drooping. I'm propped against Santo's side, treating my husband like a pillow, and I'm so full from lunch. So comfy and calm. A shriek of laughter floats up from the grounds, and I stifle a smile, burrowing deeper into the sofa.

Maybe I'll nap.

No hit men this year. There's been nothing so dramatic for a long time. Since settling down, the De Rossi empire has gone legitimate.

Well. Ish.

"Remind me why we all reproduced at the same time," Santo mutters, stroking my hair. He sounds grouchy, but *I* know better. It's his pleased-grump tone. His happy bitching.

"So we can all palm them off on Nico whenever we need a break," Allegra says. Raul grunts in agreement, nibbling on her ear. "Bit late for second thoughts now, big brother."

"No second thoughts," Santo says mildly, his thumb rubbing against my side. Hey, he doesn't need to tell *me* that. I've seen the reverent way he looks at our daughter with her ice blue eyes; the way we *all* go gooey over our kids. "But maybe we should lock the doors—trap Nico out there for a while."

Diego snorts. It's an empty threat and we all know it.

And I could sleep here so easily, could drift off and drool on Santo's shoulder in front of everyone, but I force my limbs back into action, standing up on wobbly legs. I have a plan, after all. "Come with me for a second."

My husband takes my outstretched hand right away. Whistles follow us out the door, but Santo ignores them all.

We pass oil paintings and chandeliers. Marble statues and bustling maids. The mansion hums with conversation, delicious smells drifting from the kitchens, and I squeeze my husband's hand as I lead him through the halls.

"Bored of the cold weather?" he asks when I nudge the conservatory door open.

"Make sure we're not disturbed, Rocco," I tell the man standing watch.

"Yes, boss."

The sudden blast of heat makes sweat prickle under my sweater. And Santo hasn't recognized what I'm wearing yet, hasn't put the pieces together, so I fight a smile as I lead him through the explosion of waxy green leaves.

A bird flutters overhead. The glass walls have steamed over, and I can hear the trickle of distant water.

"You're being very mysterious, Erin."

"Oh, you know me." I stop by the swing bench and wait for him to notice the pile of black fabric. The holiday sweater he wore to ruin my father years ago with a holiday card; the one with a reindeer on it. I'm wearing its twin, and I beam as Santo huffs out a laugh, shoulders dropping. "Put it on."

A dark eyebrow ticks up. "Since when do you give the orders, sweetheart?"

It's true: we both like it when he's the one bossing me around. But I want to relive our first cuddle, and I planned this weeks ago. I fold my arms and fix my husband with a glare.

"Don't make me set my goon on you."

Santo shakes his head, but he's already flicking his shirt buttons open, giving me a glimpse of that bare chest, dusted with hair.

Those muscles. Those *abs*. Oh, I remember this alright, in high definition, and I'm almost sad when he shrugs on the reindeer sweater.

301

"Sit." I point at the center of the swing bench. The mob boss gusts out a long breath but complies, and when I settle into his lap, strong arms wind around and hold me tight.

Oh, yeah. I tilt my head back against his shoulder and close my eyes; feel my heart rate settle and his body harden beneath my ass.

This is it. Santo kisses my neck, and I let out a sigh. A bird chirps high above, and I wriggle against his length, my blood heating.

Paradise.

* * *

Thanks for reading the Very Merry Mob series! I hope you loved it. :)

For a bonus story in this world, check out Ruth's Story. *Ruth sees her sister fall in love with a mobster, but where's her happy ending? ...Right here. With a gruff groundskeeper with silver in his beard.*

And for another festive treat, check out Santa Baby. *We're messing around when we call our boss Santa. But the truth is, I'd die to sit on his knee.*

Happy reading!

xxx

Teaser: Santa Baby

I know the exact moment that Jack steps out of his office. I'm sure to everyone else, nothing has changed, but to me—it's like the air shifts. Electricity crackles, and the roar of the crowd fades away, and it's just me and him and my quick, shallow breaths. He surveys the room, hands tucked in his faded jeans and a black long-sleeved shirt clinging to his broad chest, and then he looks over. Our eyes meet.

I grip the edge of the bar so tight the wood creaks.

"Gina. Clara." Jack smiles at us both as he squeezes behind the bar. It's a tight fit back here—barely enough room to open the dishwasher—and Jack's a big man. Tall and broad and so freaking *sturdy*. "How's it going tonight? You two need another pair of hands?"

"We've got it," I say quickly, before Gina can pipe up. Much as I love any excuse to be near Jack, it's Christmas Eve. He shouldn't have to work, not if we can help it. A man like him deserves to have his feet up in front of a fire—or to be drinking freshly-poured drinks at a table with his friends from the town. And if my lizard brain is screaming at me, begging for any excuse for our bodies to brush together as we squeeze past behind the bar… that's my problem, not his.

Jack's eyes land on me again, and is that a flash of disappointment? Whatever it is, he covers it quickly, nodding and rapping on the bar. "I'll leave you to it, then."

My heart sinks. He's not—not looking at me properly. Jack empties the cash register, avoiding my eye, and I've got this sickly, swooping feeling. Like I've missed a step on the stairs. Like I've misread something *important.*

"Wait, Jack."

I could kiss Gina for keeping him here a while longer. But then she reaches past me, grinning, and tugs open the drawer with his gift. He peers down into the drawer, and when he realizes what he's seeing, his eyebrows shoot up his forehead.

"Santa, huh?"

"Made me think of you." Gina's smile is sly.

Jack laughs, but there's a strain to it. Can't she hear it? Am I the only person paying attention to this perfect man? I grab a cloth and scrub aimlessly at the bar, working my frustration out on the wood.

"What do you think, Clara?" My best friend elbows me. "Want to sit on Jack's knee and tell him you've been good?"

My mouth goes dry. I stop scrubbing, still squeezing the cloth tight, eyes fixed on the bar. *Answer, you idiot.* "I, um. I…"

In the time it takes me to stumble over my words, I go from pale to bright, glowing crimson. The blush spreading hot over my cheeks—it's damning. It tells the whole freaking world that *yes*, that's exactly what I've been picturing. What I've been yearning for in the dead of night.

Gina's grin falters. She was joking, but I forgot to play along.

"Sure," I say weakly, way too late. "That'd be funny."

Funny. The way I feel about my boss is a literal joke. Kill me now. And when I gather up the courage to look at Jack, he's staring like he's never seen me before.

"See." Gina snatches the red hat from the drawer and jams it on Jack's head. She's flustered, trying to cover for me, but we're fooling no one. "Santa. Told you it suits you."

Jack starts to say something, his reply a low murmur, but a customer waves from the other end of the bar and I stumble over, light-headed with relief. I serve the man in a daze, my hands clumsy and my lips numb, and I don't look at my boss and best friend again. Not even once.

For hours and hours, I serve an endless line of customers, and I do it with dry, unblinking eyes and a blush seared into my cheeks. After a while, Gina comes to check on me, her words a soothing murmur.

"You okay, honey?"

I nod, still speechless with horror, loading the dishwasher with dirty glasses.

Gina hums, and the sound is miserable. "I didn't know, Clara, I swear. I wasn't out to cause you trouble."

It's obvious, then, how I feel about Jack. Exactly as I feared.

It takes a few seconds, but I force a reply through my tight throat. "It's okay. It doesn't matter."

But it *does*. It does to me, anyway. Jack's good opinion is the only one I really care about. And he's done so much for me, and how do I repay him?

By pining after him. Making a scene.

I'm so embarrassed. So ashamed.

When the bar closes and the last singing customer spills out into the night, we clear up in record time. Gina and I whirl around the bar like demons are chasing us, wiping down tables and stacking chairs, rounding up glasses and restocking the

305

shelves. Five minutes in, Jack comes out of his office again and leans on the doorway, watching us work. He doesn't offer to join in this time, and we don't ask.

His gaze is heavy on me. My cheeks flush brighter, and I blink back tears.

Jack's office door closes with a snap.

"It'll be okay," Gina tells me, hugging me tight at the end of our shift. We're standing in the doorway, snowflakes swirling in the moonlight, and I'm so tired I'm swaying on my feet. "He'll have forgotten it all by morning."

I nod, miserable, her dark hair tickling my nose. "Can you forget too, please?"

She squeezes me tighter. "Sure, honey. If that's what you want."

When the door closes, I'm left alone in the bar. It's silent, no sound except for the *pop* of the dying embers in the grate and the echoes of earlier conversations still bouncing off the walls.

Golden light glows around the edges of Jack's office door. I pause on my way past, fist raised, but I don't knock. I can't.

My hand drops to my side and I hurry past on silent feet. My heart aches in my chest, long after I've raced up the stairs to my room.

* * *

Check out Santa Baby!

xxx

306

Cassie Mint

About the Author

Cassie writes outrageous, OTT instalove with tons of sugar and spice. She loves cookie dough, summer barbecues, and her gorgeous cat Missy.

You can connect with me on:

🌐 https://www.authorcassiemint.com

📘 https://www.facebook.com/cassiemintauthor

🔗 https://www.bookbub.com/authors/cassie-mint

Subscribe to my newsletter:

✉ https://www.authorcassiemint.com/newsletter